ACCLAIM FOR *FIRE DANCER*

"[F]eatures the excitement of fire fighting in the Arizona wilderness."

—*Publishers Weekly*

"[I]f you're a Colleen Coble fan and liked her first series, you will not be disappointed with this one. Colleen writes with skill and makes the reader turn page after page wanting to know what happens, while fearful about what that might be. A great read!"

—Linda Mae Baldwin for The Road to Romance

"[E]xcellent writing; engaging, edge-of-your-seat story; great attention to detail."

—epinions.com

"Combine the excitement of smoke jumping with a sweet romance and edge-of-the-seat suspense and you have Colleen Coble's engaging new novel *Fire Dancer*. Coble sweeps us up in the drama of family secrets then takes us into the demented mind of an arsonist, all while weaving an intricate mystery sure to stump even the most perceptive reader. A riveting read!"

—Denise Hunter, author of *Finding Faith*

"Typical Coble . . . every page is alive with suspense as she develops her intricate plots. There has to be a sequel!"

—W. Elmo Mercer, the Nashville songwriter of songs such as "The Way That He Loves" and "Each Step I Take"

"In *Fire Dancer*, Colleen Coble creates a novel that sparks to life with the first sentence and blazes through a story so real, you'll struggle to breathe. A breakout novel you won't want to miss!"

—Diann Hunt, author of *RV There Yet?*

"Dance to the beat of a Navajo drum in this story of mysterious family dynamics. The more you read, the more enchanted you'll become with this fascinating author, whose writing deepens and delights more with every book."

—Hannah Alexander, author of *Fair Warning and Grave Risk*

"Wow! Colleen Coble has done it again. *Fire Dancer* is a page-turner with twists and turns galore."

—Carol Umberger, award-winning author
of the Scottish Crown series

"How is it possible that Colleen Coble has gotten even better? *Fire Dancer* is a combustible mix of intrigue, action, mystery, and romance—sparked by compelling characters. Colleen's love for Arizona seasons every page. The master of romantic suspense has done it again—with a flare! Pull the rip cord on *Fire Dancer* and feel the heat."

—Kathryn Mackel, author of *The Hidden*

"*Fire Dancer* is an action-packed tale of arson and intrigue and family secrets. It will keep you guessing!"

—DeAnna Julie Dodson, author of *In Honor Bound*

Fire Dancer

OTHER BOOKS BY COLLEEN COBLE

The Rock Harbor series

Without a Trace

Beyond a Doubt

Into the Deep

The Aloha Reef series

Distant Echoes

Black Sands

Dangerous Depths

Midnight Sea

Alaska Twilight

Fire Dancer

COLLEEN COBLE

WESTBOW
PRESS

A Division of Thomas Nelson Publishers
Since 1798

visit us at www.westbowpress.com

Library of Congress Cataloging-in-Publication Data

Coble, Colleen.
    Fire dancer / Colleen Coble.
        p. cm. —
    ISBN-13: 978-1-59554-139-0 (pbk.)
    ISBN-10: 1-59554-139-X (pbk.)
    1. Arson—Fiction. 2. Arizona—Fiction. I. Title.
PS3553.O2285F57 2006
813'.6—dc22
2006023025

Printed in the United States of America

06 07 08 09 10 RRD 10 9 8 7 6 5 4 3

For Chase Arnold, whose name inspired the character in this story. May you grow to be a man of integrity like your father, Allen Arnold.

PROLOGUE

OCTOBER 1991

Nibbling on a strand of strawberry blonde hair, Tess Masterson sat on the red dirt with a book on her knees and her back propped against the fence. She barely breathed, caught up in a world very much like that around her—sage, pine, and the sharply rising escarpment known as Mogollon Rim. The scent of the creosote bushes added to the sensation that she was living the story right along with the characters, riding on a horse with the wind in her face.

A truck came up the dirt drive, red dust puffing from its tires. It pulled a horse trailer. Tess got to her feet and dusted the dirt from her jeans. Her father pulled the truck and trailer to the side of the narrow lane and got out. Her mother exited the passenger side.

A broad smile lifted the corners of her father's mouth. Tess thought he was the handsomest man in the world. She wanted to

1

find someone just like him someday. The dusting of gray at his temples just made him look wise.

His green eyes, so like her own, crinkled at the corners. "Hey, birthday girl, what are you doing out here by yourself?"

Tess held up the book. *Riders of the Purple Sage* was her favorite Zane Grey novel. Her dad thought she read too much, but Tess didn't know if that was possible. "I should start at the beginning of the set, but I couldn't wait to reread this one." She'd squealed when her parents presented her with the entire collection of Zane Grey books this morning at breakfast. It was a grand present for her fifteenth birthday.

"I should have known. I think I've got something that might get your mind off books." Dressed in dusty jeans and a plaid snap-front shirt, Garrett Masterson stepped to the back of the trailer and opened it. He led out a bay colt.

Tess squealed. "Oh Daddy, he's beautiful!" She moved to touch the colt. He nudged her hand with his velvety nose. "How old is he?"

Her mother, Willa Masterson, answered with an indulgent smile. "About a year."

"What's his name?" She caressed the colt's black mane, and he nestled closer to her.

"That's up to you," her father said.

Her hand stilled. Did he mean it? His smile broadened, and she threw her arms around the colt's neck. "He's mine? You don't mean it!"

"He's yours all right, and he cost me a pretty penny. It would have been more, but I gave Sam a good deal when he wanted to use Midnight as a sire. If he's as fast as he looks, this little guy will be worth a fortune when he's grown. He'll be the first of your world-famous horses."

Tess didn't care that her father was teasing about her unlikely dream of breeding racehorses. She moved away from the colt and hugged her dad. "You're the best, Daddy. I love you." Wait until Chase Huston saw her horse. He wouldn't be so cocky. The foster boy was always trying to take her place in the family. The horse proved Tess came first to her dad and always would.

"I love you too, Tessie." His hug was fierce, then he released her.

She released her dad and moved to hug her mother. "Thanks, Mom."

"Only the best for our baby girl." Her mom planted a kiss on Tess's forehead.

"You have a name all picked out, don't you?" her father asked.

Her gaze went back to the colt. "Wildfire. His name is Wildfire."

"Well, I need to get Wildfire to his stall. He's had a busy day," her dad said.

"I'll come with you."

"You need to feed the cattle," he said. "Wildfire will be in the barn waiting for you."

Tess suppressed a sigh as her dad led the colt away. "Can I take him over to show Aunt Doty after supper? I want to take her some birthday cake. Why wouldn't she come to my party? Is she mad at me?"

Her mother looked away. "You know your aunt. She's never been one for parties."

"I'll ride over there in a little while."

Her mother nibbled on her lip. "I'd rather you didn't. Not until they catch the arsonist. I'll run you over in the truck."

Tess wished they'd catch the guy. Since someone had begun torching hay fields and meadows at the beginning of summer, her parents had curtailed her freedom. The fires were front-page news every couple of weeks. Every time Tess began to think the fire spree was over, a new blaze would appear. There'd been talk of getting a vigilante group going to patrol the back roads and catch the culprit, but nothing had come of it yet.

"Okay, Mom."

Her mother grinned at Tess's suffering tone. "Let me know when you're ready to go."

Tess nodded and ran to turn on the water for the cattle. The sooner she got this over with, the quicker she could see her horse again. Her horse. She could hardly believe it. She grabbed a pitchfork and began to break flakes of hay from the bale. The cattle came meandering over the hill as she pitched the hay over the fence to them.

By the time she finished, twilight had begun to descend, brushing the sky with purple and pink. If she wanted any time with Wildfire before supper, she needed to get a move on. She put away the pitchfork and set off, running through sagebrush and rabbitbrush toward the barn. As she neared the ranch house, she became aware of a strange sound: crackling and an odd popping. Was that smoke she smelled? Maybe the cowboys were branding. The odor intensified as she jogged past the chicken coop and through the orchard. She stepped out from the cover of trees behind the back paddock.

Black smoke roiled toward her, the scent of kerosene in the wind. Hungry flames shot through the barn roof and leaped into the sky, just beginning to darken to indigo. Tiny sparks floated around the barnyard and caused the chickens to run squawking for cover. Tess stood frozen, not sure what to do. She wanted to clap her palms over her ears to block out the horrific sound of fire devouring dry wood. Her horse was in the barn.

She started back toward the house to call for help, then stopped.

There was no time. "Mom!" she screamed. "Dad! Help! Somebody help me!" She seized the side door and threw it open. Acrid smoke burned her throat and chest. The first stall was just inside the door. Blind from the smoke, she fumbled at the latch. The colt screamed in terror, then ran past her when she succeeded in getting the gate open. Nearly sagging with relief, she stepped away from the door.

Hardly aware of what she was doing, she ran to the pump house and grabbed the hose. The faucet resisted her effort at first, then she managed to get the water flowing. The hose caught in a loop, and she untangled it, then ran toward the barn with it. She saw a movement at the window. Horror deadened her limbs when she recognized her parents. They beat on the window, their eyes wide with terror. Her father broke the window with a shovel, and black smoke billowed out, obscuring their faces.

"No!" Tess screamed and ran toward the window with the hose.

The roof collapsed with a deafening roar. Flames licked their way toward Tess, but she ran anyway until something seized her arms and pulled her up short. Her cousin Whip held her back.

"No, Queenie, you can't get any closer."

The scent of kerosene choked her. Cinders fell from the sky in a swirling black rain that singed the hair on her arms and marked her forever with the scent of fire.

CHAPTER 1

y heart dances with the leaping flames of the campfire. Mom never cared much for poetry, said she had no use for it in what she faced every day, but the cadence of words speaks to me. Kind of stupid when you consider who I am and what I do. There is more to a soul than what others see.

The flames mesmerize me. I hold my hands over the flickering light and take a deep breath I close my eyes. We used to roast hot dogs over a fire in our backyard, just me and Mom, in fall when the stars were clear and close and the air was a blade in my throat.

The Navajo witch settles beside me. I'm not afraid, even though my breath sounds in my ears. Shrouded by wolf skins, he seems to grow bigger. People have told me there's no such thing as a skin-walker. They are wrong. The hair on the back of my neck rises, almost as if it's saluting the magic of the imposing figure. The heat he radiates is as bewitching as the flames.

The witch begins to chant and drops something into the fire. It flares into the black Arizona sky. Color rises deep in the smoke, and I peer closer, longing to grasp the power that thrums around me like an unseen drum. The Navajo witch focuses his dark eyes on me, and I straighten. I *am* worthy. Suffering produces character, and my suffering is exquisite, like the hottest flame.

"You are not ready," the witch says. "I see no pain in your face."

His low, guttural voice vibrates with power, a power I *will* have, no matter what it takes. Can he not see the suffering that screams inside me? Curling my hands into fists, I force my anger back to its cave and peer into the man's unblinking stare.

"I'm ready," I say in a steady voice.

He shakes his head. "Not yet. Becoming a skinwalker takes much discipline. Many years. It is not a weapon you can grasp in your hand like a bow or a gun."

"I know." Power fills me, a sense of destiny no one can steal from me. "I will do whatever it takes."

He finally nods. "I will set you a series of tasks to do, but it will take time. One day, your soul will change at your calling."

"Tell me what to do." My voice is hoarse as I lean forward.

Instead of answering, the witch bends and picks up a firebrand. The red-hot end is in his hand, but he doesn't seem to feel the heat. My respect rises like the smoke ascending above our heads. Someday I will own his power.

He holds out the brand. "If you take it, you'll know what to do."

He who hesitates is lost, and I'm about to be found. I grasp the flame in my hand. A cry rises in my chest as the pain sears my hand, and I know I am right. Fire is my calling.

"You're not pigged in." Tess Masterson raised her voice above the roar of the DC-3's engines. Cooper Johnston, known as Coop to the rest of the smokejumpers, looked back at her and nodded. He attached the pigtail of his restraining line to the clip, then took a firm grip on the cargo-door handles. As the team's spotter, he took responsibility for making sure they hit the target.

"Guard your reserves," Coop said as he opened the door.

The jumpers all put a protective hand on their spare chute. The sudden influx of air had been known to inflate a reserve parachute and sweep the hapless jumper out of the plane and to his death when the lines tangled. The rush of mountain air blew through the plane filled with smokejumpers and their gear. Tess peered past Coop. Below her was the jump target, a heavy pine forest atop Horse Mountain on the northern cusp of Hellsgate Wilderness. A wisp of smoke wafted up through the pine treetops. The trees parted around a clearing, and she could see a line of fire crackling toward a cabin. A man on a small tractor was plowing up the meadow in an effort to stop the blaze, an effort that showed he knew something about fighting wildfire. He needed help though, and fast.

Tess watched Coop throw out the drift streamers to determine how the air currents were moving. The faint scent of smoke came to her nose, and the odor revved her adrenaline. She shuffled as she checked her lines. It was unusual to have a fire this late in the season, and all the smokejumpers were ready for some R and R. She'd been looking forward to it too, until her sister's call.

"Ready to get home?" Buck Carter asked.

Tess frowned as she glanced up into her friend's face. A wilderness outfitter in his other life, Buck had been a rock for her during her training and on the subsequent missions they'd flown together. Behind her, the rest of the smokejumpers shuffled as they prepared to jump. Ten smokejumpers, a tightly-knit cadre of firefighters—all men with the exception of Tess and Allie Stinson—who had become a family to her.

"I still don't know what she wants," Tess said.

"You have to go," Buck told her.

He always did that, read her mind before she said a word. She often wondered why there were no romantic feelings between the two of them when they were so attuned.

"Want to place odds that she'll think of an excuse to back out?" Flint Montgomery said to Buck.

Buck's wolf dog, Spirit, sat at his feet. Tess rubbed the dog's head, and Spirit practically groveled. Intelligence shimmered in his yellow eyes. Flint and Tess were two of the few full-time Forest Service employees on the team. The rest worked at other jobs when their seasonal firefighting gigs were over. Some were with the Forest Service and others were employed by the Bureau of Land Management. Raised by his Apache mother when his cowboy father died, Flint was the quiet one of the group.

Buck grinned and nodded toward the door. "You're in the first stick out, second jumper," he said to Tess. "There's time to decide on the visit later. Let's go."

The firefighters jumped in twos, referred to as "sticks." Tess forced her tight facial muscles into what she hoped was a cheeky grin. She pulled on her helmet, snapped the chin strap, and pulled down the wire-mesh mask. Tugging on her Nomex gloves, she followed Allie to the open doorway. Her vision filled with the glory of the landscape's panorama. She could see the world moving by below in a kaleidoscope of umber earth and the vivid green pine

tops. She prayed she would acquit herself respectably today. The
other sticks lined up behind them. Five sticks in all, ten jumpers,
and she had the luck to be in the first group out the door today. As
one of only twenty-seven women among the more than four hundred smokejumpers in the country, the responsibility always rode
heavy on her shoulders.

"Stay out of the water," Coop admonished. "We haven't had
any drownings this year, and I'm not about to start now."

"Yes, Mom," Tess said, rolling her eyes at Allie.

About forty, Coop usually kept his golden mane of hair corralled
in a band, and the crags and planes of his face added to his lionlike
appearance. The tough, sinewy muscles under his bronzed skin
were hard and taut. He pointed at the streamers. "Looks like there's
about two hundred yards of drift."

Tess nodded and lowered herself to the floor, dangling her feet
into the slipstream. The heat from the fire warmed her face.

"We missed the best exit point," Coop shouted at the pilot.
"Circle around for another pass."

The plane banked and began to turn back. They had a few more
minutes, but Tess stayed put. Allie joined her, irked at the delay.

"Sorry about mixing up our chutes today. Distracted, you know.
I'll straighten it out on the ground."

"It's okay. You've been preoccupied."

"You got that right. I should have quit a long time ago."

"No!" Tess gripped her friend's hand. "You're the best jumper in
the country. Think of all the lives you've saved!"

"And all but ruined my own." Allie pulled her hand away. "I gave
up too much for this."

"Daryl won't be angry at you forever," Tess said, reading between
the lines. "You'll be with him in time for dinner."

"I should have been with him yesterday. His mom *died* this morning, Tess. What am I doing here? I can't believe I let you talk me into one more jump."

Tess gave her a playful punch in the arm. "You'll get over it."

"Easy for you to say."

"Ready?" Coop shouted over the roar of the wind.

The women nodded. Coop slapped Allie on the back. From the corner of her eye past the wire cage of her helmet, Tess saw Allie lean forward and tumble from the plane. Coop slapped Tess hard on the shoulder. She propelled herself forward with all her strength.

As the roar of the wind rushed past her ears, she began to chant off the count. "Jump-thousand." The world and the sky blurred together as she tumbled through the air. At ninety miles an hour, the air rushed past her in a howl that blotted out other sound. It was like riding bareback on the fastest horse in the world.

"Look-thousand." She glanced back to see Flint tumble from the plane. "Reach-thousand." Her hand reached for the green rip cord. "Wait-thousand." Even though she'd jumped hundreds of times, she always had to resist the impulse to pull the cord now.

She glanced to her left. Allie still hadn't pulled her rip cord. Was something wrong? Tess's hand dropped away from her chute handle. She angled her body into a downward torpedo and dove toward Allie. The shriek of the wind intensified. Allie's arms and legs were splayed, slowing her descent. She kept jerking on the chute handle. She looked up, her mouth open in a scream Tess couldn't hear.

Tess hugged all appendages as close to the trunk of her body as she could. Just a little closer and maybe she could grab hold of Allie. She zipped past Allie, then stretched out her hands to slow herself.

Allie's hand brushed hers, and their fingers caught. Moments later, Allie was hugging her.

"Pull!" Allie yelled.

Tess pulled hard and her hand snapped back to her side with the handle in it. She felt herself tip forward, and a tugging sensation rippled across her shoulders. The drogue was out and struggling to open. Air filled her chute, and the resulting jerk lifted her and Allie. She looked up at the gleaming rectangle of orange and white. Silence settled as the rushing air slowed to a gentle glide. Riding on the wind, she had a bird's-eye view of the fire below.

"Thanks. I owe you." Allie's voice trembled. "Who would want to kill you?"

"What do you mean?"

"This was your chute. I saw him—"

The wind shifted and drove them toward the trees. "Look out!" They were coming down too fast. Tess tugged harder on the steering toggles. They hurtled down toward trees that reached high into the air.

"Pull right, pull right!" Allie screamed.

The gusts of wind were stronger than Tess and drove them closer to the stand of tall ponderosa pine that stretched upwards of a hundred and fifty feet. She managed to twist in the wind but was unable to resist the current. Tree branches rushed to meet them. They landed hard in the top of a ponderosa, and the impact knocked loose her grip on Allie. Allie slid away.

The chute billowed around Tess. Fighting the yards of fabric, she got the canopy out of her eyes and looked around. Her lines were entangled nearly a hundred feet off the ground. Her gaze scanned the treetops, and she caught a glimpse of white. Branches had snagged Allie's pack, and the young woman dangled above the ground. She was fighting with her harness, but the movement threatened the tree's tenuous grasp on her gear.

Tess heard Allie scream as she slid about two feet. "Tie off, tie off!" she shouted.

Allie's white face peered out of the foliage up at Tess as she reached for her letdown rope.

"Wait!" Tess shouted. She ripped off her Nomex gloves and tossed them to the ground far below. Trying to still the shaking in her hands, she managed to tie off her own lines. "I'm coming." By now several of the other smokejumpers had gathered at the base of the tree. Tess took out her climbing gear.

"I can't wait. It won't hold that long," Allie called. She sounded calm.

"Tie off," Flint called up. "It's not stable."

Allie was attempting to rappel down with her chute, which was what Tess would do, though that shortcut was a no-no. Standard procedure was to tie off to the tree for stability, shrug out of the pack, and then rappel down, but none of them liked to do it because they'd have to climb back up to retrieve the chute.

Allie reached into the pocket on the outside of her right leg. She took out about six feet of rope and passed it through the D-rings at the waist of her pants.

Was Allie's pack slipping? The straps seemed to be sliding in tiny degrees, though it was hard to tell through the swaying pine branches. Tess attached her climbing gear to a solid tree limb. She disengaged from her chute and left it behind as she began to rappel down. Pine branches slapped at her face and clutched at her clothes with sticky fingers. Her shoes were about ten feet from Allie's head.

Tess heard a ripping noise. Her horrified gaze shot to the lines just in time to see the tree release Allie's pack. Allie screamed, flailing. One hand grazed a branch, and she managed to latch onto it. She hung there with her other hand grasping toward the limb but unable to reach it. "Help me, Tess!" Her gaze met Tess's through the foliage.

Tess looped her legs around the branch and dangled upside down. Her hand grazed the top of Allie's head. Should she grab Allie's hand that was on the branch? She could touch that one. But what if she loosened Allie's grip on the tree and couldn't hold her? It would be better to try to catch her free hand. "Grab my hand!"

Perspiration dotted Allie's forehead. She made a wild swing at Tess's hand but only managed to graze her fingers. "I can't reach you. Come closer."

"There's no branch strong enough to hold us both." Tess loosened her knees and managed to gain an inch or so. "Try again."

Allie nodded, her face white as she stared into Tess's eyes. She whipped her arm up and grabbed at Tess's hand. The movement caused her grip to weaken, and her fingers fell away from Tess's hand.

Allie's hand slipped off the branch. Her eyes widened, and in their depths, Tess read resignation. "No!" she screamed. "Allie!"

But Allie was gone. She disappeared through the branches, toes pointed to the earth. The sound of snapping branches followed her descent. She hurtled through the air in the space of a heartbeat, her pack following like a bullet. The thud when she hit the ground was mingled with the sickening sound of breaking bones.

Tess sagged on the branch. She was tempted to let go, to follow her friend down. This was her fault.

"She's alive!" Flint's voice reached up through the branches.

Alive? Tess tightened her knees on the limb, then grabbed it with her hand. She managed to get upright. Rappelling down the tree, she feared what she would find at the bottom. Allie might have survived the fall, but at what cost to her future?

Buck reached up and lifted her down when she was five feet from the ground. Tess shook off his help and knelt by Allie. Her face was scratched by the branches, and one leg lay at an odd angle with the jagged ends of a bone sticking out through the material. "Call a chopper!"

"I already did." Flint dragged his EMT bag closer to Allie.

Tess moved out of the way. Flint's hands were gentle and assured as he pulled a cervical collar from his pack and slipped it around Allie's neck. "Will she live?" she asked. *Please God, let her be okay.*

Flint didn't look up. "I don't know, Tess. Pray."

"I am."

"We've still got a job to do," Coop said, his voice heavy. "There's nothing you can do for Allie, Tess."

"I talked her into one last jump," Tess said. "I'm going back with her."

Coop stared at her, then nodded. "Okay."

Tess barely noticed him herd the other firefighters off through the brush in the direction of the flames. She managed to hold her tears until she delivered Allie to the hospital, where the doctors rushed her into surgery and told Tess to go home for now.

Tess returned to her barracks. Spirit had come back with the plane, and he met her at the entrance. He followed her inside, then nosed at her hand. Taking comfort from his coarse fur, she rubbed his ears. His golden eyes seemed to reflect her own distress.

Each of them lived with the possibility of death every day, but when an accident came it was always a shock. Her eyes burned, and her throat felt thick. Allie had looked right into Tess's eyes as she fell. Did she blame Tess? She should.

Allie had been the only one to share the women's barracks with her, and her friend's things were piled around the next bunk. Tess went to Allie's bed. She picked up the koala bear on the neatly made bunk. The bear had one eye missing, and the fur was matted and tattered. It had been given to Allie when she was five, and she still took it with her everywhere. Maybe it would bring her comfort when she got out of surgery. *If* she got out of surgery.

Tess curled up on the bed with the bear in her arms and closed her eyes. She doubted if she could sleep, but it was dark when a tap on the door awakened her.

"Come in," Tess called. She sat up and put down the bear.

Coop stuck his head in the door. "You okay?"

The scent of smoke drifted in with him. "I'm fine." Tess blinked rapidly and got control of her emotions. "I didn't hear the choppers come back. Are we heading out again?"

"No, the fire's under control. You just slept through the choppers. I hope this fire is the last of the season. I just wanted to check on you and give you your fall assignment."

"I thought I was going to the Casa Grande station." Tess had been looking forward to the thought of throwing herself into something interesting like the cataloging of the pueblo artifacts.

Coop shook his head. "We're keeping you here to help repair equipment. I heard your sister needs you at home, and you're close enough to stay at the ranch if you like."

She didn't like. In fact, staying at the ranch was the last thing in the world she intended to do. In the last three firefighting seasons, she'd managed to make sure she was assigned to camps on the other side of the state. "I see." She could guess where Coop heard the gossip. Blabbermouth Buck. He'd been after her to make peace with her past. "I don't know that she needs me at home. She just asked me to come see her. I'm only staying the weekend."

A long pause followed. "You're welcome," Coop said finally. "I can see you're thankful I pulled strings. I thought you'd like to stay at the fire camp. You generally love working on equipment."

"Sorry. I'm sure I'll enjoy the work. All winter?"

He nodded. "We've got lots of parachutes to repair as well as routine maintenance and some fairly major repair on the buildings. You won't be bored."

His mention of parachutes brought back the last moments in the air with Allie. "What happened to her parachute? It was actually mine. And she said something strange, something about someone trying to kill me."

Coop's eyebrows arched. "Maybe she was joking. We haven't looked at the chute yet. I'll try to examine it tomorrow."

"Seemed a poor time for a joke. Allie had just survived death."

"You know as well as I do that Allie has a warped sense of humor." Coop hesitated and glanced at Allie's bed. "Her parents are on their way from Phoenix."

"Any word from the hospital?" Coop dropped his gaze, and her heart sank. "What is it?" she whispered.

"She's out of surgery, but . . ."

"She's not going to make it?"

"They think she'll live." He reached down and scratched Spirit on the head.

"Look at me, Coop. What's wrong with her?"

He raised his gaze then. "May be brain damage. They won't know until she wakes up."

CHAPTER 2

There had been no change in Allie's condition. Tess clicked off her cell phone and accelerated. The Jeep Cherokee slued sideways in the loose gravel on a road barely wide enough to allow it to pass. Her knuckles white, Tess gripped the leather-wrapped steering wheel and wrestled the vehicle back to the center of the road. She glanced in the rearview mirror at the horse trailer she pulled.

"Sorry, Wildfire," she whispered. Her hands and tongue felt gritty from the same ochre dust that coated the trailer's gray exterior. *Coming home.* The words sounded empty to her when she wanted nothing more than to go back to her familiar, stark barracks. She glanced at the landscape of rolling hills pocketed with caves. The turnoff to the Zane Grey cabin zipped by, and she pulled to the side of the road. She thought she remembered this shortcut, but she'd gotten confused at the fork by the river, and now she was nearly an hour late. At the top of the hill on Rim Trail, she pulled to the berm and looked down into the green valley dotted with grazing cattle and horses. Rolling down her window, she leaned her head into the wind and caught the scent of manure and grass, a calming aroma that caused her to smile in spite of her anxiety.

The ranch below her stretched as far as her gaze could see. The road split three ways here. At the end of the track to her right was the small cabin where her aunt lived on her share of five hundred acres. Straight ahead was the small house where Stevie and Paul had lived when they were first married. Tess too. But the track to the left was a lane she hadn't traveled in twelve years. She couldn't see the main ranch house from here, and she didn't want to, but that was where she must go. If only Stevie hadn't insisted on moving back in. Tess would gladly have taken the straight lane to the tiny cabin near the woods.

Tess pulled her head back into the cab, dropped the Cherokee into drive, and continued on. The lane was unchanged. She almost expected to see her dad come over the embankment on Whistles, his Arabian mare. But they were both gone, ashes now. She inhaled deeply as the Jeep crested the hill, and she looked down on the ranch buildings. There it was. Without allowing herself to think, she pressed her foot to the accelerator and drove down to the house. She wouldn't look where the barn used to be. Not yet.

Dust settled around the Jeep as she parked in front of the old adobe-style ranch house. There it was after all these years. Her gaze traveled the landscape. She'd dreamed on that porch, played in the orchard as a child, climbed the big oak tree out front. A familiar ache started under her breastbone and moved up her chest, exerting a suffocating pressure. She loved this house, yet it looked hostile to her now. The bay windows seemed to peer back at her, jeering as though they saw her pain and laughed.

Why had she agreed to come? She should have insisted Stevie tell her what this was all about over the phone. She slammed the Jeep's door behind her and wiped her dusty hands on the seat of her jeans.

"Some things never change," a deep voice behind her said. "You're still running late."

She sometimes heard that voice in the night in her dreams. Or more accurately, nightmares. Tess pinned a fake smile to her lips and forced herself to turn. "Hello, Chase," she said, determined to sound carefree and natural. Her gaze scanned his dusty boots up to the faded denim jeans and T-shirt. The fierce Arizona sun hadn't managed to wash out his vivid blue eyes as they looked her over from under his tan cowboy hat.

"You've got a new hat." Sheesh, could she say anything more lame? She wished she could spit the dust from her tongue, but it wouldn't be ladylike, and while she hardly considered herself a girly-girl, she wasn't about to let Chase Huston sense even an ounce of weakness. Why didn't he say something? He stared her down as if he were trying to look under her skin and into her soul. Tiny new lines crouched at the edges of his eyes, and she spotted a weary droop to his lips. Maybe she could hold her own against him this time.

She took a step toward him, but he didn't move. If she dared, she'd stick her tongue out at him. "Are you going to hug me or just stare?"

He unbent then, pulling his hands from the pockets of his jeans. They exchanged a brief hug, but Tess felt she was embracing a saguaro. She probably should have kept her distance, but she couldn't resist the desire to unsettle him just a little.

"I'm surprised you showed your face," he said. "I had a bet going with Whip that you'd make some lame excuse at the last minute and not show up. You're late."

"I took a wrong turn."

"More likely a shortcut that got you lost. When will you learn shortcuts are of the devil?" He flashed white teeth in a grin.

He knew her too well. She stepped away from him. She nodded toward the horse trailer. "Would you turn Wildfire out into the pasture?"

"Yeah, I guess."

"Stevie in the house?"

"In her bedroom. Your parents' old room," he amended.

Tess took two steps toward the house before his words sank in. "In bed? At eleven in the morning? What's wrong?" She didn't wait for an answer, but stepped into the shade of the overhanging portico. Hummingbirds flitted away from the feeder as she passed, and their movement stirred the brilliant cardinal flowers that attracted the hummers. Her mother had loved the little birds flocking around the porch. She clamped off the memory before it could hurt her.

Crossing the threshold onto the terra-cotta tile felt like going through a time portal. The scent of the pine boughs Stevie and their mother liked hanging around the house brought all the memories of home rushing back. Everything in her wanted to turn and leave.

She took a moment to glance around the large open living space. Dead pine needles lay littered around the bough on top of the TV, and a dry odor of decay lay under the fragrance of pine. Stevie's house was usually spotless. What was going on here?

"Stevie?" Tess stepped down the hall lined with pictures of her and her sister from birth through high school. It was as if the air itself pushed against her and slowed her movements until she reached the bedroom. An invisible barrier seemed to guard the oak door. When she was a little girl, she used to crawl into bed with her mother. Her dad was usually up and out the door by the time she and Stevie awoke. Her mom would fix him breakfast, then go back to bed for a little while. When Tess poked her head in, her mom would throw back the covers and open her arms, and Tess would scramble into them.

There would be no welcoming smile from her mother today. Tess could almost hear the crackle of the fire that night so long ago, could almost smell the smoke. She looked at the closed door. Her hand hovered over the doorknob. What would she find inside? Tess often called early in the morning, and Stevie was always up getting ready to head to the pasture. Even after Mindy was born, Stevie would be in the kitchen fixing breakfast by six.

She cleared her hoarse voice and tapped on the door. "Stevie? It's me. Are you awake?"

"Tess, get in here so I can hug you."

Her sister sounded normal, and the pressure pushing Tess away from the door eased. Tess twisted the doorknob and peeked inside. The room looked nothing like it had when her parents were alive, and Stevie lay propped against the pillows with her Bible in her hand. A gray pallor pinched the color from her cheeks, and she looked like she'd gained at least twenty pounds, but her smile welcomed Tess. She held out her hands. "Come here right now."

Tess flew into her sister's embrace. In spite of the room's warmth, Stevie's skin was cold and dry. She held Tess in a fierce hug that brought tears surging to Tess's eyes. She'd stayed away too long. Tess hung onto Stevie even after her sister let go.

Stevie grasped Tess's shoulders and pushed her away to look in her face. "You look marvelous, Tessie. I'm so glad to see you. Mindy will be thrilled. She's in the back meadow with her dad."

"I can't wait to see her." She sat on the edge of the bed and took her sister's hand. "What's wrong with you, Stevie?" she asked, keeping her voice soft.

Stevie's fingers tightened on hers. She licked her lips. "I'm going to be fine, Tessie. Don't look so scared. We've had few rough weeks, but it's getting better. I'm not dying or anything."

"You're still not saying what it is. Is it . . . " She couldn't say the word *cancer.*

"I'm fine. Really." Stevie gave Tess's fingers a gentle squeeze. "I've got lupus. Isn't that just my luck? A disease that hates heat when I live in Arizona."

"Lupus?" Tess wasn't sure what it was, though she'd heard of it. It was some kind of autoimmune disease, wasn't it?

"I know I look like the Pillsbury Doughboy, but it's the steroids they have me on. I'm feeling much better, but fatigue still knocks me down at times. I'd hoped to meet you at the door." Stevie's eyelids were half-closed, and she was beginning to slur her words.

At least it wasn't cancer. Tess patted Stevie's hand. "You need to sleep for a while. I think I'll go see Mindy and Paul."

Stevie's eyes popped open. "Did you see Chase?"

"Briefly. He was his usual charming self, though he did agree to pasture Wildfire for me. Are you sure you don't mind me bringing Wildfire home for a while? It seemed reasonable since I'm going to be living so close."

"Of course it is." Stevie's lids drooped again. "I don't know why you resent Chase so much."

You mean other than the fact he took my place? Tess didn't say the words. She tiptoed from the room and closed the door. Backing away, the heel of her boot caught a loose tile, and she started to fall. Hard hands steadied her, and the scent of aftershave—Stetson—

told her whose. Chase, sneaking up on her as usual. Jerking away, she turned to face him.

Crossing her arms over her chest, she corralled her anger and managed to speak civilly. "Why didn't you tell me she was so sick?"

"If you'd been any kind of sister, you would have seen it for yourself. But you're too busy running."

Though his words stung, she lifted her chin and managed not to flinch. "It's not like I goof off, Chase. Do you have any idea how many fires I've fought, how many lives I've helped save this year?" She winced at how boastful her words sounded.

"Tess Masterson, superhero. You still don't get it, do you? Sometimes the bravest thing we do is get out of bed in the morning and do our duty by the ones we love. It's easy to run away from responsibility."

"I've never run away!" Conscious of her sleeping sister, Tess lowered her voice. "You won, isn't that enough for you, Chase?" She stomped past him and headed for the front door. She heard his boots clicking on the tile as he came behind her.

Quickening her pace, she flung open the screen door and ran to her Jeep. His boot heels pounded after her, but she reached her SUV first and flung herself under the wheel. She clicked the lock as he put his hand on the door. He pounded on the window. Hoping to irritate him, she flashed a victory smile as she drove away in a plume of red dust. She should be bigger than that, able to rise above his jibes. Why did he bring out her childish side? Another reason to hate him.

Chase polished the metal on his tack hard enough to wear off the plating. Tess hadn't gotten anymore likeable. She'd been a burr under his saddle from the day he first clapped eyes on her. With her freckled face and reddish-blonde hair tied up in a ponytail, she'd looked him over as if he were a clump of manure on her boot. Princess of all she surveyed, apple of her father's eye, she rarely spoke to him at the supper table, and she ordered him around like a lackey when she was on the ranch. As far as she was concerned, the poor foster kid who showed up with only the clothes on his back didn't deserve to wipe her boots.

"You look mad enough to stomp a scorpion." Whip Masterson hefted a saddle onto the hook by the door, then sat down and pulled off his boot. Whip was Tess and Stevie's second cousin, and though his official title was cowboss, he ran the ranch behind the scenes of everything the rest of them did.

"I could stomp a whole nest of them barefoot."

Whip's toe poked through one of the holes in his sock. He dumped out a rock and pulled the boot back on. "Queenie here?"

"How did you know?"

"I haven't seen that look on your face in a coon's age. I reckon you two already butted heads."

"She's going to live up to her responsibilities this time if I have to hogtie her to the fence post. You only stick up for her because she's family."

Whip took a pack of cigarettes out of his shirt pocket and shook out one. "'Envy is rottenness to the bones,'" he said.

Chase rolled his eyes. Whip knew more proverbs than the preacher. "Meaning what? That I'm *jealous* of Tess? Now you're talking crazy."

"That's been the problem between the two of you all along. You each think the other got more of Garrett Masterson when there was enough to share. Cut her some slack, Chase. She had some growing up to do, I ain't denying that, but she's been doing a man's job out there fighting wildfires. You seen the news stories, same as me. Folks been talking about how fearless she is. She could have turned into some kind of la-de-da female with no thought in her head but fancy fingernails and new clothes."

"Her dad would have expected her to stay by the stuff and help work the ranch." Just thinking about the way Tess ran away made him clench his teeth and want to snarl. "Her leaving put us in a bind. The least she could do now is to stay through calving season and help us get on our feet."

"You've never seen that gal clearly." Whip blew a curl of smoke toward Chase. "Not many gals stick by the stuff in fire school. When Coop offered her the job, I figured she'd see it through. She had a powerful amount of guilt to work off. The gal's got grit."

"Grit—ha! *Abrasive* would be a better word." Chase eyed Whip. "Didn't you ever feel jealous that Garrett inherited the ranch when you had just as much right to it? Now Tess has shares and you don't, and you work harder than anybody."

"Mebbe a time or two," Whip said. "But like I said, 'A sound heart is life to the body, but envy is rottenness to the bones.' I ain't complaining about my lot."

That made Whip the better man, then. Chase stood and stalked to the wooden crate by the door where the coffeepot sat. He poured out coffee that smelled strong and stale. He gulped down the tepid liquid and grimaced.

Whip followed him to the coffee. "Give me a cup of that poison." He took the cup Chase handed over, then stared at him. "You ever heard the old adage about coaxing more bees with honey than vinegar? I seen the way you charm the ladies at the town dance. You might try a little of that on Tess. She might meet you halfway if you give her a chance."

Chase stopped with the coffee cup at his lips and stared at Whip. The old man had been out in the sun too long. "Are you talking about *romancing* Tess Masterson? I'd rather take a scorpion to my bed."

Whip took a sip of coffee and a drag on the cigarette. "I ain't talking about marrying her. But you could make a friend of her. No sense in being enemies."

"We've been enemies since she told her dad I shoved her into the manure pile."

"That wasn't no lie."

"She deserved it, after dumping the stuff in my boots! But I got punished for something that she started." Aware of how childish he was sounding, Chase cleared his throat.

"Go easy on Queenie, Chase. This is the first time in twelve years she's set foot on the ground where her parents died."

"She should have come back sooner. Stevie and Paul moved up to the main house a year ago."

"You won't get no argument from me on that. Stevie should have brought Tess here right away and made her face facts. I never did think it was too smart of them to move into that little cabin clear across the way. It don't do nobody no good to ignore pain. 'Whoever hides hatred has lying lips.' Queenie put on a smiling face, but she never has got over that fire."

"That's all in the past. The point is that we could never be friends. We've got too much baggage behind us." He swilled the last of the coffee and put the cup on the crate. "If she thinks she can just breeze in here and breeze out again when the weekend is over, she's about to find out different."

CHAPTER 3

*T*ess drove toward the back pasture, then changed her mind and circled around to the backside of the orchard. Just beyond the garden was the site of the old barn. Though grass covered the site now, she knew about the charred remains that lay under the green carpet. Three people died here that day—her parents and her uncle Giles had all been trapped by the blaze. She knew she should get out and go over to pray there or something, but her limbs refused to obey her will. What would it take to make her peace with their deaths? She didn't know if it would ever happen.

Her hand found the door handle, and she pulled it. The door opened, and the scent of apples from the orchard blew inside the Jeep. Moving like an old woman, she planted her feet on the pebbled ground. It had been twelve years since she last stood here, but not a week went by that she didn't think of that day. The rocks crunched under her steps as she moved nearer. No matter how many homes or lives she saved, she had failed to save the most important.

She stopped a good fifty feet from the mound of green, unable to get any closer. An invisible barrier blocked her advance. She didn't want to relive that day. Maybe she'd never be able to move past it. She turned and went back to her Jeep, sans horse trailer. Chase had unhitched the trailer and parked it against the side of the barn. She would have to thank him.

She drove out to the pasture past familiar hills and valleys and parked beside Paul's truck. The October sun felt warm on her arms when she got out. She'd been cold ever since she saw her sister. She scanned the horizon for her horse. "Hey, Paul," she said to her brother-in-law.

His brown hair had thinned since Tess saw him last. It was grizzled too, a bit like Spirit's with the same coarse texture. Now forty, he'd filled out some, but it looked good on him. How long had it been— five years? Six? He didn't usually come with Mindy and Stevie to see her at her home in Tucson. She put her fingers in her mouth and blew out a piercing whistle. Wildfire would be sure to hear it.

"Idiotic animal thinks he rules the pasture." Paul Granger put one pointed boot onto the fence rail. "If he breaks down the fence, it will be your job to fix it, not mine."

"He's the king and knows it." She meant it as a joke, but when Paul frowned, she hurried to change the subject. "Where's Mindy? I thought she was out here with you. I'm eager to see her."

"She fell asleep on the way out. I left her in the truck."

"I'll get her." Tess started to turn toward the battered truck sitting under an oak tree.

Paul grabbed her arm. "She's fine. If you're going to be poking around for a while, I'm not going to have you bucking my authority at every turn, Tess. It's going to be different this time, or you can just turn around and go home."

"Around for a while? What are you talking about? I have to be back to work on Monday." Tess pulled away. Maybe he could boss her sister around, but Tess wasn't about to suffer quietly under Paul's tyranny. She had no choice when she was a teenager, but she was twenty-seven now, far past the age where he had any say over what she said or did.

Paul looked away. "I guess you haven't talked to Stevie," he muttered. "You'd better talk to her. I was against it from the start."

She wasn't staying here. No way. If that's what this was all about, they could forget it. Her sister's wan, bloated face rose in her memory. If Stevie needed her, how could she say no?

She stared into Paul's face. "Against what?"

Before Paul could answer, a whinny sounded from the stand of aspen trees north of the pasture. Tess turned to see Wildfire flying across the pasture toward her. A beautiful bay, his black tail streamed behind him, and his black mane rippled in the wind. The color of a penny, his thick coat was starting to thicken with winter growth. He snorted and flicked his ears when he saw her. Dirt flung up as his hooves ground to a stop in front of her. He'd come into the promise he bore the first time she laid eyes on him.

She climbed the fence and threw her arms around him. Inhaling the earthy horse scent of him, she tangled the fingers of her right hand in his mane while her left hand held out a sugar cube. His soft lips whispered over her palm as he sucked up the sugar. Tess rubbed his neck. "Good boy, Wildfire." She tried to spend time with him every week, but firefighting made that an elusive goal in summertime. He'd wanted to run when she loaded him this morning, but there was no time.

Twisting his mane in her hand, she vaulted onto his back. Once she was seated, she turned him back into the pasture and pressed her knees against his flank. At the signal, he took off across the meadow. Cantering on the back of Wildfire, Tess was able to forget the problems she sensed were waiting for her. Around and around she galloped across the pasture with Wildfire's hooves kicking up dust behind them. If she closed her eyes, she could imagine she was rushing through the air with a parachute strapped to her back. She and the horse melded into one, and she could almost hear God's shout of delight in her head, the same sense of wonder and awe she felt when she was jumping into a fire.

When they were both winded, she slowed him to a walk under the cover of tall pine trees. "We have to go back, Wildfire," she whispered. She didn't want to leave here, didn't want to face what awaited her at the house. They turned to head back to where Paul stood watching. Tess sniffed the air. Was that smoke? She glanced around the pine-strewn ground and peered into the forest's recesses, but she didn't see anything.

Maybe it was a camper. "Hello?" Wildfire snorted and she stilled him with a touch on his neck. Straining her ears, she listened. Wind soughed in the pines, and she heard a squirrel chatter from a nearby oak tree. Still, she sensed rather than heard another presence.

Her back prickled. "Hello? Is anyone there?" Only the caw of a crow answered. A rustle past her ears made her flinch, but it was only a flock of startled blue jays. The smoke smell grew stronger, then she saw the smudge in the clear air. A small fire was beginning to burn at the base of a pine tree. She slid off Wildfire's back and ran to the tree. Dry needles had been piled up, and a match lay in the middle. She kicked the needles apart and stomped on the fire. Her boots smothered the flames.

Once it was extinguished, she glanced around. The match told her the fire had been deliberately set. But why? A riffle of white caught her attention. The wind whipped a paper nailed to the tree. "Who's there?" The skin on her neck constricted. Looking closely through the underbrush, she saw something shuffle, then a large animal moved off. She thought it was a wolf, but it moved strangely.

She reached out and jerked loose the paper. It was still white and crisp, so she didn't think it had been here long. It was folded into fourths. She unfolded it and stared at the writing. The black words printed in block letters made no sense. She looked around again, saw no one, and reread it.

LET THE DANCE BEGIN.

What did it mean? Holding it in two fingers to avoid leaving any more of her prints on the paper than she already had, she started across the pasture with Wildfire following at her heels. Maybe Paul had seen or heard something.

Her cell phone rang, and Wildfire snorted and pranced away. Tess dug it out. Caller ID indicated the fire camp. A tightness spread over her chest. *Please God, let Allie be all right.* "Tess here."

Buck Carter's deep voice was on the other end. "Hey, Tess, where are you?"

He sounded up. At least he wasn't calling with bad news about Allie. "In the field by the Bar Q. I'm about to head back to the house and see if Stevie is ready to tell me why she called me home. I just stomped out a small fire. It's weird—I think someone deliberately set it."

"Maybe just a careless camper."

"It was on our property. There shouldn't be any campers out here."

"So you haven't found out what Stevie wants?"

"Not yet."

A heavy sigh came from the other end of the phone. "You need to deal with this, Tess."

Tess bristled. Buck needed to quit pushing. "There's nothing here to deal with. It's a short visit, and then I'm getting back to work. How's Allie?" The silence stretched out between them. She ducked her head and pressed the cell phone tighter to her ear. "Buck?"

"Yeah." His voice deepened. "She's slipped into a coma."

Tess closed her eyes and pressed her fingers to her temples.

"Tess? Are you there?"

"I'm here," she whispered. "She didn't want to jump, Buck. I talked her into it. She was ready to quit, get out of wildfire work. I begged her to take one more jump."

"You didn't cause the chute to fail."

The chute. "She was wearing *my* chute. Hey, did you hear what Coop found out about the malfunction? Allie said something as we were falling about someone trying to kill me." Tess laughed at how that sounded now. "Isn't that ridiculous?"

"I don't know if Coop had a chance to check it out yet. I'll ask him. Hey, the other reason I was calling was to let you know I agreed to work with you and Flint here at the Mogollon Fire Station for the next month. My sister can outfit any hunters who come through for now. I couldn't pass up the chance for demolition. Our first job is going to be gutting and redoing the barracks."

Tess grinned at the boyish excitement in his voice. Typical guy to want to demolish something. Then his words penetrated. "Where are we all going to sleep if the barracks are gutted?"

Buck cleared his throat. "We were hoping there might be room for all of us at the ranch."

"There isn't," Tess said, her fingers tightening on the phone. "I'll call the station and tell them we need rooms. They'll have to find us something."

The signal hummed for several long moments before Buck finally answered. "Whatever you say. Stevie will be disappointed."

"I don't want to add to her burden. She was in bed when I got here and isn't feeling well. She has lupus, Buck. You have any idea what that is? I was going to look it up on the computer, but I haven't had a chance yet." *Coward.* Buck was smart enough to know she was blowing smoke. He'd see right through it. Staying at the ranch would ease Stevie's burden, not add to it.

"Lupus?" His voice was sharp. "That's pretty serious, I think."

"I thought it might be, especially with her being in bed in the middle of the morning." She saw Mindy get out of Paul's truck and come running toward her. "I have to go. I'll give you and Flint a call after I try to see Allie." She clicked off the phone and stood, realizing she'd put off the inevitable as long as she could. It was time to find out why Stevie had summoned her.

Mindy leaned back against Tess's chest as the two rode into the yard on Wildfire's back. It had been all Tess could do to talk Paul into letting her take her niece up on the horse. She would never understand his unreasonable dislike of her horse. He claimed Wildfire was spoiled and untrustworthy, but she often wondered if he saw her horse as an extension of her.

"Hold on and I'll lift you down," she told Mindy. The five-year-old looked just like Tess as a child. Reddish-gold curls hung to her shoulders, and big greenish-gold eyes topped round cheeks. Tess slid to the ground and lifted the little girl off the horse.

Mindy planted a wet kiss on her cheek. "I love you, Aunt Tessie. Why didn't you come see me before? I wanted to show you my new wallpaper. It's got horses in it."

"Your mommy always liked to go shopping in Tucson, so it was more fun to meet there."

"Daddy said it was because you were selfish. Becca calls me selfish when I don't let her play with my dolls. You always share your ice cream with me, so I don't think you're selfish."

Tess blinked back the sudden moisture in her eyes. Mindy's complete faith in her made her feel like an imposter. She cuddled her niece, then set her on the red dirt. "How about you wash up while I go see your mommy? Then you can show me your room." How was she going to make it until Monday when every nerve screamed for her to get in the Jeep and keep trucking west? She watched Mindy scamper off, then started for the house. She was waylaid before she'd taken three steps.

Lifted off her feet and swung around, she laughed when she felt the tickle of whispers against her cheek. "Whip, you old codger, put me down. I'm too big for you to be lifting around now." He set her down, and she turned to hug him.

"You'll never be that big," he said, planting a kiss on her cheek. His walrus mustache was grayer than she remembered, matching the colorless wisps of hair that escaped his cowboy hat. He still wore the suspenders she'd gotten him for Christmas twelve years ago, though they looked stained and tattered.

She made a mental note to find him a new pair. "Who told you I was here?"

"Recognized the expression on Chase's face," he said, winking slyly.

Her smile faded. "I'm not any happier about my returning than he is."

"It's time you come home, Queenie. Your sis needs you."

"Stevie will be fine. She bounces back from everything."

"Not this time." He took off his hat and slapped the dust from it. His gray hair was thinner now, and a bald spot crowned his head. "You haven't looked close enough."

Tess sank her nails into her palms. Stevie had to be fine. Tess wouldn't accept anything else. Her sister was the one stable rock in her life. Everything else she loved had been torn from her. And Stevie was the strongest person she knew. If anyone could overcome a physical ailment, Stevie could.

"From the way you're chewin' your lip, I reckon you plan to run off, but don't do it, Queenie. Not this time. You're a grown woman now. It's time you stepped up and quit lettin' your sis carry the whole burden."

Tess refused to accept that guilt. Her sister had chosen the life she lived with no expectations of Tess. Tess craved the daily adrenaline rush she got from battling the elements and taming a forest fire. "Stevie loves ranch life. She was born for delivering calves and colts. I can't come back. I've moved on."

"Girlie, you got to stop runnin' someday. Fightin' them fires just keeps you from thinkin' too hard. I reckon this is gonna make you stop and take stock. 'There is a way that seems right to a man, but its end is the way of death.'"

Her offense softened, and she kissed Whip's cheek again. He meant well with his proverbs and advice, but he didn't understand. "I'd better go talk to Stevie."

CHAPTER 4

Chase put the last of his tools in the cabinet at the back of the barn. Paul entered and blocked the sunshine streaming through the window. The displeasure on his face made Chase lock the cabinet with slow deliberation.

Paul stood with his hands on his hips and his hat tipped back from his broad forehead. "I told you I wanted those calves cut this morning. This afternoon I'd planned to have you work on reroofing the chicken coop."

"I had to take care of getting the back paddock fence repaired," Chase said, keeping his voice even. "The calves will wait. They're plenty young yet."

Paul's temper flashed in his eyes. "Stevie isn't here today to make excuses for your defiance, Huston. You have to answer to me now."

Chase didn't let himself react. The man was a church deacon and his boss, both reasons to show him deference.

Paul stopped at the barn door and turned. "And keep an eye on Wildfire. I'm going to insist Tess either sell that horse or take him with her when she goes. He's too much upkeep when no one can ride him but her."

"She won't sell him."

"It would sure help us out if she would. That animal is worth a fortune." Paul took down a bridle from the tack wall and stepped out of the barn.

"Good luck with that," Chase muttered. "No one ever told Tess Masterson what to do." He knew he was out of sorts, but he was in no mood to talk himself out of it. He'd had enough dealings with Tess to know her arrival was sure to put the household in an uproar. And Stevie always took her side, so Paul had no chance of bucking the sisters. Chase didn't either. Maybe that was the real reason for his disgruntlement.

He stopped to check on the injured horse. Stocking had cut herself last week and gone lame. His touch gentled the mare, and he rubbed a salve he'd mixed onto her wound. It was looking much better. The vet would be pleased. With a final pat on her withers, he picked up a pitchfork and went to the haymow in the back of the barn and began to muck out the horse stalls. The dirty, matted hay was easy to pitch into the wagon, but he was sweaty and smelled like manure by the time he finished. Tossing the pitchfork into the corner, he strode to the tractor to pull the wagon out of the way. A form moved from the shadows under the barn's overhang, and Chase looked up.

"Hey, buddy." His brother Jimmy stepped out into the sun.

Chase stiffened. "What are you doing here?" His gaze traveled over his brother's shiny—and expensive—boots and up the stiff new jeans. How had Jimmy afforded them? Chase wasn't sure he wanted to know.

"I thought you'd be happy to see me." Jimmy strolled toward the tractor and stopped three feet from Chase. "I should have known better." His mouth drooped.

Even though Chase knew his brother's expression was an effort to manipulate him, it was hard to evade the guilt he knew Jimmy meant to invoke. "What do you want, Jimmy?"

Jimmy wasn't really a bad kid, but he'd fallen in with the wrong crowd in his teens. He was twenty-five now, a sullen contradiction of sweetness and spite. Chase wished he could take Jimmy by the collar and shake some sense into him.

"Can I bunk with you for a few days?" Jimmy looked past Chase toward the road as if he were watching for a vehicle.

Chase caught the worried tone in Jimmy's voice. "Who are you hiding from?"

Jimmy held out his hands with the palms up. "I'm not hiding. I just thought we'd spend a few days together."

"Have you been selling meth again?" Chase watched his brother's eyes. When they flickered, he knew something bad was up. "I told you to stay away from those guys, Jimmy. You're going to end up in prison. Or dead."

"Yeah, yeah, can the sermon." Jimmy's face reddened. "So can I stay or not?"

Chase knew he should exercise tough love on his brother and refuse to help, but how could he say no to his own flesh and blood? "For how long?"

Jimmy's eyes gleamed. "No longer than a week."

Maybe he could get through to his brother in that time, get him some help. He could ask Pastor Richmond to stop by and have a talk with Jimmy. God might get through to his brother yet. If not for the grace of God, Chase would be in the same situation.

Jimmy jerked a thumb toward the house. "Her ladyship is back?"

"For the weekend. She'll be off getting adulation for her firefighting."

"I can't believe she'd actually get her hands dirty."

"To give the devil her due, she never was afraid of hard work. She can carry hay with the best man in my stockyard. What she craves is the limelight. You don't get many atta-boys on a ranch in the middle of nowhere." He shouldn't be talking about her like this. Tess wasn't as spoiled as he tried to make her sound, but they'd been enemies so long it was hard to separate the good from the bad.

"Remember that time I put the rattler under her bed?" Jimmy's grin was all boy.

"If it hadn't been dead, you would have been."

"Whoo-ee, she screamed like a Comanche."

"It was the straw that caved in the haymow," Chase reminded him. "If you'd minded your manners, you never would have been sent to Diamond's."

Jimmy's smile faded. "I hated that man," he muttered. "No one's killed him yet—can you believe it?"

Chase didn't like to hear his brother talk like that. He nodded at the backpack on the ground. "That all you have?"

Jimmy hefted it to his shoulder. "Yep."

Chase led the way to the bunkhouse and prayed his brother would stay under the radar this time. The last thing he needed was for Tess and Paul both to be on his case about Jimmy.

The aroma of chocolate-chip cookies wafted out the screen door. Tess found her sister in the kitchen sliding cookies onto a cooling rack. Mindy sat at the table. Stevie was still pale, but the red blotches on her face had faded. "Should you be out of bed?" Tess snagged a warm cookie and handed it to Mindy before grabbing one for herself.

"I'm feeling better. I just needed a nap. There's milk in the fridge." Stevie handed her an empty glass.

Tess went to the refrigerator, a mammoth commercial one that had to be at least twenty years old. She shook the milk jug to mix the cream with the milk and poured out two glasses. She relished the taste of unaltered milk straight from the cow, creamy and fresh. "Too bad I can't get this in the city." Taking the glasses of milk with her, she went to the scarred wooden table and handed Mindy her milk, then sat beside her and took another cookie.

Mindy got up and went to her mother. Grabbing her leg, she looked up. "Mommy, can I watch TV?"

"Don't grab me, Mindy." Stevie removed her daughter's hand from her leg. "You want to watch *Bright Eyes*?" Stevie disappeared through the kitchen door with Mindy.

Moments later, the TV began to play, and Tess heard the opening strum of the theme music. When Stevie returned to the kitchen, Tess pulled out a chair. "Sit down and rest. You look like a ghost." She reminded herself that Stevie was strong. "Are you going to tell me what's going on and why you called me home right now?"

Stevie sat down and took a cookie. "I'm sure you've heard of all the arsons we've had this past year. Small stuff, like empty buildings torched, some brush fires set that were quickly extinguished."

"I put out a fire a few minutes ago that looked like it had been deliberately set. In the back pasture."

"Good thing you saw it! There have been several incidents. We have a new sheriff, and he's been looking over past arson cases for a connection. You know him, Tess. Eric Curry, Brandon's older brother. You graduated with Brandon, didn't you?" She didn't wait for Tess's nod. "He noticed the fire here was ruled arson but never solved. He's got it in his head that the current fires are related to the old ones, and he's reopening our case."

This revelation wasn't what she'd been expecting. Tess had been steeling herself to resist a plea to help out at the ranch while her sister was sick. She redirected her thoughts. "What makes him think they're related?"

"Other small fires followed that one, a couple a year for the past twelve years. He thinks he sees a pattern. I say he's nuts, but he's plowing ahead with the investigation. You know something about arson investigation. Could you look at the evidence and convince him to leave us alone? I'm just not feeling well enough to deal with all that."

Tess had seen pictures of fire victims before, and the thought of seeing the photos of her parents' remains made her put down the cookie she held. "Don't ask me to do that, Stevie. You've never seen crime-scene photos. They're lurid."

Stevie leaned across the table and took her hand. "I just can't take any more, Tess. He needs to stop poking around." Her voice broke, and she swallowed hard. "Please, Tess, I—I didn't want to say anything, but my kidneys are failing. I may have to have a kidney transplant. I can't take any more right now—I just can't." She put her face in her hands and began to sob. "I just want it all to be over. I can't deal with the past and the present too."

Everything in Tess didn't want to go back to the fire that killed her parents, but she couldn't refuse her sister. "You've always been so strong, Stevie. Even when Mom and Dad died, you pitched in and ran the ranch, made sure I got into college, took care of everything. Don't you want to find out who killed our parents?"

"It's been twelve years, Tess. If there was any chance of finding the killer, I'd be all for it. But it's been too long. The trail is stone cold. I just want a little peace. Is that too much to ask?" She ran her hand over her pale face. "I'm tired of it all."

Tess slipped out of her chair to her knees and embraced her sister. "I'll do what I can, Stevie. You can have one of my kidneys if you need it." Stevie smelled like chocolate-chip cookies and fresh air, but underlying the pleasant aroma was something else, a sour smell. Her sister was really sick.

Tess hugged her tight, and Stevie clutched her in a grip that seemed almost desperate. "Thanks, Tess. I knew I could count on you." She finally pulled away and dabbed her eyes with a napkin she snagged from a holder in the center of the table.

"Is—is the ranch doing okay?" Tess wasn't sure she wanted to know. She might be expected to do something she wasn't comfortable with.

Stevie twisted the napkin. "I won't lie to you. My illness has hurt us. Chase has been struggling to get everything done, and you know how Paul rides him."

"I'm surprised they haven't killed one another yet. Have you had to pull them off one another like Dad always used to?"

A smile lifted the corners of Stevie's mouth. "A time or two. Paul never stomached the way Dad loved Chase any more than you did. And maybe it was harder for him. You always knew Dad loved you, but Paul. . ." She looked away.

"You have to admit Dad had good reason. Paul killed his prize bull."

"He didn't kill it! The bull was always getting out of the stall."

"Paul admitted he forgot to lock the gate. Dad lost ten thousand dollars, not to mention having to pay the trucker who hit it."

Stevie flushed. "He'd only worked here a month. Paul redeemed himself a thousand times over. You know that."

It probably accounted for Paul's uptight attention to every detail, much as she hated to admit it. "Yeah I know." Tess shouldn't be criticizing her sister's husband. "It's just that Paul didn't used to be quite so domineering."

"He's a good man." Stevie looked out the kitchen window. "When Sarah died—things changed."

Stevie didn't mention Sarah often. The memory of her niece's chubby face flashed through Tess's mind. Though Tess had been only sixteen, the morning they awakened to find the baby cold and lifeless in her crib was seared into her memory. So much tragedy. No wonder Stevie was tired.

"What about money?" Tess asked.

"The beef market has been down, so we're a little cash poor. We could use some extra help through calving season, but we can't afford to hire anyone right now." Stevie bit the cuticle on her index finger.

"Is the ranch in serious trouble?" Tess asked.

Stevie's gaze skittered away. "We'll be fine."

Tess spoke quickly before she could change her mind. "I could help out for a while, check out the arson investigation and see what I can find in my off time. I've been assigned to the Mogollon fire camp, so I can come over evenings and weekends."

Stevie's gaze returned to Tess's eyes, and an eager smile lifted her pallor. "Could you stay here then, since you're stationed so close?"

Tess almost said no. The last thing she wanted was to have to face that dark scar in the backyard every day, but with her sister's pleading gaze on her, she found herself nodding. "I could, I guess." She'd just told Buck there was no way she was staying, and now here she was agreeing. "I've got a couple of friends who need a place to bunk, too, since we're going to be redoing the barracks. Is there room in the bunkhouse for two more? I bet they'd help out on the weekends and after hours too." If she had their company, she could endure staying here.

"There's oodles of room." Stevie's eyes began to gleam with hope. "I knew I could count on you, Tess."

Tess saw Chase through the window. He and his brother Jimmy had just stepped out of the bunkhouse. "How's Chase going to take having me for a boss?" She couldn't wait to see the look on his face. Stevie's mouth grew pinched. She didn't say anything. "What is it?" Tess wanted to know.

"I don't need another foreman, Tess, I need a ranch hand. The ranch hands all report to Chase."

Tess was shaking her head before her sister finished the sentence. "I'm not taking orders from Chase Huston. No way."

"Why can't you just try to get along with him, Tess, just this once? He's a great guy. I've never understood why you two fight so much."

"And I've never understood how you could stand the sight of him," Tess fired back. "Our father left a share of the ranch to him, a foster kid who was in one scrap after another. He came here for what he could get, and got it too. Have you ever thought that maybe *he* set the fire that killed our parents?" She put her hand over her mouth when she saw Stevie's stricken expression.

Stevie's eyes flashed. "Chase had nothing to do with the fire."

"I know. I didn't really mean it. But where was he that day? He never explained where he was. He was supposed to be mucking out the stables."

"I blame Dad for the rivalry between you two. He never should have said Chase was the son he always wanted. It never affected me, but it made you feel Dad thought we'd failed him in some way."

"Don't talk about Dad like that. He was a good man."

"Of course he was a good man, but he was just a man. You need to let him down off that pedestal." Stevie tossed her mangled napkin in the trash. "Try to make a fresh start with Chase. I think he'll meet you halfway. You've both grown up and matured."

Tess blinked rapidly and turned her head away. "Until Chase came, Dad and I rode the ranch together—Dad took you and me along when he wanted to go brand the cattle. Chase changed everything. Dad took Chase when he wanted to go check out the back pasture for strays. It was Chase who went to town with him. I don't get why that never bothered you." She knew jealousy was wrong, but right now, she didn't care.

"I loved Chase like a brother from the first week he came, Tess. Didn't you always feel a lack that we didn't have a brother? I did. And it gave me joy to see Dad so happy."

"I'm not that big, I guess. I just saw that he took our place."

"Try to see his good points. There are plenty of them. You could be friends if you tried."

"You're asking too much. I'll work hard, but don't ask me to like him. I'll move my things into the spare room tomorrow." Tess stood and walked away. She couldn't stand listening to her sister defend Chase. The man had ruined her life. Nothing would change the hatred she felt for him. He might fool other people, but she knew the real Chase Huston. He was a conniving, cheating coyote.

CHAPTER 5

I love the mesmerizing sway of flames, the crackling sound of consumed wood, and especially the smell of the burn. The hands down at the ranch are heating the irons to brand the calves, and the wind brings the scent of smoke to me. Where there's smoke there's fire, and I relish the thought of seeing the flames. I draw deep. The aroma is like a noose around my neck, pulling me to be a spectator to its power. More potent than perfume, the scent makes my heart race. I can feel it fluttering like a bird trapped by a forest fire as my gaze alights on the campfire's flame.

Fire is like an animal, wild and untamed, and it carries the possibility of danger, like a puma that might spring on its trainer. Watching this tiny campfire, I long to set it free to run along the ground to the barn. I imagine the structure with flames licking the sky. The beauty of the fire inherent, its power masterful, spreading out to claim the landscape. And I hold the key. I lift a match to the sky. I hold the key to its power.

Only when the flame begins to scorch my fingers can I bring myself to drop the match to the ground. It smolders a moment, and I hold my breath as I wait to see if it will take hold of the dry needles at my feet. But no, the flame is too far gone by the time it lands. One tiny puff of smoke, and it goes cold. I fondle the matchbox in my pocket. There is always another opportunity. My mouth lifts at the thought, and I turn to look again at the ranch.

Tess was out there a little while ago—for the first time in years. From my vantage point on top of Mogollon Rim, I watched her lean on the fence. Her piercing whistle brought me pleasure. It's a pity my plan will cause her such pain. She should be where her smokejumping buddy is now. The Mastersons and the rest of their neighbors must pay for their sins, and I have the task of seeing justice through. Then I will forgive them. Forgiveness can't take place before justice is meted out. Justice allows forgiveness.

My gaze returns to the flame. Someday I will have the courage to dance with the fire myself. That dance will end with my death, but what better way to die than in the embrace of the thing I love the most? A cleansing, holy flame is a lovely thing.

Tess barely slept, and in the morning her eyes felt gritty and hot. She dropped Stevie at her doctor's, then drove through the Payson streets. The little burg had grown since she was here last. Highway 87, otherwise known as the Beeline, trailed north from Phoenix through the town streets. It has been billed as one of the three healthiest places to live because of the clean air, and Tess had always loved the sense of a bygone era in the town. People waved to her, and she had a sense of déjà vu, as though she had segued back in time to a place of dim memories, a time when she was a little girl and thought all of life was like a Zane Grey novel. Sometimes there was no happy ending, only a determined forging ahead to right a wrong.

The hospital parking lot was nearly full, but she was lucky enough to find a spot near the front of the building. She peered up the height of the building and wondered which room Allie was in. Clutching the vase of flowers, she went inside and was directed to the second floor.

Allie's door was only open a crack. Tess peered through the slit and saw Allie lying in the bed. Tubes and lines to machines snaked around her. Her eyes were closed. Tess's throat constricted, but she pushed open the door and stepped inside. The scent of antiseptic assaulted her as she moved closer.

Tess stood at the bed and stared at her friend. Allie's face was so bruised and swollen she was barely recognizable. A gauze bandage covered her forehead. Her lids pulsed as though she was dreaming. Tess hoped the dream was more pleasant than the reality. Tess set the flowers on the table. At the slight clunk, Allie's eyes opened. She stared into Tess's face. Her lips curved into a welcoming smile that made Tess smile in return. Buck must have been wrong. She wasn't in a coma.

But the dreamy expression in Allie's eyes vanished, and the stare grew fixed.

"What are you doing here? The nurses were told not to let you in." Tess turned to see Joe Stinson, Allie's father. "Did you want to come see your handiwork?" His dark eyes were rimmed with red, and his denim shirt looked like it had been slept in. Tufts of black hair stood on end as though he'd recently raked his hands through it.

"I'm just thankful she's alive. I'm praying she pulls out of this." Tess said.

"*Alive?* You call this alive? She told us yesterday morning she was going to quit. I asked Buck why she went out at all, and he told me you talked her into one last dive. This is your fault."

Tess recoiled. "She may pull out of it."

"Don't kid yourself."

A nurse appeared in the doorway. Tess didn't recognize her. "What's going on in here?" the nurse asked.

"Tess is just leaving. You might make sure she doesn't come in again. I said no visitors."

Red ran up the nurse's neck. "Sorry, Mr. Stinson." She held the door open and looked at Tess. Her brown eyes held a trace of sympathy.

Tess's chest squeezed as she walked out of the room and out of the hospital. That had taken all of fifteen minutes. She felt sore and bruised. Stevie had said she would call when she was done at the doctor's. Tess still had time to talk to the sheriff.

She drove to the jail and parked, pulling her sweater tight as she got out to ward off the autumn chill. The sunshine washed over her face, and she wished the brilliant light could reach inside where she shivered like a lost puppy. Walking with deliberate steps that showed none of the dread she felt, she bounded through the door and into the sheriff's office. When she told the receptionist what she wanted, the sharp-faced young woman told her to have a seat.

The office smelled of stale coffee and despair. Tess picked up a *Field & Stream* magazine and flipped through it with cold, stiff fingers, but her mind didn't register any of the text or the pictures.

She felt like she'd been here an eternity, but glancing at her watch, she saw it had only been ten minutes. When the sheriff came through the door, she sprang to her feet.

"Tess, good to see you. I would only have recognized you by your hair." Sheriff Eric Curry gripped her hand, and his gaze skimmed her face with curiosity.

"How's Brandon?" she asked. Eric was the older brother of a boy she'd gone to school with and had a crush on in sixth grade.

"Married with two kids." He led her back through a maze of offices to a room that smelled of cigars and new carpet. "Have a seat. Coffee?" He shut the door and went to a rolling cart by the door.

"Cream please." She sat in the chair opposite the desk and looked around. Pictures of T-ball players were on the walls. "You coaching?"

"That one's mine," he said, nodding toward a little boy who had Eric's blond hair. Eric handed her the cup of coffee and went around to his chair. "When you called this morning, you said you wanted to take a look at the evidence we acquired when the barn first burned. I've pulled the file for you, but I have to warn you, Tess, the pictures aren't pretty. You sure you want to see them? I could pull them out and let you just read the report. We've labeled all three deaths murder since the cause of the fire is arson."

"I have to see it all." At least her voice didn't quiver as much as she'd thought it would. She held out her hand. "I've seen my share of fire scenes."

"I know, but this is different." He still held on to the file.

"Why don't you tell me how this fire could possibly be related to the current ones under investigation. This was twelve years ago."

"I'm leaving no stone unturned in catching this guy. We've had a thousand acres burned so far this year."

"But the arsonist set fire to our barn. It wasn't a wildfire."

"There have been other structure arsons as well over the past ten years. Chicken coops, an abandoned cabin, that kind of thing. You'll see the evidence. I'm positive they're related."

"My sister is sick, Eric. She can't handle any more stress. If I can convince you the fires couldn't possibly be connected, will you drop this?"

His blue eyes looked her over. "I don't see any way you can prove that. Not if you look at the evidence with an open mind." He held out the file, then stood. "I'll be in the lunch room. Let me know when you're finished."

The file was right in front of her. All she had to do was take hold of it, but Tess hesitated. She'd tried so hard to block out the memories. A sigh eased from the back of her throat. She'd promised Stevie.

When she didn't take the file right away, Eric laid it on the desk and went to the door. "You don't have to do this, Tess."

"Yeah, yeah, I do." Once the door closed behind her, she reached over and picked up the file. It was thick and heavy, and she thought she smelled smoke. Probably her overactive imagination. She pulled her chair closer to the desk and opened the file. The first page was a picture of the smoldering ruins of the barn.

Tess slammed her eyes shut, the sounds and smells of that day rushing over her: the horses screaming, the fire crackling, the black smoke filling her throat. Three lives as well as several horses had been lost in the choking blaze. Only Wildfire was saved. Her chest felt tight as though the smoke had found a way in.

Could she have saved her parents if she'd gotten the main door open first? The thought had haunted her for twelve years. She took a deep breath. She could do this. Opening her eyes, she forced herself to examine the photo. Though it was a color picture, everything was black and white. Ash, soot, ruined and charred timbers. A dark line smeared one corner. The point of origin where the arsonist had dumped the kerosene. Tess picked up the photo and studied it, then she took the file to the window, where she examined each photo in the stack.

She almost vomited at the photos of the bodies, but she forced herself to take a step back, to pretend she wasn't seeing the remains of her own parents and uncle. She hurriedly passed them by and went on to other parts of the barn.

In one photo, a lone spur lay half-buried in the rubble. To most people, it was logical that there would be spurs in the barn, but no one on the ranch wore spurs except for Chase. Her dad hated them and wouldn't let his wranglers wear them, though he made an exception for Chase. The ones Chase wore belonged to his dad, who had been killed in a robbery at the gas station he owned. Chase had been wearing them the day of the fire. Tess remembered because she'd had an argument with him about them. She told him if he really loved and respected her dad, he'd honor Garrett's wishes. So why were they in the barn?

She laid the picture aside and picked up the next one. The main barn door lay charred and splintered in the ashes, but the padlock was clearly visible. Closed. She put her hand to her throat. It should have been unlocked. Dad never locked the barn until nine o'clock. She closed the file and went down the hall, where she found Eric in the lunch room. He was sitting by himself in the corner with a cup of coffee and puffing on a cigar.

"All done?" he asked, stubbing out the cigar. He got to his feet.

"There doesn't seem to be a list of suspects here. Is anyone under suspicion?"

"Not really. The investigators interviewed dozens of people, but nothing points to any one person. The guy is like a ghost."

"I really can't see any link between the fires." She should ask about the lock, but she didn't want to believe someone had locked it. Wouldn't believe it.

"Only because you don't want to see."

"Most fires are started with a flammable liquid, and arson targets are commonly abandoned buildings. That's no real connection."

The sheriff didn't answer right away. He took a sip of his coffee. "Still taking shortcuts, Tess? You missed the key clue." He set down his cup and took the file from her. Flipping through it, he held out a page. "Take a gander at this."

Tess took the sheet from him and scanned it. "I never knew a timed device had been used to set our fire." She wanted to crumple the paper in her hand and toss it to the trash. Over the years, she'd seen her share of incendiary devices, and they never failed to sicken her with the deliberate intent to cause harm.

"Not only yours, but ten of the other more recent fires as well. They're all constructed with the same white kitchen timer as the timing device. How can you say they aren't related?"

Tess swallowed, then found her voice. "I found a picture of the barn door."

"Yeah?"

"The padlock on it was set. Dad never set it until late. Do you know if a deputy messed with it?"

Eric grew still. "You're sure?"

"Yes."

"No one would have messed with the scene." He flipped open

the file and pulled out the report. The minutes ticked by as he scanned through it. "Ah," he said. "Deputy Joe Walker mentioned the locked barn door, but the sheriff thought it was normal, that you all used the side door."

Tess's knees went weak. She grabbed the back of a chair. "We rarely used the side door. Dad never did." She couldn't deny the evidence in front of her. Eric was right. And this monster needed to be caught. "Could I get a copy of the file?"

He nodded. "You might find something else I missed. I'll have a copy made for you. Stop by tomorrow and pick it up."

"Thanks. Tell Brandon I said hello." She hesitated. "Don't talk to Stevie about this, just contact me with any questions. I don't want to upset her." She shook his hand and practically ran outside.

Stevie wasn't waiting outside the doctor's office, so Tess parked in the lot and went inside. Doctors' offices were something she avoided whenever possible. The last time she'd visited Dr. Wyrtzen had been three years ago when she cracked her clavicle during a jump. He told her she needed to be coming in for an annual checkup, and she smiled and agreed with him. Of course, she didn't do it. Who had time for such nonsense? She'd see him when she needed to.

Stevie wasn't in the waiting room either, so Tess grabbed a magazine and sat down. She barely noticed what she was reading as she thought about the arsons. Was there any way the padlock could have been set accidentally? She didn't want to believe anyone could be so cruel, but she didn't see how the deaths could have been anything but intentional. Which changed the whole scope of the past.

"Tess?"

She looked up to see the doctor standing in front of her. "Hey, Dr. Wyrtzen."

"Could you come back with me? I need to talk to you for a minute."

She eyed his somber face. "Is—is something wrong?"

"Let's talk about it in my office."

Tess shot to her feet and followed the doctor down the hall lined with pictures crayoned by the children of his practice. She'd done one of them herself, once upon a time. Dr. Wyrtzen turned off into a room on the right labeled Dialysis Center. Stevie lay stretched out on a table. A tube ran from her abdomen to a machine. With the harsh sunlight streaming through the window onto her face, Tess saw the odd hue to her sister's skin tone.

"What's going on?" She wanted to rip the tube out and carry Stevie away from this place.

"I'm having dialysis. I've been putting it off, but Dr. Wyrtzen said I had no choice today. I'll be able to do this at home though. It won't be so bad."

Tess picked up her sister's hand. It was cold and dry. "Your kidneys are totally shot?"

"Your sister has resisted letting me talk to you about this, Tess, but I finally convinced her today. Would you be willing to consider giving her a kidney?"

"Of course." Tess squeezed Stevie's hand. "I told you I would. You know I'd give you anything, Stevie."

"It's a major surgery, Tess. Are you sure?"

Dr. Wyrtzen jumped in before Tess could respond. "Yes, it's a major surgery, but you're young and healthy, Tess. Your recovery will be rapid, I'm sure. You'll be back to smokejumping by next season."

"All that matters is that Stevie gets well. What happens once she has a new kidney?"

"She'll have more energy and will be her old self."

"The lupus?"

"She'll still have that, unfortunately. But we've got it under control. The damage was done before we knew what was wrong. I'm sending her for some alternative care that I think will help her."

"When do we need to do the surgery?"

"First we have to determine if you're a compatible donor. I want you to go to the hospital lab for tests. We'll get the results back in a few days, then we can schedule the surgery." Dr. Wyrtzen glanced down at Stevie. "In the meantime, she's going to be just fine. The dialysis will help her feel better for now, but she's going to be weak the rest of the day."

"I love you, Tess," Stevie said softly.

Tess squeezed her hand. "You're going to be all well again, Stevie. I promise."

CHAPTER 6

$\mathcal{D}$ust covered Chase's body, and he felt like he was encased in chalk. The dirt clung to his lips and coated his tongue. The job was done though. He'd rounded up all the male calves, and tomorrow he would cut them. At least Paul would be off his back. Speak of the devil, the man was strutting this way. Chase pushed his hat to the back of his head and leaned against the fence to watch the old green pickup bump over the potholes to where he stood.

Paul's tanned arm hung over the open window. He got out and slammed the door behind him. "I don't appreciate being your answering service, Huston." He thrust a note at Chase. "Whip insisted I bring it out to you."

Chase took the folded note without answering. He unfolded it and read the scrawled words. JIMMY ARRESTED. Stuffing it in his pocket, he looked up at Paul. "Were you there? Do you know the charges?"

"Running a chop shop. But what do you expect from a guy like that?"

"Spoken like a true pillar of the church. Where's your compassion, Paul? Jimmy hasn't had the easiest life." Chase straightened and went toward his horse. "He in the Payson jail?"

"Yeah. I suppose you're going to bail him out. You ever heard of tough love, Huston?"

Chase didn't bother arguing with Paul. The man had about as much compassion as a horsefly and was every bit as annoying. Chase mounted his workhorse, Bugs, and headed toward the ranch house. He heard Paul shout something, but the wind snatched the man's words away. Chase didn't care enough to turn back and find out what he'd said. It was more arguments, he was sure.

A chop shop. Chase had expected the charge to be drugs. Was that what funded Jimmy's fancy duds? He'd heard Arizona was thick with car-theft rings. They swiped the cars, then dismantled them and sold the pieces for huge profits. Jimmy was involved in some dangerous stuff. Chase wished he knew how to get through to his brother.

The day was warm and clear with a thin plume of clouds hanging in wisps along the horizon. Bugs moved under him in a loping canter that kicked up the scent of sage as he brushed through mounds of creosote and greasewood.

A cloud of dust roiled down the road behind a gray Jeep Cherokee. Tess waved her hand through the open window at him, then pulled to the shoulder and waited for him and Bugs to reach the road. She got out and leaned against the front bumper with her arms crossed over her chest. The sun hit her blonde hair and made it so bright with red highlights that he blinked. Stevie was in the passenger seat. Her eyes were closed as she leaned against the headrest.

He reined in Bugs and sat looking down at the women. Tess's fresh appearance in trim jeans and an army-green shirt made him glance down at the filth that covered his jeans and boots.

"Been mucking out the stables?" Tess asked, her nose wrinkling. "Your aroma is a bit—interesting."

He dismounted and beat at his jeans with no results. They stayed the same dull persimmon color. A bright red Band-Aid was at the bend of her elbow, and he thought of asking if she'd given blood or something, then decided it was none of his business. "You need something? I'd like to get back and shower."

"I just came from the sheriff's office," she said.

"Oh? You see Eric hustling Jimmy to jail?"

Her eyes registered surprise. "No, and Eric didn't mention it. What happened?"

"He's involved in a chop shop. So what were you doing there, checking out the arson investigation?"

She nodded. "You obviously already know. Did Stevie ask you to have him drop the investigation into the fire here too?"

"Yeah. No dice. He's sure they're connected. Did you try it too?"

"He has some pretty convincing evidence in the incendiary devices. They all used the same timer." Her green eyes studied him. "Did you know the barn was locked? That's why Mom and Dad couldn't get out."

The air left his lungs. "That can't be right."

"I saw photos."

"He let you see the files? I've asked and he wouldn't let me."

"I'm a fire professional." Her mouth took on a pinched look.

"Someone deliberately killed my parents, Chase. And Uncle Giles."

"Then we need to find whoever did it," he growled. He took off his hat and beat the dust from it out against his leg.

She scuffed a toe in the dirt. "Where were you that day? You were supposed to show up for my birthday party, but you didn't come home until two hours after the fire. You weren't mucking out the barn like you were told. I didn't see anything in the interview about where you'd been."

"So now I'm under suspicion for starting the fire. Typical, Tess. You've always believed the worst in me. I'm just a no-good foster kid, right? And now I'm a firebug as well." He turned back to Bugs and mounted. "I should know better than to think you might grow up and get that chip off your shoulder about me."

She stepped forward and grabbed the bridle before he could leave. "I didn't mean to imply I suspected you. I have another question about something in one of the photos."

He couldn't ride off without jerking Bugs's head, and the horse had a tender mouth. "Get it over with."

"One of your spurs was in a photo. You were never without those spurs. How did they get in the barn?"

The spurs. He didn't like to think of that day. "I don't owe you any explanation. Let go of Bugs."

"Not until you tell me." Her greenish-gold eyes narrowed.

"It's none of your business."

"They were *my* parents, not yours."

"And that's the whole bone, isn't it? It sticks in your craw every time you remember that they loved me too, and that's the only reason I'm here. There's room for both of us, but you want it your way." Her face went white, and she stepped back, dropping her hand from the bridle. He pulled Bugs's head around and dug his heels into the horse's flank. Bugs leaped away, and Chase didn't look back.

The dust Bugs kicked up was just a smudge in the distance. Tess didn't know how long she sat on the bumper and stared after Chase. She hated the way he made her sound petty. Did he really not see how inappropriate it was for her father to leave him a share of the ranch instead of leaving it all to his own kids? An honorable man would have bowed out and refused to take the share. Chase had been a leech, refusing to let loose once he got it in his hands. And when Tess had suggested he had no right to any property, her own sister had taken his side. She wouldn't be surprised if he had aspirations to boot them all out eventually. The three of them—she, Stevie, and Chase—had equal shares, so he would have to buy them out, but that would never happen as long as she had breath.

There had to be a way to figure out what the spurs meant and where Chase had been when he was supposed to be at the ranch house. Why was he so reluctant to tell her? Probably pride, she decided. He didn't want to have to answer to her. As far as he was concerned, she was still the little brat in pigtails.

Stevie stuck her head out the window. "Tess, are you going to sit out there forever? I need to get to bed. I'm wiped out."

"Coming." Tess started back to the Jeep when she heard a low growl from the ditch beside her. Guttural and menacing, it didn't sound like a dog or even a wolf. Whatever it was, it made her pulse leap and caused her to jump into her vehicle and slam the door. Her pulse galloped in her throat, and she told herself not to be ridiculous. Nothing here would hurt her. But the growl resounded in her head. She'd never heard anything like it. She peered through the window, but there was nothing in the ditch but grass waving in the wind.

Stevie opened her eyes. "What's wrong?"

Tess contained her fear. "There was a wolf or a wild dog out there. I decided to get out of its way." Had it been her imagination? There is nothing out there. She started the Jeep and ran her window down a few inches, but the noise didn't come again. Maybe it had been a bear cub. There were black bears in the area, but the growl didn't sound like any bear she'd ever heard.

She covered the last few miles to the ranch in minutes. She'd been too overcome with nostalgia to really notice the landscape when she first arrived, but now her gaze took in the worn look of some of the fences, and the weeds that grew high along the lane. In her father's day, the weeds never got so tall. Stevie had said they were short handed, and Tess supposed tending to the weeds was the least of their worries. She'd do all she could while she was here.

When she arrived at the ranch, she caught sight of Mindy riding her pony, Pepper, in the corral. Dressed in a red fringed cowboy shirt and hat, she looked adorable. Tess's lips curved in a smile as she and Stevie went to stand at the fence just as Mindy lassoed a calf. Stevie leaned against the fence with an obvious effort to smile.

"She's good," Tess told Stevie. "I could show her some rope tricks. With her posture, she should enter the junior rodeo competition."

Stevie nodded. "Chase is helping her train for the junior rodeo. He's quite the rodeo darling around these parts."

Chase again. Tess managed not to grit her teeth. He'd always been good with a rope, and he could cling to a horse's back like a burr. Tess had always respected his horsemanship. "When's the competition?"

"Next Saturday."

"Watch me, Aunt Tessie." Mindy nudged her horse faster and weaved among a series of barrels. She and the pony moved as one and finished the course without knocking a barrel over.

Tess clapped and whistled, and Mindy beamed a smile their way. Her curls bounced as she jogged around the course again.

Stevie turned her head and stared at Tess. "Any luck with Eric?"

Tess knew she should tell her sister the truth, but was Stevie strong enough to deal with it? "He showed me the evidence, and Stevie, even though I tried to dismiss it, it's pretty strong. I can see why he thinks the cases are related."

Stevie bit her lip. "All arson fires can be similar. I'm sure ours had nothing to do with the others."

"Are you trying to protect someone, Stevie? You seem awfully eager to stop the investigation. I would think you'd want to find out who killed our parents. And it wasn't a simple case of fire. It was murder."

"Murder?" Fear crouched in Stevie's eyes. "Is that what they're calling it? Why not manslaughter?"

"Someone locked the barn door, Stevie. They trapped our parents and Uncle Giles inside on purpose."

Stevie gasped. "I don't believe it."

"I saw the picture of the locked door. We have to find the killer. He can't get away with it."

"What good would it do, Tess? It wouldn't bring them back. I want to try to forget it and move on with my life. It takes all the strength I have to raise my daughter and run the ranch. I've worked hard at putting the past behind me. I don't want to relive the nightmare again." She shook her head. "You don't know what it was like back then listening to all the gossip, the whispers. I don't want to go through it again."

"Whispers? What do you mean?"

"People suspected Paul had something to do with it."

"Why would anyone think that?"

"He and Dad argued the day before," Stevie admitted.

"What about?"

Stevie leaned against a post. "Paul was never Dad's pick for me. We'd been dating for several years, and he told Dad he was going to ask me to marry him. Dad told him he'd fight any marriage between us."

"I've always thought that was why Paul and Chase never got along. Chase wanted to marry you."

Stevie laughed. "Don't be silly. He's my brother. That's the only way we've ever thought of one another. Is that the reason you don't like to come to the ranch?"

"Of course not." She wasn't jealous of Chase's relationship with her sister. How ridiculous.

"You used to have a crush on Chase."

"I was *twelve*, Stevie. I saw through him soon enough."

Stevie's eyes didn't waver from Tess's face. "I think you avoided home because you blame me for something."

Tess stared into Stevie's face and shook her head. "I love you, Stevie. I've just been busy with my work. I never meant to hurt you."

Stevie hugged her. "I'm so glad you're here, and we had this conversation."

Tess returned the hug. "Me too. I didn't realize we had this between us." But did she? Or had she just not wanted to face it? For years she'd told herself she loved her sister with a deep commitment, but now she wondered. She didn't want to think about it.

"Why didn't you date anyone but Paul? You generally listened to everything Dad said." Tess remembered Stevie as being compliant as a teenager. There'd been no temper tantrums, no sneaking out at night.

"No girl listens to her parents about boys. Besides, we were going to have Sarah."

Tess had never heard Stevie mention her unplanned pregnancy before. It had been a taboo subject. Did Stevie ever wish she'd listened to her dad? Though she never voiced any dissatisfaction with her marriage, Paul was hardly the ideal husband. Still, Tess supposed Stevie loved him, and he stood by her, which was more than some men did.

"You don't talk about Sarah much," Tess said.

"I find myself thinking about her a lot lately. She would have been eleven this year. It doesn't seem possible. Our lives would be so different if she'd lived." She looked down at her hands. "Paul and I drifted apart when Sarah died. I think I blamed him, and he sensed it."

"In what way?"

Stevie shrugged. "He was the last one to check on her. He gave her a bottle at three and came back to bed. Maybe he didn't prop her right. Maybe the milk was too warm. He always resented her, right from the start."

Tess wanted to pooh-pooh the idea, but she remembered how possessive Paul had been of Stevie in the early days. "The doctor said it was SIDS."

"The doctors say a lot of things. All I knew was my baby died." Tears swam in Stevie's eyes.

Tess touched her hand. "I'm sorry, Stevie. She was a darling baby. I loved her too."

Stevie gripped her hand. "I know you did. But can't you see,

Tessie? Supposedly God won't give us more than we can handle, but I'm at the end of my endurance. I just want all the pain to go away. Just let it go, all this arson business. I want a little peace."

"I want to find out who did this, Stevie. We have to stop that monster."

Stevie squeezed her eyes shut, and Tess wondered if her sister really thought Paul could have had something to do with the fire. Surely not. While Tess could imagine her hot-headed brother-in-law arguing with her father and maybe dropping a cigarette and throwing a punch, locking the door was a deliberate act of malice.

A shiver ran over her at the thought. Usually she was the one most likely to be in the barn. Either her or Uncle Giles. Could the killer have wanted to hurt her? She shook her head. And what about her uncle?

Stevie opened her eyes. "What are you thinking?" Stevie said. "You've got that look in your eye that usually gets us all into trouble."

"What do you know about Uncle Giles? He never did marry, did he?"

"I don't think so. Girl, you jump from subject to subject so fast you make me dizzy. What's Uncle Giles got to do with anything? He's dead."

"He never came around, not for years. There was something between him and Dad." She tried to remember the day she'd first seen her uncle. She was twelve and was sitting on the porch swing letting Stevie try to braid cornrows into her hair.

"Ouch!" Tess put her hand on her head when Stevie yanked it.

"Sit still, I'm almost done."

A red car drove up the driveway. Tess was ready for any distraction to get her sister's hands out of her hair. Stevie shouldn't bother trying to fix her up. Tess glanced at her flat chest. Her mom told her to be patient, but that virtue had passed Tess by. She often despaired of having a figure or attracting any male attention when she looked at her mom and big sister. She looked like a boy, even though she was nearly thirteen, and all the cornrow hairdos in the world wouldn't change that.

A red car came slowly up the dirt lane. Tess had never seen it before. It stopped by the front porch, and a man got out. He looked so much like Dad that she blinked. She shook off Stevie's hands and stood. "Hello," she said.

"You must be Tessie." His gaze went to Stevie. "And Stevie, all grown up. You've outgrown your pigtails." His tone suggested he disapproved. "You must be eighteen now. I think you were only Tessie's age the last time I saw you."

"Hello, Uncle Giles." Stevie's lips were tight, and she didn't look at the man.

Her uncle. Why hadn't she ever seen him before? Tess couldn't even remember hearing his name before. "You're hurting my hand," she whispered to her sister. Stevie didn't loosen her grip.

Her dad stepped through the barn door. "Giles, what are you doing here?"

Giles turned. "I thought it was time we mended fences, Garrett."

Her dad's grim mouth didn't lift in a smile. His gaze went to his daughters. "I guess you'd better come inside," he said.

Stevie said something, and Tess shook off the memory. "I never knew what caused the breach between him and our parents, did you?" Tess asked her sister. "I liked Uncle Giles. Whatever it was, they seemed to put it behind them." She chewed on her lip. "What if someone wanted to kill me?"

"You were a kid. No one would have wanted to hurt you. If someone was a target, it had to be one of the adults."

"Maybe Uncle Giles? He might have had enemies. I should see what I can find out about his past."

"Leave it alone, Tessie! You never listen. I asked you to dig out something to get him to drop the case, not get us in deeper. Just let it go."

But Tess couldn't. If someone had deliberately murdered her parents, she would find them and bring them to justice.

CHAPTER 7

y old home looms above me, and I slip on the gravel as I get out of the car. It is a huge monstrosity that always makes me think of lurking monsters in the closets. I never could watch *Psycho*. I hated this place when I was a teenager, and dread still coats my throat. I go to the door and let myself in. "Uncle Ben? It's me."

There was no answer, which is typical. Ben Diamond lives for my visits, but he doesn't like to let on. But really, who else comes to visit him? I'm not even sure why I come. Maybe to reassure myself that I've won. He didn't break me. He never will.

The sour smell of the house never changes. It brings back memories I don't have time to linger over. The odor is strongest in the hall, as if all the misery and evil in the place collects there. Ben is in his tattered green recliner as usual. Stretched out with his mouth drooping open, a bit a drool slips from his lip along with a strong garlic odor. Four coffee cups are on the table beside him, as well as a half-eaten plate of spaghetti. The garlic bread beside it looks as hard as the back of Ben's hand, which has flown my way many times. But never again.

I jiggle Ben's stockinged toe. "Wake up." The harshness of my voice should rouse him. You get further with him if you don't show weakness. I learned that quickly during my stay in this god-forsaken place.

He snorts midsnore, then raises a puffy eyelid. "When did you get here?"

Instead of answering, I shove the foot of his recliner down. His gray head bobs, but the action makes his eyes look less sleepy.

"You didn't have to do that," he whines.

Try as I might to prevent it, my lip curls. When did my fear of him vanish? If I'd snarled at him as a teen, his wrath would have been swift. I still have the scars on my back from some of his "correction."

"Where is the old box of pictures?"

"Why?" He thrusts out a belligerent lip.

"Where is it?" I repeat. If he knew me now, he wouldn't push me.

He eyes me and seems to see my determination. "In the attic," he says. A crafty smile touches his mouth.

He has put it there deliberately, no doubt about it. "Go get it," I say.

"You get it. I can't navigate the steps anymore. It's in the closet under the eaves." He reaches over and picks up the remote control. Punching a button, he turns on the TV, though he still sees me from the corner of his eye.

The TV blares out. He always has the volume loud enough to wake the dead. My gaze goes through the doorway to the kitchen.

The back stairway runs to the second floor and continues on to the attic. The thought of climbing through that darkness is daunting. Is it worth it? Heat from the gas log radiates in the room, but my icy muscles don't warm. He continues to watch from the corner of his eye. He loves playing games with me, and unfortunately, he's won this round.

My fingers curl into my palms with the need to hit him, but instead, I turn and step through the doorway. This should only take five minutes. My lungs labor to breathe by the time I reach the second floor. The switch is just inside the door. When light illuminates the stairway to the attic, it chases away the shadows except for those caused by cobwebs that drape the opening. When was the last time anyone has been up here? The soft touch of the cobwebs makes a shiver course along my back. My breath huffs in and out, drying my lips. I plunge up the final flight of steps, willing myself not to think, not to remember.

My gaze finds the closet under the eaves. Screams still linger, trapped in the dark corners of the attic.

My first fire flared here, there in the back of the closet. Its warmth and glow kept me sane when the door was shut and locked, kept my screams from erupting from my throat. Confined to an old metal tin, the fire never did any damage, but my fascination with fire grew as I watched it push back the darkness of the nightmares. My hand creeps into my pocket and fondles the Zippo lighter there. There is plenty of flammable material up here, enough for one last fire that will take away the memories.

My hand pulls out the lighter and flicks it. The welcome flame bursts into view. It trembles in my fingers. No. I drop the lighter, and the flame sputters out. Not yet, though the fire clamors to be my dance partner.

Chase leaped down from Bugs's back. He fumed over the suspicion in Tess's eyes. How could she think he would harm her parents? The girl didn't have a clue how he really felt about them. She and Stevie had arrived back at the ranch before him, and Tess now stood talking with Mindy. She should have felt the heat of his stare, but she didn't turn. Just as well. He'd likely have blasted her with his words, and he didn't want to give her the satisfaction of knowing he was still angry. Besides, Mindy didn't need to see him make a fool of himself.

He turned his back on Tess and went to the house. He found Stevie in the living room with the phone to her ear. She held her finger to her lips and motioned for him to sit down. He didn't want to sit. Pacing in front of the fireplace, he waited for her to end the call.

"I see. Yes, I'll tell Chase." She clicked off the phone and laid it on the table beside her. "That was Emilio. Whip told me what happened with Jimmy, so I called him."

Stevie's attorney. At least Stevie had gotten right on the problem. "Does he know how serious this is?"

"He's at the jail now. The police raided a garage in Payson this morning and found a bunch of Jimmy's things along with his wallet and ID. His prints are all over the stolen vehicles."

"Stupid, stupid," Chase muttered. "No wonder he was hiding out here. I should have known."

"I think he's going to have to do time for this one, Chase. At least that's what Emilio said."

Chase's eyes burned. He should have done something sooner to straighten up his brother, but nothing he did or said seemed to get through to Jimmy. "I'd better get in there, try to post bail." He didn't have much in his account. Every dime lately had gone to keeping the ranch afloat. He might have to take out a loan, if he could get it. He couldn't let his brother rot in jail even if it meant taking a second job.

He became aware of Stevie's gaze. She grabbed her purse from the floor and pulled out her checkbook. He shook his head. "I don't want your money, Stevie. I'll figure something out."

She ignored his protest and handed him a signed blank check. "Get him out of jail, and then bring him here. We'll get him on a horse and see if we can straighten him out."

He stared down at the check. "I'll pay you back, I swear."

Tess told Stevie she was going out for a while and headed to her Jeep. She wasn't sure where to check first. She didn't know any of Uncle Giles's friends, but she knew he used to hang out at the Rim Café. The café was on Highway 280 on the west end of Payson. It had been various things over the years: a tool shop, a filling station, a saloon, and now a café that served the best chicken quesadillas Tess had ever eaten.

She stepped inside the nearly empty restaurant and seated herself at the counter. The place had the same shiny red barstools. Tess twirled herself on the seat as she remembered coming here with her dad when she was a little girl. The owner, Buddy Havelin, always gave her Hershey's Kisses from his pocket. They were generally misshapen and warm, but oh so gooey and good.

Buddy came out of the kitchen wiping his hands on his large blue apron. "Well, Tessie Masterson, I haven't seen you in a coon's age. Come give your Uncle Buddy a hug." He grinned and opened his arms.

Tess hopped up and went around the counter to nestle in his embrace. It was like being swallowed by a bear that smelled of roast beef and onions. He was nearly as big as he was round, and a head bald as a javelina's topped his seven feet. He'd always reminded her of a giant pirate. "Hey, Uncle Bud. Are you busy?"

"Never too busy for my favorite girl." He fished in his pocket and produced a Hershey's Kiss that was flattened on one side.

Tess grinned and took it from his open palm. "I thought you might have quit carrying them." She popped it into her mouth and it melted almost instantly, flooding her mouth with the taste of chocolate.

"I buy enough of them I should own stock." He sat on one of the stools. "Your sister doesn't look good, Tessie."

"She has lupus. Her kidneys are failing, and she's on dialysis now." Stevie had told her she didn't have to keep it a secret.

Buddy scowled. "I thought it wasn't good. Anything I can do?"

Tess shook her head. "She just needs less stress. I'm going to give her a kidney, and she'll be fine."

"Is that why you're in town? You didn't come in here wearing that somber expression for nothing."

"Did you hear the sheriff is reopening the investigation of the fire that killed my parents?"

"I mighta heard something about that floating around."

"Stevie wanted me to get Eric to drop it, but I think Eric might be right. If there's a chance someone deliberately killed my parents, I have to know."

"And how does Stevie feel about that?"

Tess shook a teasing finger at Buddy to warn him away from that snakehole. "Let's just say I'm an independent investigator. I wanted to talk to you about my uncle Giles. Did he have any enemies?"

Buddy scratched his head. "Well, Giles always marched to the beat of a different drummer. We were buddies since Woodstock. I grew up, and he didn't. And that's all there really is to say about him, Tess. Let the dead rest in peace."

"Eric isn't content with that," she pointed out. "He'll be around to ask you questions, if he hasn't already."

"He already has, and I told him the same thing. Now I'm with Stevie on this. There's nothing to be gained by stirring up the past. It won't bring back your parents, and it might make things worse. You ever thought of that?"

"Justice is always better."

He smiled then. "You're young, Tessie. When you have a little more life under your belt, we'll see if you feel the same way." He stood. "Life isn't always about what we deserve, Tessie. Sometimes it's about what we don't."

"You're talking in riddles." She couldn't hold back the hint of impatience in her voice. "Did my uncle get something he deserved?"

"Don't we all eventually?" He handed her another piece of candy, then sauntered back to the kitchen.

Tess blew out an exasperated breath. Glancing at her watch, she saw it was only two. Maybe Coop was around the fire camp. From here, she was only fifteen minutes away. Coop worked at the Bar Q years ago, when she was just a kid. Maybe he remembered something about Uncle Giles. She got back in her Jeep and drove out to the compound.

Encompassing fifty acres, the fire camp stretched from the road to the pine forest. Several large hangers, aircraft-maintenance shops, a runway, the smokejumper standby shack, and a helicopter staging area lined the road to the facility. She stopped at the fire-coordination center, called "the head shed" by jumpers. The shed sat in the shadow of the training towers to the north, rising forty-five feet into the air.

She entered the head shed and looked around. "Hey, where is everyone?" she called.

Coop came out of an office. His smile broke out when he saw her. "You're not due in until Monday."

"You know me. I can't stay away." A paper clip lay on the counter, and she picked it up and toyed with it in her fingers. "Um, Coop, was my uncle Giles around in the years when you worked at the ranch?"

"Sure he was."

"Did you like him?"

His faded blue eyes blinked. "Sure. He was an okay guy. He was a good boss."

"I've wondered if someone hated him. Could someone have wanted to kill him?"

Coop's long blond hair swung in its ponytail as he wagged his head from side to side. "I always thought that was all just an accident. I never saw any evidence of enemies. I guess it's possible though. I was hardly his best friend or anything. I was just a teenager then."

"Someone locked him in the barn. But how would the murderer even have known he was in there? None of us knew it until the fire was out."

"What does the investigation say?"

"There seem to be some holes," she admitted. "The only autopsy reports seem pretty cursory."

"You want me to take a look at the evidence?"

"You take a good hint. You're a good friend, Mom."

He rolled his eyes, then grinned. "You don't have to hit me over the head."

Tess could have hugged him. There was no better arson investigator than Coop. "Did you ever look at Allie's chute?"

His smile faded. "Yeah. Someone cut the suspension lines, Tess."

"That was my chute," she said slowly.

He nodded. "What was it she said as you were falling?"

She wrinkled her forehead, trying to think. "That day is so blurry. Something about who would want to kill me?" Tess still couldn't take it all in. She had no enemies. "It doesn't make sense."

"I've notified my superiors. They'll be investigating, but this kind of thing is hard to figure out. Anyone could walk in and mess with a pack."

"They would have to know something about skydiving," she pointed out.

"Yeah, but that's not hard to come by." He fingered the gold ring in his ear. "When do you get the arson files?"

"Eric is supposed to have copies of the file ready for me tomorrow. I'll drop them off after I get them."

"Maybe we can look over the evidence together. With the barracks being closed, I'm probably going to hole up in the bunkhouse. That is, if you'll have me."

"Flint and Buck are staying with us as well, so the gang will all be together."

He grinned. "Think you can stand us all?"

It wasn't all of them. Her smile dimmed when she thought of Allie. "Allie's dad threw me out at the hospital," she told him.

"I tried to see her too. Got stopped at the nurse's station. I guess we're all persona non gratis."

"She needs her friends."

"Her parents will see that soon enough."

"What if they don't?"

"It's not your call, Tess. Or your fault. Get over the guilt. I believe in karma, you know? What goes around comes around. It will all work out."

"I hope so." She missed Allie. There was so much going on in her life right now, and she wanted to talk it over with a close friend.

"You sure there's no problem if I bunk at the ranch?"

"I can't wait for you guys to get there. It will make my own stay easier." She wished she could get over her aversion to the ranch. It strained family relationships. But every time she saw the empty spot where the barn should be, she remembered how she failed to save her parents. She deserved fire and judgment.

Chase parked across the street from the jail and sat looking at the stone building. How many times had he been down here to bail out Jimmy—twice, three times? No matter how much trouble he got into, Jimmy never seemed to learn. The Lord knew Chase had messed up his own life often enough. If not for Garrett Masterson, Chase figured he'd be behind bars somewhere himself. When he'd come to the ranch, he'd been a sullen fourteen-year-old boy with a chip on his shoulder the size of Spider Mountain. Garrett had seen beyond the sneer and the uncaring attitude Chase had used to fool everyone else.

He got out of his truck. As he crossed the street, a Ford Explorer slowed and stopped to let him pass. The vehicle then pulled to the curb, and the window came down. Dr. Tally stuck his head out. "Hey Chase, how's Stocking?"

Chase paused to talk to the vet. "Doing fine. That new salve really helped."

"You've got a way with the animals. My assistant is leaving in a month. Any chance I could tempt you into taking the job? I'd like to retire in ten years. I'd pay for you to get your veterinary license. A gift like yours shouldn't be ignored."

Everything within Chase rose at the offer. All through high school, he'd planned to go to college and get his vet license, but when Garrett died he chose to step up and be a man. But he had never lost the longing to heal animals. The smile that had started to his lips died. He couldn't leave now, not when Stevie was counting on him, not when things were so bad. If the ranch wasn't struggling, he might have considered it, but without his help, it would surely fail.

He gave a shake of his head. "It's a great offer, Sam. I wish I could take you up on it. The ranch needs me right now."

"The ranch always needs you, my boy. You need to figure out what you really want and chart your course. Garrett Masterson was a good friend. I don't believe he would want you to waste your life working the ranch when you've got a yen and a gift for healing animals. God didn't give you that gift and expect you to squander it."

Squander it? Chase had never thought of it quite that way before. "I have plenty of chances to use it on the ranch. Hardly a week goes by that I don't have to nurse some cow or horse."

"That's not the same, boy, and you know it if you're honest with yourself." He shot Chase a piercing look from under craggy white brows. "Think about it. I'll hold it open for you until Katie leaves." With a little salute, the vet ran his window up and pulled away from the curb.

Chase stared after the Explorer. If wishes were horses, beggars would ride, he reminded himself. Things were what they were. He turned and went up the steps to the jail. Eric was coming down the hall when he entered.

The sheriff stopped when he saw Chase. "Hey, buddy, I'm sorry I had to do this."

"Why didn't you call me first, Eric? I had to find out after the fact."

"I left a message on your cell phone. You leave it home again?"

Chase clapped a hand on his shirt pocket. "Yep, I guess I did."

"I had no choice, Chase. You here to spring him?"

"Can I?"

"I think he's a flight risk. I wish you wouldn't bail him out."

Now was the time to exercise the tough love he'd been telling himself he needed to show. "For how long?"

"Until the trial."

"Eric, that will be months away. I can't let my brother rot in jail that long."

Eric rolled his eyes. "You ever look at the cells? He's perfectly comfortable. It will do him good, and it will count toward time spent. He's probably going to jail, you know."

Chase winced. "How about I leave him in overnight and spring him in the morning?"

"He's been in overnight before."

"I'll let him stay a week, then I'll get him out. That's surely long enough to make him think about the course his life is taking."

"You're a softie, Chase. Too much so for your own good." Eric shrugged. "It's your call. But I think you're making a mistake."

"Jimmy has no one but me. I want God to show him his love through me." But Garrett hadn't been soft on Chase. He needed to remember that. He tended to remember only the love Garrett poured out on him and not the discipline and the firm hand that was occasionally necessary.

"When the children of Israel were hardheaded, God punished them. There needs to be a balance between grace and accountability, Chase."

An ancient Cadillac pulled up in front of the jail. The color of a robin's egg, it was meticulously clean with shiny whitewalls and a hood ornament of a stallion rearing. Doty Masterson rolled down her window. "G'morning, Chase, Eric." Her blue eyes, rimmed with smile lines, twinkled from under an ancient well-used straw hat.

The only surviving child of Bessie Masterson, Doty was a familiar figure around town. Her striking similarity to her brother Garrett pained Chase. "Miss Doty." He tipped his hat to her. "How are you today?"

"I won't waste my time with chitchat. I've come for Jimmy." She pulled the car into a parking space but left the rear end extending into the road. "How much bail, Eric?"

Eric looked at Chase. "A thousand dollars."

"I thought we were going to leave him in jail for now," Chase whispered.

Eric shrugged. "Haven't you learned by now not to argue with her?" he said softly as Doty rummaged in her purse.

"I'm not deaf," she said. "Why would you leave that boy in jail? I thought better of you, Chase."

"It was my idea," Eric said. "I thought he might learn something."

"Would Chase have learned anything if Garrett hadn't taken him in?" she retorted. "That boy just needs a firm hand, and I'm just the one to do it, seeing as no one else will." She got out of the car and handed the check to Eric. "I want it set up so he's required to live with me."

"I should tell you to see a bondsman, but I'll take care of it for you," Eric said, cutting his glance to Chase. A half smile lifted his mouth, and he rolled his eyes again.

"Don't think I can't see you mocking me, Eric." Doty's words were severe, but her eyes gleamed with kindness. "Go get that boy for me. We'll see what he's really made of." She glanced at Chase. "My intuition says he might be the man his brother is if he's given half the chance."

CHAPTER 8

*A*fter church, Tess changed her clothes and went to the barn to saddle Wildfire. He huffed when he saw her and jumped around his stall in his eagerness. She fed him a lump of sugar, then saddled and mounted. She didn't tell anyone else where she was going because Stevie would object.

She rode out of the barn and headed out the back lane. The land cried out for moisture, and her stallion's hooves kicked up puffs of red dust. Tess shaded her eyes with her hand and looked to the sky, but only a few small clouds clung to the west side of the blue bowl over her head. No rain anytime soon.

There was a shortcut to her aunt's—a narrow, little-used trail that led through ponderosa pine and pinyon trees. The pine scent was thick and cloying as she rode through the box canyons that blocked out any hint of breeze. Vegetation had narrowed the path, and there was barely enough room for Wildfire to squeeze through in places. Cougars prowled the high crags and rocks of the canyon, and they sometimes got bold. She nearly lost her horse last time.

With the path so narrow and rocky, she didn't dare urge Wildfire to a faster gait. Bald eagles cried overhead, and the chatter of a squirrel in a tree ahead was cut off with a squeak. Her horse snorted and sidestepped. She could feel him quivering under her knees. Something had spooked him. A vulture sat atop a tall pine, but the bird shouldn't bother Wildfire. She reined in the horse and listened. The still air held a hint of menace in it, and she struggled to understand why. A slight sound disturbed her, and she strained her ears. The faint growl came again. Wildfire snorted and shuffled in the path. His muscles strained under her in his eagerness to move away.

Casting an uneasy glance into the rocks that jutted out over the path, she let out the reins and prayed he wouldn't stumble. Mountain lions still roamed these parts, and while they didn't usually attack humans, it had been known to happen. It didn't sound like a cougar though, more like a dog or a wolf. With every thud of the horse's hooves on the rocky path, she expected to see a tawny shape leap toward them. Just ahead, the canyon walls receded, and the pine forest dissipated. If she could reach that spot, they should be safe. A movement to her left caught her eyes. A dark blur ran beside them. She hunched lower in the saddle and didn't dare lose her concentration by turning to see what it was. Wildfire raced along the path, his urgency fueling her own.

Horse and rider burst into the sunlight. A howl went up behind her. The fury made her shudder. What was that animal? It was too big to be a cougar. Maybe a wolf? If it was, it was the biggest one she'd ever seen. Even though she'd only caught an impression of its size, it seemed huge. Thankful they'd escaped the danger, she paused at the lane that turned onto her aunt's property. Did she really want to do this? From here, she could see a puff of smoke from the chimney, and the wind carried the scent of a wood stove. Her aunt kept the house about ninety degrees all the time. But there was no one else to answer the questions Tess needed to ask. Wildfire nickered as if to ask what she wanted to do, and Tess turned his head toward the house.

Her Aunt Doty terrified the whole family. Her real name was Dorothy, but when Tess's dad was little, he couldn't say it, and his mispronunciation became Aunt Doty's nickname. A few months before the fire, she'd quarreled with her brothers, taken her five hundred acres of inheritance, then moved to this tiny cabin on the far edge of the Masterson property. As far as Tess knew, her aunt had never set foot on the Bar Q again. If anyone wanted to talk to her, they had to beard the lioness in her den.

Approaching the house, she saw the sheriff's car driving away. Though she waved at Eric, he didn't smile, and her gut tightened. Was something wrong? She urged Wildfire faster and ducked as they went under a pinyon tree.

Her aunt was in her garden. Doty wore a flowered housedress under her jacket, a red straw hat, and mud-encrusted black Wellingtons. She bent over her rose beds, raking mulch over the canes. Her head turned when Wildfire neighed, and she straightened and turned to watch Tess approach. The fingers of her tan cotton gloves were stained with red. For a wild moment, Tess imagined her aunt burying a body in the flower garden. The chuckle that escaped at the thought held an uneasy speculation. There'd been talk in the family for years that Doty once killed a boyfriend with a shotgun. It was supposedly a hunting accident, but no one was ever sure. And her aunt had never married.

Only when Doty straightened did Tess see Jimmy. He knelt beside a basket of potatoes. Continuing to dig up the tubers, he didn't acknowledge Tess. Doty came forward with the rake still in her hand. Her gray hair was corralled in a braid that reached to her waist, but her blue eyes were just as shrewd as ever.

She wiped the moisture from her brow with the back of her hand. "Took you long enough to come see me. I heard you got back to town several days ago. I was going to carry you off after church this morning, but my car was being temperamental." She tipped her head and looked closer. "What's wrong, Tess? You look wild-eyed, and your horse is lathered."

For some reason, Doty had always indicated a liking for Tess. Maybe she saw a hint of her own adventurous spirit in her niece. Tess dismounted and went to hug her aunt. "Sorry, Aunt Doty. A lot's been going on." Her aunt's sinewy arms hugged her close. Her dress held the lingering odor of wood smoke and mothballs. Tess could feel every rib in her aunt's back. She didn't want to scare her aunt about the animal, but maybe Aunt Doty had seen or heard it. "A big cat or something chased us for a while."

Her aunt released her, but her hard fingers dug into Tess's shoulders. "A big animal? A wolf, but bigger?"

Tess nodded. "You've seen it?"

Doty's lips tightened. "No." She glanced back at Jimmy. "Keep working, boy. I'll be back to check on you later." She turned and went toward the cabin. "I bought some Earl Grey tea when I heard you were back in town. Come inside."

Tess let Wildfire loose to roam the orchard, then followed Doty into the small cabin. There would be no sense in asking more questions about the wolf or whatever it was. When her aunt got that blank expression on her face, there was no budging her. The heat

of the interior washed over her. It was hard to breathe. She fanned
her face. "How do you stand it so hot, Aunt Doty?"

Her aunt ignored her and put the kettle on to boil. "I made
chocolate-chip cookies this morning. They're still warm."

She held out a plate, and Tess took two. "Thanks." She bit into
one. No one made cookies like her aunt. Full of black walnuts and
stuffed with chips, the cookies were each as big as her hand. She
glanced around the one-room cabin. A cot was pushed up against the
wall with a faded red, white, and blue quilt over it. Her aunt had
whitewashed the logs since Tess was here last, and the light color
brightened the room and made it look bigger. "I like the paint." She
didn't mention the sleeping bag in the corner. Was Jimmy living here?

"The dark logs were too depressing." Her aunt sat in the cane
rocker by the stove. "You're biting your lip, Tess. And you're not
looking at me. You've got something on your mind. Spill it."

Tess forced her teeth to let go of her bottom lip. "Did you hear
the sheriff is reopening the fire that killed my parents?"

"Yep. You probably saw him leave. I told him to hightail it and
quit bothering me."

Tess suppressed a grin. No wonder Eric looked peeved. A knock
came at the door. Her aunt muttered and got up. She jerked open
the door and caught Chase with his fist raised to give the door
another rap. His gaze shot past Doty to Tess in the armchair.

"Don't just stand there, get in here. You're letting out the heat,"
Aunt Doty snapped.

Chase's mouth was dangling open. He shut it and stepped
inside. "Letting out the heat would be a good thing." He fanned his
face with his hand. "Hey, Tess." He stuck his hands in his pockets.

"You're looking at her like a calf at a new gate. She won't bite.
Sit down, I was just pouring the tea."

With an uneasy glance at Tess, Chase did as he was told. He sat gingerly on the faded floral sofa with his hat on his knees. Doty poured three cups of tea and passed them around. Chase lifted his from her hand, took a swig, and grimaced. Tess hid a grin. He hated tea, preferring coffee that was strong enough to dissolve the spoon. What was he doing here?

He must have sensed her curiosity. When Doty went back to the cabinet to get sugar, he whispered to Tess. "I stopped by to check on Jimmy."

Her aunt returned and settled into the rocker. "You're not drinking your tea, Tess."

"Sorry." Tess took a swallow. "It's good."

The cup rattled in the saucer as her aunt put down her tea and fixed her gaze on Tess. "Now tell me what's on your mind. Why are you disturbed by the sheriff reopening the case?"

"Stevie doesn't want it reopened. Her health can't take it. I told her I'd poke around, but I looked at the evidence. Eric is right—it looks like our fire might be connected to the other arsons. But more than that—it was murder. Someone locked the barn door."

"And you have questions for me. Fire away."

Tess loved her aunt, but she never knew how she'd take things. All she could do is spit out what she needed to know. "Why did you quarrel with your brothers? It was only a few weeks before they died that you moved out here."

"I wondered how long it would be before you asked me about the argument." Aunt Doty didn't seem offended by Tess's question. She sat in the chair with her booted feet crossed at the ankles.

"I know it's probably none of my business, but I had to wonder if there could be any connection to the fire. Not that *you* would set the fire," she hastened to add.

"I should hope you wouldn't think that." Doty said. "But breaking a confidence is what caused the argument. I can't do it again. It's not my secret to tell."

"Whose confidence? I don't understand."

"If I told you that, it would be the same as breaking the confidence. I still feel I had to do what I did, but I won't compound my sin by spreading gossip."

"Is there any chance this . . . gossip could be related to the fire?" Tess had been so sure she was onto something. Now her confidence slipped away. There seemed to be a closed door at the end of every corridor.

"I don't see how, Tess."

"But both your brothers were so angry. That kind of rage had to have something big behind it. I remember that argument. The screaming was so loud it woke me up. Mom was crying, and so were you." It had been the one and only time she'd ever seen her aunt cry. "I came out of my room to find you dragging a big suitcase out the front door. I tried to get Mom to tell me what had happened, but she told me it wasn't my problem."

Doty pressed her lips together. "The culprit didn't want to admit his sin when I confronted him, and the other one didn't believe me. Sometimes the bearer of bad news gets shot. That was me. But it's done. There's no use crying over spilt milk. I don't regret what I did. I couldn't just say nothing. Not when it was such a great evil."

"Something my father did? Or Uncle Giles?"

"Your father never did anything wrong," Chase put in. "He was a wonderful man. So was Giles." A frown settled on his forehead as if it were taking up permanent residence.

Tess sent him a quelling glance. "He was still a man. He wasn't perfect. Same with Uncle Giles."

"He was as close to it as any man I've ever met."

Tess ignored him. "What about the relationship between my uncle and Dad? He never came to see us for years after that. I didn't even know him that day he showed up again when I was twelve. He moved into the bunkhouse, but my dad rarely spoke to him. It was weird."

"I'm not saying any more," her aunt put in. "Now drink your tea."

Either her father or her uncle had done something Aunt Doty regarded as a great evil. What could it be? Fraud? Murder? Tess couldn't believe it could be something that large, but from her aunt's manner, she knew it was big. Big enough for someone to decide to kill them all in one big fire? It seemed far-fetched.

"Did Uncle Giles have any enemies? I've been wondering if the arsonist meant to kill him."

"Quit pestering your aunt," Chase said.

She shot him a quelling glare. "She's *my* aunt, Chase." She turned back to Aunt Doty.

Her aunt stirred her tea. "We've discussed this quite enough, Tess. Now drink your tea."

From the finality of her aunt's tone, Tess knew she wouldn't get any more out of Doty. But her aunt's reaction was enough to send up more red flags about her uncle. She finished her tea, and they talked about the things that had changed in the area since Tess was a child. An hour later, she hugged her aunt good-bye. Chase followed her out the door, stopping briefly to say good-bye to Jimmy. Then he hurried to catch up with Tess.

"What good did you think that would do? You just upset Doty."

"Look, this is my family and my business, Chase. Not yours."

"You take every opportunity to remind me I'm just an interloper here."

"It's the other way around," she fired back. "You were the one who made me feel like an outsider in my own house."

"Whether you like it or not, I love your family. And they love me. I'm not the homeless foster kid you kicked around when we were younger. I'm here to stay. Deal with it." He stalked toward his horse, which was tied to a tree by the cabin. The horse shied as he approached, but he grabbed the gelding's reins and mounted, then looked down at Tess. "You hurt your sister by running off the way you did, and you'll answer to me for that."

"She's *my* sister. I wouldn't hurt her for anything in the world."

"You hurt her all the time. But it needs to stop." He dug his heels into the horse's flank, and they bounded down the dirt road.

Tess stood staring after him. For the past four years she'd been careful to call Stevie every week. She took Mindy on outings and sent her presents. They met in Tucson or Phoenix once every couple of months for dinner. There was no reason for him to insinuate she'd neglected her sister and caused her pain. Stevie understood her aversion to the ranch. Of course she did.

Tess sat at the sewing machine with yards and yards of parachute material billowing around her. Flint, Coop, and Buck hunched over their own sewing machines. Spirit lay sleeping on the floor beside Buck. It was rather endearing to see the men laboring over such a humble task. The walls around her held pictures of various smoke-jumper teams that dated all the way back to the 1940s.

Her dad and his partner's picture hung just over her left shoulder. Some days she couldn't look at it, and today was one of them. The picture showed a twenty-year-old Garrett Masterson with a carefree smile on his sooty face. He had an arm around his jump buddy, and they both wore the exhausted yet exalted air of firefighters everywhere. She had one like it over her bunk. When she found it at eighteen, she'd known she was supposed to do this.

She looked over at the men. "You guys are better at this than I am. You should let me go pack parachutes."

"No way," Buck said. "All for one and one for all. The sooner we get through the sewing, the quicker we can go do something fun. Like demolition." He grinned over the top of his sewing machine.

The door opened behind them, and Buck's fiancée, Esther Sanchez, walked in. Tess liked her, but she often wondered if the woman wore a suit to bed. Maybe she felt the pressure to keep up appearances; her father was a state senator. Today's outfit was a black double-breasted number with red buttons. Her perfume was nearly overpowering. The French roll at the nape of Esther's neck looked pinned tight enough to give her a headache.

Buck's face lit with a smile when he saw Esther. He got up from his sewing machine and kissed her. "I didn't know you were stopping by." Spirit followed him and thrust his muzzle toward Esther, who recoiled slightly before finding her smile again.

"I've come to whisk you away for lunch," Esther said. "Daddy has a table ready for us."

Buck's smile faded. "I can't leave now. I have a ton of work to do here today."

Esther smiled brightly. "We'll only be gone a couple of hours. Can't you work later to make up for it? A photographer is coming to take our picture for the paper. I want to announce our engagement right away."

"You should have asked if I could go before making all these arrangements," Buck protested. "Let me see what I can do." He went over to confer with Coop in the corner.

Before he returned, a siren began to blare, and the loudspeaker called out, "Anderson, Bailey, Carter, Douglas, Evanston, Johnston, Masterson, Montgomery, Stanley, Wilson, report to the ready room."

They looked at one another for a moment then sprang to their feet. "A fire!" Coop exclaimed. They all began to smile and high-five.

Tess used to think it strange the smokejumpers got so excited when they got a fire call, until she faced down her first dragon. Firefighting got into the blood. It was a test of stamina, determination, and commitment. Every time they faced down the red monster and came out alive, they underscored their fortitude and added another layer of mystique to their legends.

"Sorry, baby, I have to go," Buck said. "Stay, Spirit," he said to the dog.

"What will I tell the photographer?" Esther protested.

Buck hesitated, and Tess shoved him. "Come on, Buck. We have to move." He ran back and kissed Esther quickly. "Sorry, honey. I gotta go."

Tess spared a moment of sympathy for the other woman. Relationships were hard to maintain in this work, as Allie could attest to. Tess ran toward the ready room, a storage room that opened onto the tarmac. Tess kicked off her boots and grabbed her fire-retardant clothing. Carrying it to a changing area, she quickly slipped into the yellow shirt and green pants, then pulled the ocher-colored Kevlar jumpsuit over the other clothing. Her personal gear pack was already ready to go. She stuffed a couple of Snickers bars, tortilla chips, and frozen water into the kangaroo pockets on the legs of her jumpsuit, then stepped into the body harness, grabbed her parachute and pack, and was running to the plane within eight minutes.

Coop had checked with the operations desk, and he briefed them on the mission. "There's a fire in Tonto. It's small right now, but up the mountain. They don't want to chance it getting to the outskirts of the city. We're going to jump in, put it out, and we'll be back at the fire camp in a few hours. Piece of cake."

"It's not threatening any towns. They should let it burn itself out," Buck grumbled.

It was a common argument among the smokejumpers. They'd all come to understand the wilderness would be better for the burning off of brush now and then. The huge timbers of bygone eras flourished as the undergrowth burned away, which is what let them attain their mammoth stature. Over the past few years, the park service had begun to see the wisdom of controlled burns, but they were between a rock and a hard place when fires burned close to towns or residences, as more and more people escaped city life for the wilderness.

They settled back against the cargo boxes of the C-130 Hercules. The roar of the plane engines filled her head. The plane's hold was like a womb to her, a place to feel safe and relaxed before the thrill of the jump.

Ten minutes into the flight, Coop unzipped his gear pack and took out a packet of freeze-dried food. "Lunch anyone?" he called above the roar of the engines.

"Good idea," Tess called back. She unzipped her own pack and rummaged inside. She frowned when her hand touched something unfamiliar. The hard coldness of it shocked her hand. "What in the world?" She pulled the pack to her and peered inside. A jumble of freeze-dried food packets, extra batteries, earplugs, and her hardhat lay in a colorful jumble. Something didn't belong, and her gaze homed in on an incendiary device that lay atop her flares. She could see the clock moving. It was ticking closer to the ignition point. There were only seconds.

"Coop!" She stood and backed away. She didn't know how to disarm one of these, but Coop might.

"What's wrong?" Coop shouted. He peered into her pack, then ripped off his motorcycle-style helmet and looked closer. He took three steps to the door. "Guard your reserves!"

Tess held a protective hand over her reserve chute. Coop opened the door. Air rushed into the cabin with a clamor. Should she take out the device?

When she didn't approach the door, Coop looked back. "Throw out the whole thing! There's no time."

She grabbed it up and leaped to the door. Coop took the pack from her hand and launched it into the air. A loud *whump* hit Tess's eardrums. A bright flash of orange against the blue sky followed the sound, and she flinched. The smokejumpers crowded around the doorway and watched the burning pack spiral toward the ground like a small comet. The flames grew smaller and finally began to burn out as it fell to earth. A small clearing in the green treetops below opened, and she saw the glimmer of blue. The remains of the pack dropped toward it.

"It's landing in the lake," Flint said. "Close call."

"Too close." Tess's hands were shaking, and she steadied them against her leg. Who hated her enough to try to kill her and the whole crew? Was it directed at her in particular or at the smokejumpers in general?

CHAPTER 9

"Easy, boy." Chase ran his hand over the horse's quivering side and down the back right leg. A nasty cut had scabbed over, but dried blood caked the fetlock down to the hoof. It looked like a bite. A coyote maybe? He couldn't tell. He washed the cut and applied antibiotic ointment, then bound the leg. Patting the horse, he fed her and put the medical supplies away.

"What's wrong with Muffin?" Paul asked from behind him.

Chase didn't look up. "Looks like he got bit."

"Did you get the back fence repaired?"

"Yeah."

"How about the barn roof?"

Chase slowly straightened. "Look, Paul, let's have this out right now. You've made it clear for years you don't like me. Just because Stevie isn't around to run interference doesn't mean you can treat me like a lackey. I'm part owner too. Which is more than I can say for you." As soon as the words registered on Paul's face, Chase knew he'd gone too far. When would he learn to keep his mouth shut?

The color moved up Paul's face and stained his cheeks. "You enjoy shoving that in my face, don't you?"

An engine rumbled by outside then died. Probably Tess and the rest of the smokejumpers back. Just in time to prevent a full-blown shouting match. Paul stalked off, and Chase turned to watch the Jeep park. The men were supposed to move into the bunkhouse with him, which was no problem. It easily held twenty men, but only three were there now: him, Whip, and Coop. He shut the barn door behind him and stepped out into the night air. The men were carrying packs toward the bunkhouse, but Tess came toward the barn. A strong odor of smoke accompanied her. A beautiful wolf dog followed her.

"Test fire today?" he asked. He rubbed the dog's ears. "Whose dog?"

"Buck's. Spirit is a good dog, aren't you, boy?" She patted her leg, and the dog left Chase and nudged her hand. Ash smudged her face and coated her hair. Her eyes drooped with weariness. "We had a wildfire. Arson again. We caught it early, though, before it had a chance to get close to town."

"How do you know it's arson?" he asked.

"We found the device." She hesitated. "Don't tell Stevie, but someone put an incendiary device in my pack too. Coop threw it out of the plane just before it exploded."

He felt like a horse had kicked him. She'd almost died today. "Why was it in your pack?"

"I've wondered that all day. I only caught a glimpse of it, but it used the same kitchen timer as the arsons Eric's been looking into. Whoever it was could have taken out ten smokejumpers." Her gaze met his. "I also found out that someone cut the lines on my parachute, the one Allie grabbed by mistake. It sure looks like someone is out to get me. But I have no idea why."

A muscle in his jaw twitched. While he often said he could strangle Tess, it was all talk. "Could the wildfire have been set to lure you all out?"

"I thought of that." She shivered. "I don't know where to look next, Chase."

The appealing look she slanted up toward him made him wish he had the answers. "Has Coop looked over Eric's evidence?"

"Not yet. He's going to look at it tonight." She made no move to leave him.

He sensed there was something more she wanted to talk about. "Wildfire was looking for you. I fed him."

"Thanks. I suppose I should stop in and see him before supper." She set her pack on the ground, then put her hands in the small of her back and stretched. "I'm so tired." She dropped her hands and straightened. "Do you really think I've hurt Stevie?"

He could cite plenty of instances to prove what he'd said yesterday, but he found he didn't want to hurt her. She'd been through quite a day. He rummaged in his mind to think of something less painful.

A short laugh burst from her lips. "Why Chase Huston, I think you're actually trying to spare my feelings. This is a red-letter day. I can take the truth."

He'd never doubted her strength, except when it came to facing the past. Childhood monsters were the hardest to dispel. "I caught her crying on her birthday last month when you didn't show up for the party." He heard Tess give an audible gulp. There were other instances he could pull out, but he didn't think he needed to. She got the picture.

"I could tell you why I didn't come, but it would just be an excuse. The reality is I didn't want to come. I wish they'd never moved into the big house. It was easier when they were living at the smaller place."

"Paul decided they needed more room. Mindy was still sleeping in the loft over there." Until a year ago, they'd lived in a small house on the other side of the property. Whip and Chase had rented the main house for years. When Stevie and Paul moved in, he and Whip were transplanted to the bunkhouse, but neither of them minded. They would both take on the world for Mindy. Besides, they could have taken over the small house the Grangers vacated, but they both wanted to stay close to the livestock.

"I slept in the loft all through my teen years. It was fine."

"A little girl has toys. She wants to invite friends to sleep over. There's no reason they shouldn't live in the big house. Stevie humored you too long. She should have made you face it sooner."

"Maybe you're right." She ran a hand over her face. "I just can't stand to look at where the barn used to be."

He understood. Sometimes when he stood in the moonlight near the grass-covered site, he felt like he was close to Garrett.

A breeze lifted her hair, and she brushed a strand from her eyes. "Do you think we should examine the site for clues? I don't want to, but maybe it's necessary."

"What kind of clues do you mean? It's covered over now, Tess. I doubt there's anything left to see without excavation. Not even Eric's been out here for that." The discouragement of her posture softened him. "But we can go look around if you want."

Taking her arm, he escorted her toward barn. The fragrance of her hair drifted to him as the breeze blew a strand across his lips. The new intimacy between them felt strange and yet somehow right. Weird.

The grassy field appeared. Prickly pear cactus, sage, wheatgrass, and columbine had grown up over the once-gaping scab. The healing effect looked almost artistic, and Chase supposed it was. God was the physician and painter, brushing soft green strokes across the black and bringing new life to what was once ruined. Tess's grip on his arm nearly made him wince. He glanced at her from the corner of his eye and noticed her pallor.

"You okay?" he asked.

"Fine." Her clipped tones warned him not to probe.

Chase stepped onto the site. Tess hung back, and he left her at the edge of the barn. The bodies had been found where the tack room used to be. He realized Tess had finally followed him.

"The bodies were here," she said in a remote voice.

With a quick glance, he saw Tess was in firefighter mode. With a detached expression, she surveyed the site, then squatted and began to move rocks around—not an easy task with the tenacious roots adhering to some of the stones. He knelt and helped her.

They kicked their way through the rocks, but found nothing noteworthy. Tess dusted her hands onto her jeans. "Well, that was a waste of time."

"Hey, we worked in harmony for an hour. That's an accomplishment in itself."

Her teeth gleamed in her face. "It's a red-letter day," she agreed.

Chase found he rather liked seeing a smile of approval on her face. Odds were he wouldn't see it much, and the thought disappointed him.

Coop and Tess sat on the sofa with the files spread out before them on the coffee table. Buck and Flint sat in the armchairs. Tess had insisted they wait until Mindy was in bed. "Thunder Road" was blasting out of the CD player she'd put on the floor.

Coop winced. "Does that have to be so loud? You'll wake Mindy."

"I think better with Springsteen music, and Mindy could sleep through an earthquake." But she reached over and turned it down. Spirit jumped onto the couch and put his head on her lap. Coop picked up a paper and began to scrutinize it. The other men each took a handful of pages and began to study them as well. As they finished, they passed the papers to the next person.

Tess rubbed Spirit's ears as she waited. "See anything, guys?" she finally asked.

"Give me a minute. We just started going through them." Coop picked up an autopsy report and began to read through it. He set it aside and began to study the interviews.

"I see they didn't interview one person they should have," Coop said finally.

Tess turned. "Who?"

"Maxie Zahi. Wasn't she the housekeeper here?"

"She was until about a month before the fire. She quit and went back to the reservation." Tess pushed Spirit off the sofa and moved closer to the file Coop held. "She wouldn't have been here to see anything."

Coop nodded. "But she might know who hated the Mastersons enough to set fire to the barn."

"That's true. I haven't seen her in years," Tess said. "I was hurt when she left so abruptly. She never came to see me either, though she came to the funerals."

"It might be worth chatting with her. There's probably nothing she can add, but you don't want to leave any stone unturned."

Tess bent over the scattered papers. "Do you see anything else?"

"Did you know they only found one of your dad's boots?" Flint put in.

"I didn't notice that!" She took the paper he held out and glanced at it. "Maybe the other one was lost in the debris."

"It might not be significant," Flint agreed. He slanted a glance her way. "I spoke to Allie's parents today."

Tess looked over the top of the paper. "They actually talked to you?"

"If you can call it that. They told me she was still in a coma, and no, I couldn't come to see her."

Tess yearned to see Alice. Besides wanting to talk to her friend, she thought Allie might have the missing link to who might be behind the incident on the plane. If Tess ever got a chance to ask her.

Chase parked his truck behind Tess's Jeep. Dust clouded the parking lot as pickup trucks and SUVs pulling horse trailers rumbled through the lot jockeying for closest positions. Horse whinnies and the shouts of children filled the air as they got out and started toward the corrals. Mindy clung to Chase's hand as they skirted the vehicles. Tess walked beside them. He hadn't seen much of Tess this week. She had been putting in long hours at the fire camp.

"You nervous?" he asked Mindy. He squeezed her fingers when she nodded. "You're going to do great. Just remember what I told you about keeping your back straight and your head up. Focus on where you want Pepper to go, and signal to him with your knees." From the corner of his eye, he could see Tess listening to him too.

"Here come your parents," he told Mindy. She pulled her hand from his and ran to greet Stevie and Paul. Coop and Whip were behind them with Mindy's pony. Darkness smudged the skin under Stevie's eyes. She wore a wide-brimmed straw hat and long sleeves to protect her from the sun. A red blotchy rash covered her cheeks and was the only splash of color in her pale face. Stevie and Paul joined them. Coop and Whip nodded a greeting but kept heading to the stockyard with the pony.

Chase caught sight of Eric and two of his deputies making his way toward them across the crowded parking lot. He smiled and waved at them, but Eric's sober look never changed.

Stevie was smiling in spite of her pallor. "Are you entering the barrel racing, Tessie? I forgot to ask you."

"No, I'm not ready." She waved away the dust that was blowing in the air.

Chase had seen her practicing yesterday. "Scared of losing?"

Before she could answer, Eric penetrated their circle and directed a look at Paul. "I'm sorry," he said. "You're under arrest for arson." He began to read him his rights.

Paul went pale. "What are you talking about?"

Stevie gripped Eric's arm. "There must be some kind of mistake."

Eric nodded to his deputy, who pulled a pair of cuffs from his back pocket. The man asked Paul to put his hands behind his back. Paul complied with a dazed expression.

"You can't be serious," Chase said. "Paul wouldn't have anything to do with setting a fire."

"I can't ignore the evidence, Chase." Eric passed his hand over his damp forehead. His eyes looked grim.

"I asked you to keep this from happening," Stevie whispered. "You never listen, Tessie."

"What's the evidence?" Tess demanded.

"There's time enough for that after we book him." Eric nodded toward the deputy, and he took Paul's arm and led him toward the waiting car. "He'll have to stay until he's arraigned on Monday."

"Call our lawyer, Stevie," Paul called as he was led away.

Stevie nodded and began to fumble for her cell phone.

Tess sprang after Eric, and Chase was right behind her. "Just a minute," Tess said. "Eric, why are you doing this?"

Eric waited until he had Paul in the back of the car. He slammed it and turned to face them. "The Wilson's barn burned early this morning. We found evidence outside linking Paul to the crime."

"What kind of evidence?" Chase asked.

"I can't talk about it. But you know I wouldn't do this without something pretty solid, Chase. You know it too, Tess. I'm sorry, but you've got major trouble on your hands. He'll be in at least overnight while we're questioning him. I'm sure his lawyer will show up, but don't bother trying to get him out until after the judge sets bail." He nodded, then walked around his car and got behind the wheel.

Tess had her hand to her throat. "We have to fix this," she muttered. "What are we going to do, Chase?"

The appeal in her face touched him. Would she even accept his help if he offered? "I think we'd better find out what the evidence is first."

Stevie ran up to them, closing her cell phone. "It has to be fabricated," she said. "Paul would never do something like this. Mom's and Dad's deaths about killed us both. The last thing he would do is cause someone else the same hurt."

Chase didn't need to be convinced, but it was true that Eric wouldn't arrest a friend without compelling evidence. And while Paul wasn't Chase's favorite person, he couldn't see him as a firebug. He had a feeling it was going to be an uphill road to extricate Paul from this mess.

CHAPTER 10

I still haven't crossed the last threshold. The lamp on the street casts a sickly yellow glow, and it hums and flickers. The night scene is straight out of *The Howling*. Dark enough to hide a beast's movement. I've chosen well. An old Chevy stands on blocks beside me, but it's the only car in sight, so I don't bother to crouch. Darkness shrouds the other houses. Old Mrs. Walker is the one I've worried about. Her insomnia has her up drinking tea at all hours, but even her curtains are drawn tonight.

All the incantations and potions in the world won't work until I take the final step. Do I have courage to follow the prescribed method? My fingers fondle the knife at my waist. Testing the edge with my finger, I feel the razor sharpness. Yes. Invincibility is a cloak around me. The shuttered windows of the house mock me as if it doesn't believe I'll enter the power of my calling.

You're just a coward, a puny coward. You want to hit me? Go ahead, just try it. See if you're brave enough. Laughter rings in my head, and I clap my hands over my ears.

His laughter will mock me no more. "Shut up," I whisper. The key is suddenly in my hand, and I approach the front door. He will be in front of the TV as usual. I should taunt him with what I'm about to do, but I'm not sure I have the courage to go that far.

The bushes haven't been trimmed in years, and they hang over the walk in straggly, unruly abandon, almost determined to keep me out. They can't protect him. I start past them, then see where a moonbeam illuminates a fat black widow hanging in her web. I stop and stare. Black widows fascinate me. Totally self-centered and focused on their own needs, they have no remorse. I want to be like this spider, without pity. It's the only way to have power. I need to put to death emotions like compassion and regret. Even understanding. Why should I care if anyone understands or approves my actions? Does God worry about the mortals he executes judgment on?

Tess's face swims into my head. The rest of the Mastersons would be easy for me to eliminate, but Tess is different. We have a soul connection, like brother and sister. She just doesn't know it yet. I take out my knife and touch the tip of it to the spider's web. She reacts immediately and races along the silken strands toward the disturbance. Her commitment to seizing her prey enchants me. When she draws near enough, I cut the web and watch her fall to the ground. Even there, she races toward me with utter carelessness for her own safety. She is almost to my leg before I stomp her. I close my eyes and feel her power enter me. Who needs sympathy or understanding when I have power?

My key slips into the lock with a grating sound. The door opens

with a soft creak. The foyer is dark. I pass through it, knowing I will
be reborn on the other side. The glow of the TV from the living
room spills into the darkness on the other side of the hall. Feeling
my strength grow, I move toward it.

He slumps in the recliner with his mouth open and a snore issu-
ing from his mouth. My knife is out, clutched in my hand like a deli-
cate scalpel. The steel lays across his neck where the pulse beats
strongly. My spirit wants to shrink back, to stay on this side of the
threshold, but the spider's implacable determination pushes me on.
I let the spider take me, and my mind blanks out. When I am myself
again, it's done. No more pity. No further need to justify myself. I
am new, an enemy to reckon with.

I spit out the copper taste in my mouth and kneel to light the
incendiary device.

Tess lay in her bed looking at the ceiling. Moonlight filtered through
the lace curtain and made patterns on the quilt that covered her.
Paul, an arsonist? It didn't seem possible. She ran through in her
mind all the common attributes of a firebug. He'd been a teenager
when the fires started. He had a lot of inner rage and a persecution
complex that even his faith had failed to eradicate. Maybe he'd been
unwilling to let go of his bitterness. Kind of like her and her attitude
toward Chase. She moved restlessly, then threw back the quilt and
sat up on the edge of the bed. Her mind was spinning too fast to
relax. Maybe some chamomile tea would help her sleep.

She pulled on her robe and opened the door. Moving down the
dark hall, she listened outside Stevie's door. At least her sister wasn't
crying herself to sleep. Tess continued on down the corridor and

stepped into the living room. As she was walking toward the kitchen, she saw a movement at the window and saw Chase standing there staring out the window.

"You okay?" she asked. He jerked. "Sorry, I thought you heard me come in. Can't sleep?"

"Nope. I was looking through the books. I don't know how we're going to save Paul."

She didn't either. Eric had found Paul's keys outside the burned barn. They'd taken imprints of some boot prints, and she had a feeling they were going to match the ones Paul wore. The other arsons had happened in the night, which left no good alibis for him either. Eric would say Paul could have easily slipped away while Stevie slept.

"You know this will bankrupt the ranch, don't you? There's no money to fight the case without selling it."

She hadn't even considered losing the ranch. "What about a mortgage? I could help pay it back."

"It's already mortgaged to the hilt."

"I suppose you think this is your opportunity then," she said, raising her voice. "You've been watching for the right time to take it over. This isn't it. I'll figure out something."

"That's enough," Stevie said from the doorway. She stumbled into the living room and sank onto the couch. Flicking on the table lamp, she leaned back into the sofa. The rash on her face had spread, and her eyes were sunken dark pools in her face.

"Sorry we woke you," Tess said. "But we're not giving up the ranch."

"No, we're not, not if we can help it. But, Tess, you've got it all wrong. If it wasn't for Chase, we would have lost the Bar Q a year ago. He hasn't taken a dime in wages in six months."

Tess looked from her sister to Chase and back again. She recognized the ring of truth in her sister's words. "Things are that bad? Why didn't you tell me?"

Stevie spread out her hands. "What could you have done? There was no reason to worry you when you had your own life to live."

"Quit mollycoddling her," Chase said, stepping away from the window. He scowled at Tess. "The truth is we knew you'd never give up your precious firefighting to come help out anyway, so what was the use? You've always done exactly what you wanted in spite of what anyone else needed."

"That's not fair. I could have given Stevie money every month. In fact, I have some saved I'll give you now. Nearly five thousand dollars."

"A drop in the bucket," Chase scoffed.

"Chase." Stevie sent him a warning look before smiling at Tess. "That would be great, Tess, if you're sure you can spare it. It would retain the lawyer. We've just had a string of bad luck lately."

"What kind of bad luck?" Tess eased onto the chair across from her sister.

Stevie pushed the hair back out of her face. "Sick cattle, grass fires that have burned up more hay than we can afford to lose, mechanical problems on equipment. You name it, we've had it." Her voice was weary.

"I didn't know." Tess hated to see her sister's defeated air. "We'll figure this out." She glanced at Chase. Though she was afraid the words would stick in her throat, she knew she owed him an apology. "I'm sorry for misjudging you, Chase."

He reared back his head, and his eyebrows rose. "An apology from Queenie? What's next—a unicorn showing up?"

"Chase," Stevie warned.

"Sorry."

"You don't sound sorry." She shouldn't have said anything.

His frown relaxed, and he put his hand out toward her. "The ranch needs us—all of us."

His gaze was direct and steady, and he gripped her hand. She decided to take it as sincere. Withdrawing her fingers, she dropped onto the couch beside her sister. "What are we going to do?"

"I know Paul had nothing to do with that fire!" Stevie burst out. "You've got to help clear his name—both of you."

Tess wasn't quite sure how to accomplish the task, but she nodded. "We'll do what we can, won't we, Chase?"

His gaze held hers. "You bet."

The warmth that swept over her was about as welcome as a furnace blast on a summer day. Attraction to Chase Huston? Impossible. But the sensation refused to be dispelled. Tess averted her gaze, aware of the heat spreading up her neck to her cheeks. She stood and walked to the window. If Stevie or Chase saw her red cheeks, she'd never hear the end of it. She must be tired or something. Tess had never denied the fact that the man was attractive—she'd seen the girls flocking around him. But to actually feel an awareness of him as a man wasn't something she wanted to experience.

She leaned her hot face against the cool glass and stared out at the front yard. The security light at the peak of the barn illuminated the drive. Moisture from the glass condensed on her forehead. Something moved in the shadows, and she squinted as she tried to make it out. From out of the darkness, Wildfire pranced, his head high. "My horse is out!" Tess turned and ran to the door. She heard Chase's boots pound behind her.

She burst through the door, then forced herself to slow and approach the stallion with deliberate steps. A short rain had fallen earlier in the evening, and her bare feet plunged into cool mud. She grimaced and moved closer to the horse. "Hey, boy, you looking for me?" She felt around in her pocket for sugar, but all she came up with was lint. Tess held out her hand anyway, speaking in a coaxing voice. Wildfire stepped toward her, arching his neck. His velvety lips nuzzled her palm. She ran her hands over his mane. "Easy, boy." Gripping his mane, she vaulted onto his back as Chase reached them.

"You're the only one he'll let do that."

"He loves me."

Chase nodded. "When I go to feed every morning, he's looking for you. How often do you see him in the summer?"

"Often enough." If he was trying to make her feel guilty, he was doing a good job. She clung to Wildfire with her knees and guided him back toward the barn. Chase jogged alongside the horse. "How on earth did he get out?"

"He's a master escape artist. Paul gripes about it almost daily ever since you came. Haven't you had problems in the other places you've boarded him?"

She shook her head. "The other places have had metal fences and stalls. He's gotten out a couple of times, but I only found out after the fact."

Tess reached the interior of the barn and dismounted. Holding on to Wildfire's mane, she guided him inside, pausing to flip on the barn light. She led him to the stall. The gate was standing open, and she was sure she'd closed it. Examining the latch, she couldn't find anything wrong with it. It seemed to close firmly.

"This is the first time I've known him to escape the barn. The latches are harder to get open," Chase said. He put one booted foot on the bottom rung of the wooden stall. Dust motes jarred loose began to settle to the floor.

She sensed him standing close. She averted her eyes. "Could someone have let him out?"

"Why?"

The scent of his cologne—Stetson—made her feel . . . She had to stop noticing things about Chase. Chase of all people! Maybe she was getting sick. She turned to leave and bumped into him, but he didn't move to get out of the way. She felt the gate at her back.

"How did we get so much at odds, Tess?"

She heard the note of wistfulness in his voice and marveled at it. Chase so seldom showed any vulnerability. She hated him for hundreds of reasons, but right now she couldn't summon a one to mind. "We're both adults now. Maybe we can put it behind us and work as partners."

"That might just choke you." His lips twitched as if a smile wanted to make its appearance.

"It might, but I'm willing to give it a try." Her glance darted to each side of him. She had to escape him before she did the unthinkable—like step into his arms or something. Good grief, what was wrong with her?

He studied her face. "You seem different tonight. Are you okay?"

"I'm fine, fine." She was a babbling idiot, she decided. Clamping her teeth against any further outbursts of insanity, she curled her fingers around the gate behind her and prayed for him to step away. She could smell saddle soap under his cologne. He must have been oiling the saddles. She stifled a giggle. Only she would find saddle soap appealing.

He finally stepped back. "Well, I guess I'll turn in. You'd better get some rest. We've got a lot of work ahead of us tomorrow."

She drew in a relieved breath and followed him from the barn. As they neared the front of the barn, she noticed his brother sitting on a bale of hay. "Jimmy, have you been there the whole time?" It was a good thing she hadn't succumbed to the temptation to kiss Chase.

"I was just sitting here." Jimmy hunched his shoulders.

"Why aren't you at Doty's?" Chase demanded.

"Her cabin was hot, and I was bored. She's about to work me to death." His fingers played with the strands of straw on the bale he sat on. His mouth was pinched.

Tess couldn't decide if he was scared or just nervous because Chase was grilling him. "You want something to eat?" she asked.

Jimmy's head jerked up. "The ice princess is actually offering me food?"

"That's enough, Jimmy."

Tess's warm feelings seeped away. Jimmy had resented her from the first, just like his brother. The two of them ganged up on her when she was young. The day Jimmy was removed from their house and sent to the Diamonds had been a happy day. Her smile faded, and she went toward the door. "Fine. Do whatever you want."

"Wait a minute, Tess. Jimmy, you owe her an apology. She was trying to be nice."

"That's rich, coming from you. You call her the ice princess all the time."

Tess didn't want to hear more. She slid the door out of the way and ran toward the house. Her eyes burned, but the Huston brothers weren't worth her tears. She heard Chase shout her name, but she hurried on. She was a fool to think they could forget the past. While she knew they'd never gotten along, to hear that Chase called her names hurt more than she would ever have guessed.

The slick mud slowed her steps. She stumbled over a rock and went down on one knee. Dull pain radiated up her leg and finally drew tears. She swiped at them. Warm hands touched her shoulders, but she shrugged them away. "Leave me alone, Chase."

He lifted her to her feet and pulled her against his chest. "It didn't take much for you to override our cease-fire."

With her face buried against the rough texture of his denim shirt, she lost all inclination to snipe back at him. His hands smoothed her hair. She'd never dated much in high school, preferring the company of her horses and books to that of boys. So the onslaught of emotion coiling in her stomach was a sensation she didn't know how to battle.

"Hey, you're getting my shirt wet," Chase said, a laugh rumbling in his chest. He pulled her away and cupped her face in his hands.

The warmth of his palms enveloped her head. Wanting to look away but unable to tear her gaze from his, she stared up into eyes as blue as an Arizona sky. His smile mellowed, and he bent his head. She closed her eyes, expecting to feel his mouth on hers. Instead, he dropped his hands and stepped away. She ought to feel cold with his warm hands gone from her face, but more heat spread over her cheeks. He must have thought she was inviting his kiss. Would he think she'd thrown herself at him?

She couldn't stand to read the answer to the question in his eyes. She turned and ran to the house.

CHAPTER 11

hat had almost happened with Tess? Chase punched his pillow and rolled over on the cot. He'd nearly kissed her, and he had an inkling she would have welcomed it. Best not to think about it. Trouble with a capital T lay in that direction. Getting involved with Tess Masterson would be about as smart as picking up a diamond-back. He rolled on the cot again, kicking at the covers.

"You're bound and determined to keep a body awake, aren't you?" Whip's voice spoke out of the darkness. "Quit your thrashin' and get some shut-eye."

"Sorry. I can't sleep."

Whip's feet thumped on the bare wooden floor of the bunk-house, and he clicked on the wrought-iron lamp shaped like an old milk urn that sat on a barrel beside his bed. It illuminated the names of the ranch hands who had all signed the wall over the years—

Hank, Martin, Jon, Whip, Ralph, Coop. The names covered the wall. He shook a cigarette into his fingers and lit it. The smoke curled around his head as he sat there in his underwear and a gray T-shirt that used to be white. "The good Lord pesterin' you about somethin'? 'He who answers a matter before he hears it, it is folly and shame to him.' So you'd better tell me about it since I ain't getting any sleep until I give you my piece on it."

"Just worried about everything that's going on."

"We're in a heap of trouble," Whip agreed. "I got a bit of green set by if you need it."

"Thanks, Whip, but we'll figure something out. You're already living on your good looks."

Whip snorted and took another puff. "No wonder I'm poor." His teeth flashed behind his handlebar mustache.

"What are you two gabbing about? You're keeping me awake." Coop stood in the doorway with his blond hair loose on his shoulders.

"Trying to figure out how to get the ranch out of the mess we're in," Chase said. "You got any bright ideas?"

"I'm fresh out." Coop dropped into a chair by the door.

It felt right to see Coop here again. Coop's mom had worked as housekeeper for the Mastersons until she died when he was in his teens. He'd gone off to school soon after that and lost the rough cowboy edge to his speech. He reminded Chase of some hip mountain man. Coop was happiest when he was hiking some remote mountain trail that no Native Americans had ever seen.

Coop propped his bare feet on an empty crate they used as a table. "You think Paul did it?"

Chase shrugged. "I sure hope not. It would kill Stevie. You think he's guilty?"

"I think someone did a good job of pointing the finger at him."

"He's annoying, self-righteous, and sanctimonious, but that's no reason to frame him for arson and murder," Chase said.

"I seen murder done for less," Whip said.

Coop shrugged. "I suppose that's where we should start—with any incidents in Paul's past that might make someone want to hurt him," he mumbled.

"Mebbe the fella wants to hit the Mastersons where it hurts. Could be it's not even Paul they're aiming at," said Whip.

"Maybe it's Tess." Chase's stomach soured.

Coop winced. "You heard about the lines on her chute being cut?"

"Yeah. Any bright ideas?"

"What's this?" Whip sat up straighter. "What happened to Queenie's chute?"

Chase told him. "And someone put an incendiary device in her pack. That's two attempts on her life now."

"Unless the entire smokejumping team was the target for the device," Coop said, his face thoughtful.

"What about the chute? It was Tess's special one."

"True, but someone might not know that."

"You seem mighty concerned about Queenie," Whip observed. "I seen her hidin' her face in your chest. I think that's the closest I ever seen you two."

Chase tried to keep his face from betraying emotion, but the muscle in his jaw twitched. He looked away from Whip's inquisitive gaze. "She was just upset about everything."

"And it's always been your way to comfort her." Whip said the words with great solemnity.

Chase couldn't help but grin at Whip's droll tone. "Okay, you got me there. We haven't exactly been on the same crew. A truce was called tonight."

"Think it will hold?"

"Probably not," Chase agreed. "She gets under my skin."

"You ever think there might be a reason for it?" Whip lit another cigarette and crossed one bony leg over the other.

"You're barking up the wrong tree, Whip."

"If you two are going to talk about love, I'm going to bed." Coop stood with a yawn and went down the hall.

Chase got up and flipped out the light, then flopped back on his cot. He could see the glow from the tip of Whip's cigarette. The chortle from that direction told Chase the old coot was laughing at him.

Doty had one hand on the Troy-Bilt tiller and walked to the right of it. She didn't seem to notice Tess's Jeep stopping outside the cabin Sunday afternoon. Doty was always sharper than she seemed though, so Tess got out of the vehicle and waited. Sure enough, Doty turned off the engine and stepped out of the garden. Mud clumped on the bottom of her Wellingtons.

"Why are you doing that?" Tess asked. "Jimmy should help you."

"I set him to running tomatoes through the food mill. Too nice a day to be inside. Winter will be here before we know it."

"How's it going with Jimmy?"

"Fine." Doty gave her a shrewd glance. "You didn't come out here to talk about Jimmy."

"Did you hear that Paul was arrested yesterday? We have to go to town tomorrow to bail him out."

Doty betrayed no surprise beyond a slight lift of her eyebrow. "How's Stevie taking it?"

"About like you'd expect." Tess wasn't quite sure how to segue into the reason for the visit.

"Come inside."

Tess followed her to the cabin. A strong aroma of tomatoes slipped out the door. Red splattered the floor as well as the big white apron wrapped around Jimmy. He had a blob of tomato on one cheek and in his hair.

When he saw them, he threw down the towel. "I'm out of here," he said. He untied the apron and tossed it to the floor, then stalked to the door.

"You're not done, James," Doty said. "Come here, let me show you what you're doing wrong."

To Tess's surprise, Jimmy allowed her aunt to steer him back to the counter. The two worked over the mill. Jimmy's shoulders began to relax, and Tess could see how the older woman's calm, direct instructions caused the anger and frustration to seep out of Jimmy. Her aunt had always had that effect on her too. She remembered the time when she was ten and was supposed to stir the pasta while her mother was on the phone. It had boiled over, and she was crying. Aunt Doty had calmly helped her clean up the mess, then shown her how to add a bit of butter to the pot and where to turn the control to keep the fire low.

Maybe Doty really could get through to Jimmy.

Her aunt left him working at the mill again and rejoined Tess. "I'm not going to give you any money, Tess. I imagine that's why you're here."

Tess sank onto the chair. What were they going to do now? It was going to take a lot of money to get Paul out of this mess.

"Stevie has just enough to get through the winter with none to spare for lawyers. She needs your help."

"I'm not sure he's innocent."

"You can't believe he's an arsonist."

Doty glanced away. "Darkness is in the heart of every man. I've learned never to put blinders on. I've been disappointed too many times." She looked up again, and her gaze locked with Tess's. "Get me some evidence to prove he's innocent, and I'll reconsider."

Breakfast trays rattled past Tess as she stood outside Allie's hospital room Monday morning. She'd come early so she could go with Stevie to the jail as soon as the sheriff's office opened. Her life seemed pulled in a million directions, like she was a clown at the rodeo trying to keep all the balls in the air.

She rapped on the door and stepped inside without waiting for an answer. A sheet was folded across Allie's waist as she lay in the bed in pink silk pajamas. The woman beside the bed looked up. Allie looked so much like her that Tess knew she had to be Allie's mother.

"Mrs. Stinson? I'm Allie's friend, Tess."

The woman's smile disappeared. "I know who you are. What do you want? Haven't you done enough?"

"How is she?"

The frown eased. "She's showing signs of waking up."

"How wonderful!" Tess stepped into the room. "I'm so glad. In spite of how you feel, I love Allie. She's my best friend. If I could take her place, I would."

Mrs. Stinson studied Tess's face. "I believe maybe you would."

"Did you hear the lines on the chute had been cut?" Tess blurted. "Allie was wearing my chute. The accident was intended for me."

Mrs. Stinson put her hand to her mouth. "What are you saying?"

"Allie knew. Just before we crashed she said something about someone trying to kill me."

"It wasn't an accident?"

Tess shook her head. "If Allie awakens, maybe she can tell us what happened and we can catch whoever did this. Will you call me if she comes out of the coma?" She fumbled in her purse for a piece of paper and wrote her number on it. "Here's my cell number. Please call."

The older woman nodded. "All right. Thank you for telling me the truth. And pray for her, Tess."

"I will. I have." She backed out of the room and closed the door behind her.

The first part of my plan has fallen into place. The look on the Mastersons' faces as Paul was led away on Saturday was priceless. And I crossed the final threshold. *He* is dead, and all traces of who I used to be have been destroyed. The power and confirmation from on high has been sweet.

My car is parked across the street from the jail. Is Paul suffering in there, wondering what's going to happen to him? Two days is a long time to stew in one's own failings. Soon he'll discover his boot prints were found at the scene, an easy enough illusion for me to create. My web is sticky with revenge and impossible to escape. The thought brings me no pleasure or pain. Saturday night burned away the last vestiges of emotion. Other than the ones that linger in the box in the backseat.

I drop the gearshift into drive and travel along the street at two miles an hour below the speed limit. The car purrs along the empty streets as I drive to the school and park the car among all the rest in the lot. I'm invisible in plain sight. I sit there listening to the engine tick as it cools. I close my eyes and hear the sounds of children in their classrooms. The wind is blowing, an omen from God that this is right and good. I take my things from the back seat. I shiver, but it is from the anticipation, not the wind that cools the perspiration on my forehead.

The woods march right up to the back of the school. The scent of pine seems a confirmation of my plan. Fresh and invigorating—a new beginning. I hardly need to glance around to ensure I'm alone. I have the senses of the wolves now. They and the other animals of the forest are with me, urging me on. The pine needles are soft beneath my knees, a carpet that welcomes me. Lifting out the incendiary device, I set it aside. The top of the box resists my prying fingers at first, but I lift it off and riffle through the pictures inside.

My mother's face looks back at me. She rarely smiled, but then what did she have to smile about? These pictures depict the only good times in my past, my last claim to feelings like love and friendship. They tie me to who I once was, but not for long. Once I activate the device, my past will be incinerated, and I will be free.

My lips hold my smile for several long minutes as my fingers toy with the lighter. I can light it right now and watch it rush toward the school. There are many memories here too, most of them bad, but a few I like to cherish. But if I am to be reborn, it must be done. The lighter is alive in my hand, hot as molten metal. The fuse ignites, and I have a new name. *Skinwalker*.

The sheriff's office bustled with activity after the busy weekend. Tess had just enough time to run by the bank and make a deposit into the Bar Q account before meeting Stevie and Chase in the waiting room outside the jail. Stevie was sure Eric would help them get Paul out this morning. Tess wasn't so sure. They were asked to wait and went to the room they were pointed to. Utility chairs with blue upholstery circled the space, and heaps of magazines and books covered the surfaces of the three tables in the room. There was only one other occupant, a woman of about fifty with gray permed hair. The room reeked of the cheap perfume she wore.

The woman looked up when they entered. She shook her head and put down the paper in her hand. "It's terrible about that arsonist. He has to be stopped. Another murder."

"Murder?" Tess's gaze met her sister's. "Has there been another fire?"

"Last night. Ben Diamond's house burned down with him in it." The woman got up and went to talk to the receptionist.

"Let me see that." Chase grabbed the paper. "Ben Diamond was Jimmy's foster dad."

Tess put her hand to her mouth. Jimmy matched the profile for an arsonist.

Chase tossed the paper to the table. "I wonder if Jimmy knows."

Neither of the women answered, and he looked at them carefully. "Jimmy wouldn't do something like that."

"He's been in a lot of trouble, Chase. Are you sure?" Tess asked.

"I don't believe it." Chase's mouth took on a stubborn cast. "Do you realize how many kids have gone through the Diamond home? Hundreds."

"I know," Tess said. Ben Diamond and his wife had been foster parents for thirty years before the state discovered the kids were being mistreated and removed the children. "I'd still like to talk to him about it," Tess said.

"And we will. But it's not him." Chase stood and went to look out the window. He thrust his hands into his jeans and turned his back to them with an air of frustration.

A door opened, and Eric motioned to them. Stevie stepped toward him first, and Tess followed with Chase on her heels. Eric ushered them into his office. Tess dropped into the chair.

"You can let Paul out of jail," Stevie said. "He's obviously not the arsonist. We heard the guy struck again last night. The Diamond house burned, and Ben Diamond is dead."

"I wish I could," Eric said. "The evidence is strong, guys. The Diamond house is a different case. The device used isn't the same."

Tess spread her hands, palms up. "Eric, you know Paul. He can't be the one you're looking for."

Eric twiddled a pencil between his fingers. "We got the boot casts compared to Paul's boots. It's a match. He'll be arraigned in about an hour."

"That's not possible," Stevie whispered. She passed her palm over her forehead. "I'd like to see my husband."

"That much I can do." Eric rose, took Stevie's arm, and they went toward the door. He glanced back at Tess and Chase. "I'll be right back." He closed the door, leaving the two alone.

The silence that fell between them made Tess get up from her chair. She walked to the window and looked out. Her mind raced for something to say to break the uncomfortable silence. Chase joined her. "I was talking with Whip, and he had an interesting thought on all this. Have you ever considered the arsonist might be someone who is trying to hurt your family through framing Paul and threatening you?"

She turned to look at him and took a step back. "I don't have any enemies, and neither does Stevie nor Paul."

"I think Whip might be right. Think about it. We'll be hard pressed to keep things running with having to worry about Paul's legal battle."

She wrinkled her brow as she thought about it. The Mastersons were well respected in the area. Whenever they went to town, people waved and stopped to talk. She couldn't think of a single instance where they'd made an enemy. "There's just no one, Chase."

"A rival in the beef business?" he suggested.

"You'd know that better than I would," she pointed out.

"Yeah, I guess you're right. Your sister is always careful to be fair."

"And Paul?"

"He's a demanding man, but also fair."

"Stevie is the real head of the ranch. Anyone who wanted to hurt our family would target her, and she has only friends."

"I don't think I've even heard her argue with a salesman." Chase took off his hat and rubbed his hair before clapping it back on his head.

"If someone wanted to hurt me, why target Paul? Why not frame me?"

"Unless the real arsonist hates Stevie for some reason. Hurting you or Paul would devastate her."

"What about the Wilsons? Have you ever heard Stevie argue with them?"

"Not in my hearing."

"Maybe it's Jimmy."

He shook his head. "No way."

"Think about it. The fires started when he was in his teens. Statistically, that's when most arsonists begin setting fires. Ninety percent of the time, an arsonist is male. He often has an absent or abusive father. Jimmy was sent to the Diamond house after he was taken from our place. He fits the profile."

"I was a troubled kid too. Am I under suspicion?"

She raised her gaze and studied him. The sun and wind had begun to weather his face. When he was old, he would still be handsome with the strong lines of his cheeks and chin. His blue eyes held hers. She tried to find her earlier hostility, but it was gone like the summer dust devils. There was still the matter of his spurs, though. "You're no arsonist," she admitted.

A corner of his mouth twitched before the grin spread across his face. "That pained you, didn't it?"

"Not as much as you might think," she said, her spirits lifting at their banter. The awareness between them couldn't be her imagination, could it? Surely Chase felt it too.

The door opened, and Chase stepped away from her.

Eric entered the room, but Stevie wasn't with him.

"Coffee?" Eric asked.

"No thanks. So what's next in the investigation?" Tess asked.

Eric poured a cup of coffee and went to his desk. "I know it's hard to hear, Tess, but I think we have our firebug. I already told you the boot prints came back as Paul's boots. We have his keys at the site. We have a witness to an argument last month between Paul and Mark Wilson."

"I hadn't heard that," Tess said. "What argument?" She glanced at Chase and saw confusion on his face too.

"They'd been bidding on a lot of calves. Mark bid up the price before finally dropping out, but not until it was higher than Paul wanted to pay. He got stuck with the calves and wasn't too happy about it."

"He could have dropped out as soon as it went over his personal ceiling," Chase said. "Why would he blame Mark?"

"The bidding got pretty hot and heavy. I think Paul was following the thrill of the hunt without stopping to think of the consequences. They traded insults for fifteen minutes until Paul stalked off."

"That hardly seems reason enough to burn his barn," Tess pointed out. "Have you considered maybe someone wanted to frame Paul? Someone could have worn his boots and dropped his keys. You've only got circumstantial evidence."

Eric's smile was condescending. "Do you know how many times I hear that? The reality is that the person who leaves the evidence is generally the culprit. You're grasping at straws, Tess. I expected better from you."

"Don't patronize me," she snapped. "You're grabbing at the easy answer instead of looking for the truth."

His smile turned to a provoked scowl. "Do you have any proof, any potential enemies you can even point to as a possibility?"

He knew she didn't. He could tell by the careful tone, oh so calm and reasonable as if she were a child. "Not yet."

Eric gave her a hard stare. "There's nothing wrong with standing up for your family. Just make sure you're not letting loyalty blind you to the truth. Paul was at the Bar Q when the barn burned too, and it's common knowledge he and your dad argued over Stevie the day before. What if he killed your parents, Tess?"

She didn't want to believe the killer could be someone as close as Paul. She wouldn't believe it. "You have no problem if I poke around and ask a few questions, do you?"

Eric stood. "I'm not trying to ramrod Paul. If you find any

evidence indicating he's innocent, I want to know about it. But if you find evidence pointing to him, I want that as well, Tess. It has to go both ways. Agreed?"

She glanced at Chase. He gave her a slight nod. "Okay." She hoped she hadn't promised to help convict her brother-in-law. "But Stevie is sick, Eric. She needs Paul at home."

"Sick?" For the first time Eric looked uncertain.

"She has lupus, and her kidneys are beginning to fail." She hated to go for a pity defense, but it may be the only way to bail Paul. "I'll personally guarantee he won't run."

Eric glanced at his watch. "Stevie's time is up. I have a few questions for both of them. To tell you the truth, I'm wondering if they're in it together." He disappeared through the door.

"In it together?" she whispered to Chase. "Is he nuts?"

"Eric's a dedicated man, but I'm beginning to wonder if he's being overzealous. I heard a rumor the other day that he was going to run for mayor. Maybe solving a big case would cinch his election."

"Can you talk to him? Find out where he's coming from on all this. He can't believe what he just said."

"He's playing it close to his chest these days."

Tess nodded, but before she could say anything more, Eric came back with Stevie in tow. Tess tried to catch her sister's eye, but Stevie didn't turn her way. She was probably afraid she'd cry if she did. Stevie sat in the chair and laced her fingers together. She looked pale, and her strawberry-blonde hair hung in wisps around her face.

Eric opened his desk drawer and drew out a bag. "I've been going through Paul's belongings and wondered if you might identify some things for me, Stevie." He unzipped it and dumped the contents on the desk. A jumble of keys, gum, a wallet, receipts, a pocketknife, and an address book fell out. He plucked up the address book. "Some of the phone numbers in here are for hardware stores, places where he could have bought the supplies for the incendiary device."

Stevie raised her head. "Eric, he's a *rancher*. Of course he'll be doing business at hardware stores."

Eric nodded. "One of the stores listed here is in Flagstaff. Why would he go so far for supplies? We've traced the serial number on another arson to a hardware store in Flag. It looks pretty suspicious, Stevie. The only alibi he has for any of the arsons is he was sleeping. There's no way to corroborate that."

"Let me see it." Stevie held out her hand. She studied the book, then smiled. "This is Paul's brother's store."

Tess reached over and took the book from Stevie's hand. She held it out to Eric. "Please, Eric, let us post bail."

Eric chewed on his lip, then finally nodded. "I'm not a complete ogre. Our families have been friends a long time. I'll recommend bail. But watch him, Chase. If he runs, I'm holding you all responsible."

CHAPTER 12

*S*tevie and Chase exited the building ahead of her. Tess could smell the smoke as soon as she exited the jail. She gave an appreciative sniff and looked to the horizon. Black coils snaked above the trees. "Looks like the school!" The scent of smoke always got her adrenaline pumping. She and Chase ran toward his truck. "We'll be back!" she shouted to Stevie. "Go to the arraignment, get the bail taken care of, and we'll meet you back here." Her sister nodded, and Tess kicked up her speed a notch.

Chase reached the truck first. "I'll drive."

"The guys won't want to miss this." Tess got out her cell phone and called Flint's cell. He didn't answer, so she left a message about the fire. Rolling her window down, she stuck her head out and stared at the billowing smoke. The smell got stronger, and her trained nose picked up the scent of an accelerant. The oily taste of kerosene coated her tongue. If this was arson again, Eric would have to agree he had the wrong man, and this nightmare would be over.

Cars, pickups, and SUVs jostled for parking space outside the school. Black smoke billowed around them, and the choking fumes made Tess cough and wish she had her mask. Cinders rained down. Men shouted orders for water, and in the distance Tess heard the fire siren. She hopped out of the truck and ran toward the building. The fire hadn't reached it yet. The trees behind the school were ablaze, and the flames had raced along the dry grass toward the building. Even now the fire was at the back wall of the school. The blackened wall had blistered paint and would begin to burn any second.

She stood spellbound by the fire's beauty for a moment. It both drew and repelled her, something she'd never understood.

"There's no way to fight it until the fire department gets here." If only they had access to a lake or stream. Chase carried buckets in the truck, but they were useless without water. Moments later, the fire truck screamed into the yard. People jumped out of the way to let it maneuver closer to the blaze. "Come on!" she shouted to Chase.

Tess jogged alongside the truck until it stopped. "I'm a smoke-jumper," she yelled over the noise of shouts and raised voices. "What can I do to help?"

A fireman handed her a Pulaski, and she ran to the east edge of the fire. The firemen would wet down the building. She began to dig, tearing up the dry sod until all that was left was unburnable soil. Focused on the task, she only gradually became aware of someone working alongside of her. She took a moment to glance to her left and saw Chase digging as well. He wasn't as experienced, but he was doing a good job.

"Thanks," she called to him. He gave her a grin.

The firemen had the blaze under control in an hour. Tess returned the Pulaski, then wandered toward the woods. "I think I'll see if I can tell how the fire started," she said. "I wish Coop were here. He's the expert."

"Maybe he'll be along when Flint gets your message." Chase followed her into the woods. "Should we be messing with the scene?"

"I know what not to touch." She stepped over a smoldering log. The ground was still hot, and she stomped out an occasional ember. "Look," she said, pointing to the point of origin. "There's an incendiary device!" She stooped and looked at the device without touching it. "It's a different device than the others."

"Here comes Eric," Chase said.

Tess waved to the sheriff. She stood and stepped back when Eric reached her. "It was set, Eric. Now maybe you'll believe us when we tell you Paul is innocent. He couldn't have set this fire." She knew better though. He'd notice right off that it was a different device.

Eric knelt and examined the device. "You know as well as I do, Tess, that crazies come out of the woodwork all the time. It's probably a copycat arsonist. The device is different. If it were the same, I might have been tempted to believe you. But this just makes Paul all the more likely."

Tess's gaze met Chase's. They would have to fight for Paul's freedom every step of the way. What a shock to discover she considered Chase a friend now.

Eric walked away to talk to a deputy. Chase and Tess started toward the truck. Chase took her hand when they reached a big log and helped her over it. His fingers were warm and soot-covered, but she didn't mind the dirt and found out she didn't mind his help either. When he let go of her fingers, it was all she could do not to reach out and take his hand again.

They drove to the courthouse and found Stevie and Paul ready to go. They crammed into the truck, and Stevie leaned back with her eyes closed. None of them spoke on the trip back to the ranch. Tess couldn't figure out why Coop, Flint, and Buck hadn't come to join in the fun of putting out the fire. They were supposed to start the demolition today, so maybe they just couldn't get to the phones. At the ranch, she noticed her Jeep was missing. She'd left her keys for the men.

Tess hopped out of the truck and helped her sister to the house while Chase and Paul went to attend to chores. "I'll start dinner. You want to lie down?" she asked her sister.

"No, I want to be with you. There's stuff for beef stew," Stevie said.

"That I can make." The women went to the kitchen. Tess made Stevie sit down at the table, then busied herself chopping beef and onions, and soon the ingredients were sizzling on the stove.

"I can smell the fire on you. Was it bad?" Stevie asked.

"A brush fire was threatening the school. It didn't take long to stomp out. Beautiful though. This guy knows what he's doing."

"You sound like you admire him."

"Of course not! But he understands fire." She told Stevie about the incendiary device.

Stevie had seemed almost robotic since they got home. Tess studied her sister's face. She stirred the beef and onion. "Are you okay? You've been a little strange."

Stevie picked at a hangnail. "I still can't believe Eric would believe Paul could do something like this. I need to call Pastor and let him know I'm home." Going to the junk drawer, she rummaged through it. "Where on earth is the phone book?" She turned and grabbed the plastic bag of Paul's belongings that Eric had given them. "Maybe

Paul has it in his address book." She picked up the small leather book and flipped through the pages.

Tess heard her quick inhalation. "What's wrong?"

Stevie was white and swaying. She put out her hand and then grabbed the edge of the counter. "Nothing, I'm fine."

"You're not fine." Tess grabbed her sister's arm and guided her to a chair at the table. "What's wrong, Stevie?"

Stevie bit her lip and threw the book down on the table. "He told me he'd quit seeing her, but this is a new address book I just got him for his birthday, and she's in here. I thought I saw her name when I was looking at it in the police station."

No wonder she'd made an excuse to look at the address book again. Tess was sure Stevie knew the pastor's phone number by heart. Stevie had said *she* in a tone of voice that spoke of betrayal. "Who?"

"Joni Kojo."

Tess sat down beside her sister. Paul and the church secretary? Stevie had to be wrong.

Stevie stared at the book as if it were a snake, then picked it up and flipped through the pages. She pointed out the entry. "There's a note that says, 'October 16 4:30.' That's today, in about half an hour."

"Let me make sure I have this straight. Are you saying Paul is having an *affair*?" Of all the people she would suspect of having an affair, it wouldn't be Paul. She wanted it spelled out clearly.

"Yes."

"Maybe he's meeting on church business." Had Stevie's illness made her paranoid? Tess studied her sister's face and saw only determination and a weary acceptance.

Stevie sighed. "I've known about Joni for over a year. When I confronted him, he promised to break it off."

Tess couldn't believe what she was hearing. While Stevie and

Paul didn't seem to have some great love affair of a marriage, she'd always thought they were happy.

Stevie tossed the book back on the table. "I won't have it. A man who will have an affair is capable of anything. I'm going to see my lawyer."

"What about counseling?"

"I'd never trust him again. He promised—"

"Promised what?" Tess prompted.

"We've had some—difficulty since Mindy was born," Stevie said. "In the bedroom. I told Paul he could go if he wanted. He said he wasn't leaving. He promised it wouldn't make a difference."

Everything Tess thought she knew about her sister's marriage was crumbling. "Can you talk about what's wrong?"

Stevie got up and went to the window. "Whip should be bringing Mindy back soon. They went for ice cream."

"Talk to me, Stevie. I've always thought you doted on Paul."

Stevie's smile was sad. "I've doted as much as I'm able. I'm not the touchy-feely kind of woman, in case you've never noticed."

Which was why Stevie had never been a doting mother. Oh, she took care of Mindy's needs, but Tess had always noticed a reserve in Stevie's manner. Stevie was private and had never talked about things like this. Tess felt a new sense of closeness with her sister. It just went to show that there was no way to gauge a marriage from the outside looking in.

Stevie looked away. She went to the stove and began to stir the beef and onions.

Tess tried to think of any boys Stevie had dated, but there were none. Paul was her only boyfriend, and she seemed crazy about him. It made Tess even more sympathetic to Stevie to know that her sister had an Achilles heel.

Paul announced he had to run to town for a minute, and Chase told him he could handle checking on the cattle. Buck and Flint drove up in Tess's Jeep as Chase prepared to head to the pasture, and within minutes Coop pulled in behind them in his own truck. All three men, dusty from demolition work, asked to come along, so he found them horses. The four rode over the hills and valleys, and being in the open air blew the smoky smell out of Chase's hair. They found a fence down and cattle out in the back pasture. The men rounded up the strays, and he repaired the fence.

"It looks like someone cut this fence," Coop said, stooping beside him. "Look."

Chase squinted at the wire. "You're right. I hadn't noticed. We've had vandals occasionally these past few years. Good thing we were close by." But was it a vandal? All the assumptions he'd made about their past bad luck were now up for reassessment. He wiped the moisture from his forehead and climbed back into the saddle. Cattle dotted the hillside, their golden coats standing out against the green grass.

"The herd looks good—healthy and well-fed," Flint remarked. He and Buck flanked Chase.

"They should bring a decent price at market. All we need is a little luck, and we'll be able to pull the ranch out of the hole," Chase said. "Thanks for getting these bad boys rounded up." He nodded toward the woods. "Right through there is the re-creation of the Zane Grey cabin. It burned in the 1990 Dude Fire."

"We missed out on that one," Buck said. "It was a beautiful fire." His tone was hushed.

Chase didn't think he'd ever get used to hearing the three of them talk in admiring tones about wildfires. "You smokejumpers are sick. I saw the joy on Tess's face today when she came back from working that fire. I don't get it."

Flint grinned. "You just haven't been up close and personal like we have. Fire is magnetic. When it's crowning in the tops of the trees and the air is filled with the sound of it, something in my heart pauses at the beauty. I think we've got it wrong in the park service. The forests are dying now because we're stopping God's way of clearing out the weak stuff and the underbrush."

Chase had heard the argument before. "But then the homes burn."

Buck shrugged. "We should establish a no-build zone to keep out residents. Our forests will be at risk until we figure it out."

"You won't get far with that. People like to build near the wilderness," Chase said.

Flint jabbed a thumb toward the woods. "I'd like to see the Zane Grey cabin."

"I'll show you." Chase urged his horse into a trot down the hillside and through the trees. He dodged branches that tried to knock off his hat and guided Bugs around fallen trees and across mats of soft pine needles.

When they finally paused in front of the little hunting cabin, Chase's gaze went to the vehicle parked at the back. He'd swear it was Jimmy's flashy Pontiac Solstice. There weren't many of them around here, and he couldn't imagine another one in the area the same victory red color.

His gut tightened, and he dismounted. Holding his finger to his lips, he eased along the yard toward the window at the side of the building. It was too high to see in, and he couldn't hear anything. He crept around to the other side and eased up the steps to the wraparound porch. A board creaked under him, and he froze. Staring at the door, he strained to hear, but there was no sound. He stepped lightly and tiptoed around to the window. The faint sound of voices came to his ears.

Peeking through the window, he saw Jimmy with two other men. One was dressed all in white—white jeans and denim shirt—even down to his boots, which were coated with red dust. The other man was dressed in grease-stained jeans and a T-shirt. The man in white handed Jimmy a briefcase. Chase gritted his teeth. Would his brother never learn? Chase looked around for a weapon and found nothing handy. Surprise would have to work in his favor.

He glanced back at the other men. They had dismounted and were staring at him. He motioned for them to join him. Once they were creeping up the steps, he went to the front door. He tried the doorknob, and it opened easily. He threw it open, shouting at the top of his lungs. Behind him, he heard Flint shout an Apache war cry, and the sound of the rushing bodies told him he'd have backup. He leaped into the room, grabbing a chair that stood by the door. The men were fumbling at their belts when he hit them with the chair.

They went down, but the grease monkey managed to get a gun out. "Get back," the man snarled. He staggered to his feet with the gun on Chase.

"What are you doing?" Jimmy shouted.

He grabbed Chase's arm, but Chase shook him off and faced the gunman. He grabbed the briefcase and tossed it onto the man in white, who was groaning and holding his head. "Take your money and get out of here."

"No!" Jimmy made another futile grab at Chase's arm.

The men eyed the three smokejumpers, who approached with their fists clenched. "Stay back," the gunman barked. He yanked the other man to his feet, then grabbed the briefcase. The two ran out the other door. It swung in the breeze and banged back against the wall.

"Wait!" Jimmy started after them, but Chase grabbed his arm. A button popped off Jimmy's denim shirt.

"You're not going anywhere," Chase told his brother. It was all he could do not to shake some sense into Jimmy. The kid seemed determined to self-destruct.

Jimmy moaned and sank onto the board floor. "I'm dead," he groaned. He picked up the button from his shirt and dropped it into his pocket.

"Why aren't you working at Doty's? Does she know you've left her property?"

Jimmy tipped his hat back from his head. "What's with the twenty questions? You caught me. Just shut up with the lecture."

Chase narrowed his eyes. "Ben Diamond's house burned last night. He was in it."

Jimmy's mouth gaped, then he smiled. "Couldna happen to a nicer guy," he jibed.

"Someone set the fire."

Jimmy took a step back. "And you think I set it? You have a lot of faith in me."

"Have you done anything to inspire my confidence? Every time I bail you out of jail, you end up in trouble again. When did you see Diamond last?"

"When I turned eighteen and got out of his house. I'm not sorry he's dead, but I didn't do it."

Chase wanted to believe him. He really, really did.

CHAPTER 13

Tess turned from the window and faced her sister. "What are you going to do?" She found it hard to wrap her mind around the fact that both the ranch and her sister's marriage were in jeopardy.

"I'm going to go to her house. Right now. If he's there, it's over." Stevie's lips pressed together. "Will you come with me?"

Tess nodded. "If you need me."

"Paul has a smooth tongue. He'll try to talk his way out of this."

"We'd better leave a note for Whip. He'll be back with Mindy shortly." Tess scribbled a note and put it on the table, then put the partially cooked stew in the refrigerator. Tess kept glancing at her sister. Stevie really wasn't up to this, not after the ordeal she'd just been through with Paul. "Where does Joni live?"

"I'll direct you."

They stepped into the yard. Tess noticed Paul's truck was missing.

142

Stevie saw too. "I knew it," she whispered.

They got into Tess's Jeep and drove toward town. Stevie told her where to turn, and fifteen minutes later they pulled onto a tree-lined street across from the park.

"There's his truck," Stevie's voice trembled. "I'd kept hope until now. Stupid, stupid."

The old green pickup was no lie. Tess pulled in behind it, then looked at the small white house. The curtained windows hid all signs of life. They could approach the front door without being seen. The afternoon sun had paled, and early streetlights flickered on. The hum from a defective one sounded loud through Stevie's open window.

Tess put her hand on the door handle. "Are you sure you want to do this?" she asked Stevie.

"No, but I have no choice." Stevie opened her door and got out. She closed the door without a sound and leaned in through the window. "Joni talked to me about it a year ago and cried when she promised she'd quit seeing him. You can't trust anyone."

Tess got out too, letting her door fall shut softly, though noise didn't seem to matter. Not now. Even if Paul heard them, there would be no way to explain his presence here. Her face grim, Stevie stalked up the walk to the front door. Tess hurried behind her.

They approached the well-cared for house. Banks of mums and neatly trimmed shrubs lined the bed under the picture window. Ignoring the doorbell, Stevie doubled her fist and pounded on the red door. Tess could smell beef on a gas grill from somewhere. A dog barked down the street. At first there was silence behind the door, then Tess heard a thud and whispers. She and Stevie looked at one another.

"Open up, Paul!" Stevie pounded again. "I know you're in there."

A few moments later the door swung open, and Paul stood in the doorway. His hair was standing up, and his shirt was untucked. He was barefoot. "Uh, Stevie, what are you doing here?" He began to jab his shirt into the waistband of his pants.

"You're pathetic." Stevie's voice hardened.

Paul's head jerked up. "Let's not put on a show for the neighbors. I guess you'd better come in." He stepped aside.

They entered the house. A candle burned on the lamp table and perfumed the air with cinnamon. The living room was small and crowded with overstuffed furniture, making it feel welcome and comfortable in spite of its cramped quarters.

"Where is she?" Stevie demanded.

"In the bedroom." Paul looked away, then went to the side chair and sat down to put on his shoes. "Let's get it over with. This is your fault, too, Stevie."

"*My* fault? How can you sit there and blame me for your behavior?" Stevie made no move to sit down. She folded her arms across her chest.

"You sure you want to get into this in front of your sister? She thinks you're perfect." Paul's lips twisted in a sarcastic grimace. "It might taint your image."

Stevie swayed, and Tess reached out to steady her. Tess glared at Paul. She wished she had the right words to puncture his cocky attitude, but Stevie needed to fight this battle for herself.

Stevie shouted an expletive. She snatched up a vase and flung it to the floor. The sound of ceramic shattering seemed as loud as a cannon in the room.

"Cute, Stevie. Real mature." Paul reached down and pulled on his boots. When he sat back up, his shoulders were straight and his gaze more direct. "When was the last time you were glad to see me when I came home? Every time I try to hold you, you act like it's all you can do to kiss me. A man can only take so much of that."

"So instead of talking to me about what you perceive as my shortcomings, you cheat? Is that any way for a Christian to act? How do you think Pastor Richmond would accept that excuse?"

For the first time Paul's bravado cracked. He looked down. "I'm not proud of it, but God knows a man has needs, Stevie. I feel like a ghost in my own house. Most of the time you barely acknowledge my presence. I know what I'm doing is wrong. But *you*? You can't even admit your sin."

"What sin is that, Paul? The sin of being a faithful wife or a hardworking rancher? You never take responsibility for your faults. It's always someone else who made you do what you do. When are you going to grow up and act like a man?"

"Like you act any differently. You shut yourself off from me. Mindy too. Our baby girl is the only reason I've stuck around this long." He reached out and grabbed her arm. Stevie jerked it away. "See? You flinch if someone touches you—even Mindy." He stood and towered over her. "Brick by brick you've built up that barrier until I can't even see you behind it anymore."

"I like to be touched, I just don't like to be *grabbed*. Besides, this is not about me—this is about your *adultery*. Whatever I did or didn't do doesn't excuse that."

"You've never been a real wife. What else was I supposed to do?"

"I'm not going to listen to this." Stevie went toward the door. "You can stay here in your little love nest, Paul. Don't bother to come home."

Paul moved to intercept her. He slammed the door she'd opened a crack. "So that's your answer? Don't face the problems, just kick me out?" He glanced at Tess. "You must be rubbing off on her, Tess. Running is your typical behavior, not Stevie's."

"This isn't about Tess, it's about you and me. I gave you a chance once, Paul. You promised you'd break it off, and now here you are. You obviously think I should just let you have your mistress and life can continue. I'm not willing to live like that."

"I'll fight you for my share of the ranch. For Mindy too."

Stevie laughed. "Your share? You have no share. It belongs to me, Tess, and Chase. And what judge would award you any of the ranch or our daughter? You have no job, no income other than what I've provided."

Even Tess was pained by the hardness in her sister's voice. She reached out and touched Stevie's arm. Stevie pulled away.

Paul seemed to shrink a bit. "I can show I've faithfully worked it for twelve years. I should get something out of it."

"You had a free ride. That should be enough."

Paul's face reddened. "I'm not going to take the blame for this one, Stevie. It's on your shoulders. You think the Mastersons are so perfect. Typical. Your grandpa stripped his brother of his inheritance and left Whip without a dime, but I won't play dead like Whip did."

"Whip is happy doing what he does," Tess said, jumping in to defend her family. "He would hate the responsibility of ownership. It was Grandpa's property to do with whatever he wanted."

Paul turned on her. "You can say that when you carry a chip on your shoulder as big as the Rim about Chase? Leaving the ranch the way he wanted was your father's choice too, but I don't see you accepting his decision with good grace."

"That's different," Tess said, curling her fingers into her palms. "Chase isn't family."

"Which makes it even worse what your grandfather did. It's about time you Mastersons learned you don't rule the county, that there are consequences for your actions."

"I'll be glad to deliver *consequences,*" Stevie said, her voice quiet. "I'm not sure I ever knew you, Paul. Maybe you *are* guilty of arson."

He paled. "Don't think you can pin that on me."

Stevie shrugged. "I think you'd better figure out a way to prove your innocence because I'm not sure I believe it anymore."

Tess slipped her arm around her sister's waist and could feel Stevie shaking. Stevie leaned against her, and her trembles began to still.

"I want to go home," Stevie whispered to Tess.

"Step out of the way," Tess told Paul.

He stared at her. "I'll be home in a little while."

"You won't get in." Tess stared him down. "And your things will be in the barn." He still hadn't moved. Tess reached past him and yanked on the doorknob. The door hit him in the side, but he didn't budge. "Get out of the way, or I'll call the sheriff and tell him you're detaining us against our will. This time when you end up in jail, we won't bail you out."

His eyes narrowed, but he moved away. "This isn't over. You can't just throw me out and ignore the way I've kept the ranch afloat. You would have been bankrupt except for me."

"It's not much better than that now," Stevie muttered. "And you're the one who broke your marriage vows, Paul."

"It depends on how you look at it," he shot back. "I never got any love or honor from you."

A movement in the hall caught Tess's eye, and she caught a glimpse of Paul's girlfriend tiptoeing to the bathroom. Joni's bleached and permed hair stuck up in wisps. She was cute in a kittenish sort of way. Wasn't she at least ten years older than Paul too?

Paul followed her gaze, and color stained his face. He stared back at his wife defiantly. "Joni has more warmth in her little finger than you've got in your whole body."

"Get me out of here." Stevie stumbled toward the door. She barely got past the steps when she went to her knees and vomited into the bushes.

Tess rubbed her sister's quaking shoulders. "It'll be okay, Stevie," she whispered. "Take deep breaths."

"I can't believe he would try to blame me for his adultery," Stevie muttered. "Typical male. It's his own fault he can't keep his jeans zipped."

"Let's get you home," Tess murmured. She helped Stevie to the car. The drive home passed in a silent blur. There were no words to soothe the hurt of betrayal. Nothing anyone said had been able to erase the hurt Tess had felt at the reading of her father's will. When you love someone, you expect them to love you back the same way—with a singleness of heart. Tess had never considered herself a jealous person, but she found out differently when she sat in the lawyer's office and heard her father felt no different about her, his own flesh and blood, than he felt about Chase. Betrayal came in all shapes and sizes.

She turned the last curve before the ranch and saw horses tied at the rail. "The guys are back. What are you going to tell them?"

"Nothing."

"They'll see us take Paul's things to the barn."

"I'll even ask them to help me."

"I think we should tell them so they can help stop him from coming in the house. We might need all the support we can get."

"Fine. I need to sleep." Stevie leaned back against the headrest.

"Let's get you inside first."

"Mindy needs to be told. Paul was going to take her to see a movie tonight. She'll wonder when he doesn't come home."

"How much do you want to tell her?"

"You handle it. I trust you." Stevie's words slurred, and her lids began to sink to half mast.

Stevie's withdrawal as a parent on this matter stunned Tess, but her sister might not wake up before Mindy started asking questions about Paul. It might just have to have to fall on Tess after all.

Tess went around to the passenger side and half-carried her sister to the bedroom. Firefighting would be easier than the emotional storm she was going to have to endure in the days ahead.

CHAPTER 14

Tess pulled the covers around her sister. Stevie looked so shrunken lying in the bed. Her eyes fluttered behind closed eyelids as if her dreams were violent. For as long as Tess could remember, Stevie had been the strong one—the almost-parent who was there to support and comfort her. Tess wasn't sure how to act, how to step into the role Stevie had always held.

She tiptoed toward the door. Maybe she could salvage the beef stew she'd started. The sun was sitting on the horizon, and she could hear the men arriving at the barn. They'd settle the horses, then come inside and expect to be fed. Then she'd have to talk to Mindy.

"Don't go." Stevie sat up and rubbed her eyes. "I don't want to be alone."

"I thought you were asleep." Tess turned back and sat on the edge of the bed.

Stevie's strawberry-blonde hair was a tangle around her face, and she pushed it out of her eyes. The skin around her eyes looked almost bruised. "What happened to the time, Tessie? It seems like just yesterday we were kids without a care in the world."

It was Tess's fault their lives had changed. She should have gone for help for her parents sooner. She smoothed her sister's hair. "You were always worrying about me, Stevie. I don't know what I would have done without you. You worried whether I would fall off the horse, if I had on the right dress for Sunday school. You even worried whether Uncle Giles was looking at me too mean. You can't help yourself. But it will be okay."

She shuddered and closed her eyes. "I'm so tired. I still can't believe Paul would blame me for his stupidity." When she opened her eyes again, her voice was stronger. "Do you think I'm wrong, Tess?"

"No. He wasn't even penitent and didn't try to tell you he'd break it off with that woman."

"I've always liked Joni. That makes it doubly bad. They both know it's wrong. I suppose I should call our pastor."

"For counseling?"

Stevie shook her head. "I'm beyond that. Our marriage is over. Paul is a church deacon, and Joni is the secretary. Pastor will want to exercise church discipline."

"You don't sound happy about it." Maybe she was petty, but Tess would have reveled in seeing Paul's downfall.

"It's going to rock the church. I'm sorry about that." Stevie reached for the cordless phone on the bed stand.

"I'll go get supper ready while you're doing that." Tess went to the door and hurried down the hall. The men would be in any minute. Listening to their voices, she thought they seemed agitated. Their voices were raised, and it sounded like Chase was yelling at someone. She went past Mindy in the living room, where Whip had turned on *Bright Eyes* for her again, then stepped outside and followed the sound of the voices.

"Is something wrong?" she asked.

Chase stopped midshout. "We caught Jimmy at the Zane Grey cabin. He was taking money for some car parts." His voice was strained.

Tess glanced at Jimmy, then back at Chase. "Did you call Eric?"

"No. I gave the money back to the two yahoos Jimmy was with, and they got away."

"Eric still needs to know about this. Jimmy can tell him who they are."

Jimmy began swinging his head wildly. "No way. I'm already dead. If I go squealing to the cops, those guys will stomp me." He took off running, but Flint chased him down and hauled him back. Jimmy stood with his head hanging.

"I can't turn him in." Chase folded his arms over his chest. "Eric will throw him in jail and toss the key."

"Would you rather he end up dead from the company he keeps?" Tess demanded.

"He's my brother. I have to help him."

"Sometimes the best way to help is to stand out of the way and let him suffer the consequences."

Chase stood staring down at her. "How did you get so hard, Tess? Was it the fire? You judge everyone and everything by such high standards. I've often wondered how you can go into wildfires like that when any one of them might kill you. Is it your way of judging yourself?"

She felt like he'd slapped her. "We're not talking about me. If you won't call Eric, I will."

"Yeah, the ice princess has to stick her nose in everyone else's business," Jimmy said, his face red and his voice low. "This has nothing to do with you, your majesty. I wasn't even on your precious Masterson land."

Tess lifted her chin. "If we won't uphold justice, who will, Chase? We're nothing better than savages if we don't follow the rules."

"Even God believes in mercy."

Tess didn't answer. Where was God's mercy when her parents were in that barn? Their deaths had to have been payment for sin. While she didn't know of anything her parents had ever done wrong, she knew no one was perfect. Or maybe the punishment was for her. She'd never been sure. All she knew was that judgment was always extracted.

Buck was shifting uncomfortably, shooting a glance at Chase. Maybe Chase was right—this wasn't her business. But wrongdoing never stayed hidden. The cell phone attached to her waistband rang, and she glanced at the caller ID as she answered. Aunt Doty. Maybe she'd figured out Jimmy was missing.

"Tess?" Doty said gravelly. "Have you seen James?"

"He's here." Tess told her aunt what had happened.

"I'll be right there."

"No. We'll bring him to you."

Chase glanced at Jimmy out of the corner of his eye. His brother slumped against the truck's passenger door. "How do I get through to you, Jimmy? Do you *want* to go to prison?"

"You don't get it," Jimmy muttered. "I'm in too deep. I just needed to do this one thing to get out."

"This one thing? It's been one thing after another. When does it stop?" Chase parked the truck outside Doty's small house. A soft glow winked from the windows. A shadow moved across one window, and he saw Doty's face peering out. Moments later the door opened.

Doty stood framed in the doorway, her wild hair flying up in the wind. Her expressionless face didn't bode well for Jimmy. "What do you have to say for yourself, James?" she demanded as the men approached the door.

"Sheesh, I'm not a kid!" Jimmy said. "I don't have to answer to you."

"You answer to me or you can go back to jail. I signed surety for you, and one of the stipulations is that you live here under my authority. Which will it be, James? Me or jail?"

"Same difference," Jimmy muttered.

Doty poked him in the chest. "You've got decency inside there, boy, and it's struggling to get out. The past can stay in the past if you'd quit dragging it out every day. No one can make the choice but you. I won't coerce you, but I won't cover for you either. Choose your path, son. Be a man." She jerked a thumb toward the room behind her. "I didn't do your work for you. It's still waiting." She turned and went back inside, leaving the door gaping open.

Jimmy looked at Chase. "I don't have much of a choice," he muttered. He stomped to the door, then cast one pleading glance at his brother. "Can't you take over as surety for me? I can stay with you."

For a moment, Chase was tempted to give in. He wasn't sure he'd be any happier about being bossed around by Doty. He finally shook his head. "Sorry, Jimmy. You walk all over me. Let's see if Doty can make better headway."

Tess finished setting the table, then looked out the window over the kitchen sink. "That's Paul's truck."

Stevie audibly gulped. "He has a nerve to show up here. At least Mindy is in bed." Tess had fed her and put her down half an hour ago. She'd chickened out and just told the little girl that her dad was going to be gone a while. Stevie dried her hands on a towel with calm deliberation, but she was breathing fast. "Would you come with me, Tessie?"

"Sure." Tess held open the kitchen door, and they both stepped outside. Paul was striding toward the house, but he stopped when he saw the two women.

He eyed Stevie. "I hope you've cooled off and come to your senses, Stevie. We can get through this." His gaze went to Tess. "Could I talk to my wife in private please?"

"I have nothing to say to you. Tessie stays with me." Stevie folded her arms across her chest. "Your things are in the barn, Paul. Take them and leave."

"I told you, I'm not going anywhere. This is my home too. Besides, I need some money."

"Your little mistress can support you like I always have," Stevie jibed back.

"That's unfair. I've worked hard on this ranch, Stevie. Even Tess would agree to that." He looked to Tess for confirmation.

Tess looked away. She didn't want to side with him in anything, but what he said was true. He'd never been a slacker on the ranch, at least not during the time she'd spent in their home when she was a teenager. She said nothing. She was here to support Stevie.

"Just take your things and go," Stevie said.

"You can't throw me out. I'll sleep in the bunkhouse." He wheeled around and stalked off.

Tess watched him slam the door to the bunkhouse. "Should I call Eric?"

Stevie shook her head. "He can't do anything unless I see a lawyer and have papers drawn up. Right now, Paul has the right to be here. There's no restraining order or anything." Stevie sounded weary.

"I could call Emilio."

Stevie rubbed her forehead. "Let it go for now. I don't know what to do anymore. He's still Mindy's father, even if he is a lying, cheating jerk. If he'd promise not to see Joni again . . ." Her voice trailed off.

Tess wished she knew what to tell her sister. Paul still wasn't penitent. Until he was, he would assert his rights to do whatever he wanted.

"I'm going back in," Stevie said. "You want to call the men for dinner?"

"Yeah, I'll get them." Tess headed toward the bunkhouse, but before she got there, she heard the rumble of another car. "Now what?" she muttered under her breath. She squinted in the darkness, then she recognized Esther Sanchez's Porsche.

Esther stepped out of the car. She was wearing jeans and a suede jacket. Her long brown hair had escaped its bun and was pulled back in a careless ponytail that made her look approachable.

"Hi, Esther, I wasn't expecting you. Can you stay for dinner? We're about to eat."

"Hi, Tess. You sure it's no trouble?"

"We have plenty. I was just about to call the men for dinner." She'd expected Esther to try to whisk Buck away. She stepped to the bell in the yard and rang it. "They'll be right along. Come on inside."

Esther followed her to the kitchen. "Something smells wonderful. I'm starved."

"Have a seat." She was going to have to entertain Esther until Buck arrived. "Did you have a good day?"

Esther shrugged. "It was okay. Dad and I looked for a house in Phoenix today, but I didn't find anything I liked." She bit her lip. "You know, I'd like to be friends with you, Tess. I'd like to understand Buck's world more. I feel like an outsider sometimes." Her voice held a trace of wistfulness. "You all seem so close, so content."

"We're doing what we love." Tess studied the beautiful face opposite her. "You're getting a great guy. Buck is the best."

Esther's face lit up. "He's so real. And he doesn't let me push him around. I'm not used to that, but I like it. He's secure in who he is. I wish I had that much self-confidence."

"You seem to have everything. I've never noticed you lack confidence."

Esther's laugh tinkled out. "I put on a good mask. I always feel like I'm not measuring up. When I'm on Buck's arm, I feel like I've conquered the world. He's so handsome and totally male. My girl-friends are jealous." Her dimples flashed. "Hey, I was talking about you to my dad, and he said he went to school with your uncle. Giles, I think?"

Tess gave Esther an appraising look. Her father might be able to help in Tess's investigation. "Do you suppose your dad would talk to me about him? I'm trying to get to the bottom of the fire that killed him and my parents twelve years ago."

Esther smiled. "I'm sure I could arrange it. When would you like to see him?"

"Sometime this week?" Tess suggested.

"I'll arrange lunch. I'm glad to help."

It might be a wild-goose chase, but it was worth a shot. How well did Senator Sanchez know Uncle Giles? Their graduating class was probably quite small. Maybe they socialized after school too. If only she could figure this out.

Light shines from the kitchen window and illuminates Tess as she moves about preparing supper. Once or twice she glances around as though she feels someone watching her, but her gaze never penetrates the darkness to where I stand under the juniper tree.

They will be having dinner soon. It's time for the second part of my plan. Stealing away from the house, I walk through the grass, dry as straw, to the back pasture. The snakes will be sleeping tonight, so I tread boldly over the uneven ground.

This pasture, this stretch of rich hay that is nearly ready to harvest, is Chase's pride and joy. With a few snips of the scissors, I secure clippings in a plastic bag that I stick back in my pocket—for my stash of trophies. I reach into my pocket and fondle the lighter—my talisman, worn smooth by my fingers. Pulling it from my pocket, I flick it and hold the golden flame over the dry grass. It will blaze quickly, and I can envision tongues of fire gobbling eagerly at the ripe hay.

Such a beautiful fire I will summon. I am a god in my own right.

CHAPTER 15

*C*hase stared into the flames flickering in the fireplace. They sat in the living room drinking coffee, but no one had said anything for at least fifteen minutes, exhausted by the events of the day. Whip decided to turn in, and Buck excused himself to walk Esther out. Spirit whined when he went out the door but stayed put.

The somber mood was as heavy as a summer monsoon. There had to be something he could do about Jimmy, but good ideas eluded him.

Whip burst back through the door. "There's fire out there. I can see the glow. Looks to be the hay field."

Chase shot to his feet. The smokejumpers were right with him as they jostled for the door. Stevie stood in the doorway. "Stay with your sister," he told Tess.

She shook her head. "This is my job. Whip can stay."

Stevie waved them off. "I'm fine. Get going."

Chase turned and looked at the horizon. The ominous glow of red told the tale. Whip was right. The last of their hay was afire. Their winter feed supply, up in flames.

Coop called in the fire as Tess drove Chase's pickup to the site. The hay field was already half-gone by the time they arrived.

Coop took charge. "Flint, you and Buck take the right flank while Tess and Chase hit the advancing front of the flames. Whip, you're with me."

Tess nodded and grabbed a shovel and pickax. If only she had a Pulaski. She raced to the front and began digging up the hay in a line about fifteen feet from the fire. Luckily the wind had died, and the fire was burning slowly.

She glanced around and saw Flint and Buck nearly to the head. The sight gave her renewed vigor, and she began to dig harder. They had a chance to win this. The thought had no sooner crossed her mind when a gust of wind blew up and drove the flames toward Coop and Whip.

"Look out!" Tess shouted.

Coop's head came up, and he grabbed Whip's arm and pulled him to the side as the flames swept past. The men advanced and began to chop at the fire again.

Soot smudged their faces, and Tess knew she looked as bad. Fire-fighters summoned by Stevie poured in from town, but even with all the manpower, it was nearly dawn before the last of the fire was out and the field stood in smoldering ruins. The charred remains of the winter feed lay around her as far as she could see. Even the first colors of dawn failed to brighten the black and gray landscape. Her eyes stung from the smoke and heat, but the pain was nothing compared to how she was going to feel when she had to face Stevie.

Chase put his arm around her shoulders as they walked toward the truck. "I gotta hand it to you, Tess. You really know how to work these fires. We even saved a little hay."

She looked at the smoking fields again. "We didn't save much." Stevie would be heartbroken. It was different for Tess—she had another life outside these fences. Stevie's sense of worth was wrapped up in these acres of rolling hills dotted with cattle. "This was the last of the hay. We'll have to buy feed all winter."

Chase sighed. "Do we know what caused it yet?"

"Not really. I found the point of origin, but there's no incendiary device on this fire."

He nodded toward the clear sky. "There's been no lightning. It looks like it smoldered for a while before the wind started spreading it. A passerby could have tossed a cigarette."

"Out here? Only family and our ranch hands come out this far." Tess wanted to find an understandable reason. Who would deliberately destroy their hay? What did this guy want? He attempted to kill her, framed Paul, and fired their hay.

Chase slammed his right hand into the palm of his left. "We have to find this guy."

"But how?" Tess tossed her tools into the back of the truck, then went around to the passenger door.

Chase slid in behind the steering wheel. "He's been keeping us off-kilter by constant problems. We need to get proactive and start digging harder into the fire that killed your parents. It's not been our priority, and it needs to be. Eric reopening the case is what triggered all this."

"That's what I've been thinking too, but maybe it's just coinci-dence." She should have been exhausted, but her nerves tingled with the desire to ferret out the truth. "I can't figure this out by myself, Chase. I need your help."

"You've got it. Don't you want to sleep?"

"I just want a shower. Where do we start?" Knowing she wasn't alone recharged her.

"How much do you remember of that day? I remember it was your birthday."

She wished she didn't remember it at all. "It was, and my par-ents had gotten me a set of Zane Grey books. I was out reading in the pasture when Mom and Dad brought out Wildfire."

His expression softened. "That's why you never come home for birthdays."

"I've never had a birthday cake since then," she admitted. "It would choke me." Maybe no one would remember her upcoming birthday with everything that was going on.

"I'm sorry."

She could tell he really was sorry. "It's okay. I've learned to live with it. What do you remember?" Did she dare ask him again where he was that day? The truce they'd agreed to was still fragile, and she didn't want to ruin it.

"I was visiting Jimmy that day."

Her head came up at his admission. "That's all? Why have you always told me to mind my own business when I've asked what you were doing?"

He gripped the wheel and didn't look at her. "I jumped Jimmy's foster dad, and he walloped me. I ended up getting stitches. He agreed not to call the cops if I just said I got into a fight. I didn't want to confirm your opinion that I was a juvenile delinquent."

"You jumped Ben Diamond? Were you protecting Jimmy?"

His lips twitched. "How far we've come, Tess. A week ago you would have assumed I deserved what I got."

She let the smile come to her lips. "I know you better now." And she did.

"You've known me since you were ten." His voice was deep with amusement. "You've suddenly gotten to know me better in the past few days?"

The attraction between them sharpened. She couldn't look at him. Where had this developing emotion come from? It wasn't welcome. Her life was carefully ordered and planned. There was no room for someone like Chase Huston.

"You're finally being nice to me," she muttered.

His hand slipped across the seat and squeezed hers.

"Maybe you're right. I've goaded you as much as you've irritated me. I'm glad it's over. You make a much better friend than you do an enemy."

She laced her fingers with his, but she still couldn't look at him. The heat spreading over her chest and stomach would be sure to show in her face. What would it be like to kiss Chase? The thought had played hide-and-seek in her mind ever since the other night when she'd thought he was going to. She'd made such a fool of herself, but instead of it pushing them apart, it seemed to hurtle them toward each other.

The sun peeked over the charred remains of the hay field.

"So what do we do first?" she asked. Her hand felt like it was pulsing in his, throwing off sparks. Could he feel anything, or was it no less platonic to him than holding Mindy's hand?

"We need to talk to some people who knew your parents and your uncle."

"What about Maxie Zahi?" Their Navajo housekeeper had been with them for ten years before the fire. "Coop mentioned it might be good to talk to her."

"Good idea. Let's try it."

She would have done whatever he agreed to, but she couldn't tell him that. All she could do was nod.

CHAPTER 16

The computer center in Payton doesn't look busy today. Amanda Nelson waves at me as she Rollerblades past on the sidewalk, and I wave back, stepping out of the way. It's clear no one sees the change in me. Entering the building, I inhale deeply. I love computers, the hot electronic stink of them, the hum of power under my fingertips, the secrets I can dig up. What's hidden always has more power to harm than what is visible. But sins always show up. Always.

The bank of computers stretches across the east wall. The one in the back will do. It faces the door so I can see anyone approaching. The paper in my pocket has everything I need. Most people are way too quick to write down their banking passwords. The computer hums its siren song under my fingertips, and the invitation vibrates up my hand as if it recognizes me and is there to do my bidding. The screen comes up, and I put in the stolen password and wait.

The balance is lower than I expected. It won't take much to drain them. It is almost a disappointment to know my actions will have so little effect, that I'm merely hurrying the inevitable along. With two clicks, the money is transferred to an account I've set up. From there, it wings its way to another account, then another before finally landing in a bank account in Switzerland. Perfect.

How long will it take for them to discover they have an overdraft? A day, two days? Anticipation is food to the heart, and I find I'm very hungry. I stretch, then walk out the door in search of food. A cat outside a shop hisses at my approach and scurries away. The animals know what I am.

The Navajo Nation lands were some of the most beautifully stark landscapes in the country. Chase steered the truck along the dirt road past an undulating landscape that reflected the sun in patterns of pink, gold, and red. "There's her hogan," he said, pointing out the six-sided structure at the end of a long lane. It was part of a cluster of buildings that included three trailers and a ramshackle clapboard shack. Several old cars sat on bare rims. He turned the truck into the track. It bottomed out in a pothole, and he slowed his speed to a crawl.

Squawking chickens fled from the truck tires as they rolled to a stop beside the hogan. The dwelling's entrance couldn't be seen from the driveway. As was the custom of the Diné, as the Navajo called themselves, the opening faced the rising sun to welcome the new day. The wooden structure looked like a windowless cabin with a round roof. When Chase and Tess got out of the truck, several goats and sheep came toward them to investigate. In the distance, a small herd of horses grazed on the hillside. There were no fences anywhere in sight.

"It's an hour earlier here," Chase said, looking at his watch. The Navajo Nation observed Daylight Savings Time, unlike the rest of Arizona. "I wasn't thinking. We're coming right at lunch time. We should have waited a while." But he and Tess hadn't been able to wait.

"Maxie will be glad to see us. If we're lucky, she'll have fixed fry bread."

"Always thinking of your stomach." His gaze lingered on her. Tess was the most fit woman he'd ever seen. She was always active. Though she was small and feminine, she could lift heavy saddles and packs with ease.

They went around to the other side of the hogan and approached the door. He rapped on it firmly, but it was almost a full minute before the door swung open and Maxie stood in the doorway.

Nearly sixty by now, Maxie's glossy black hair was streaked with more gray than the last time he'd seen her. Her weathered skin looked a little more leathery. The stoic expression she turned on them was the same one she'd worn all the years he'd known her. The Diné didn't believe in exuberant shows of emotion. They rarely touched anyone but family, whom they fiercely loved and supported.

Tess and Chase were almost family, so Maxie gave them both a brief handshake. "You look well, Tess," she said, stepping away from the door to allow them entry. "You, too, Chase. How is the ranch?"

They stepped inside onto the dirt floor, packed hard with use. The scent of cooked onions filled the home. Several cots sat against the walls, and pairs of boots and moccasins lined up under the beds. The quilts on the beds brought a bright splash of color to the wood walls. Tools, ropes, and other implements hung from the rafters, and a cookstove sat in the middle of the one-room dwelling.

"Fry bread, Tess? I know you love it." A flicker of a smile passed over Maxie's face.

"I wouldn't say no." Tess followed her to the stove. "Are your children home?"

"They've already eaten and gone to town," Maxie said. "My granddaughter Mary is outside with the sheep."

"Susan's daughter?"

Maxie inclined her head. "Yes." She swept her hand toward the stove. "Eat."

Tess began to ladle the cooked hamburger and onions onto the piece of fry bread, then added green chilies and cheese. She handed the plate to Chase and fixed herself another one. They sat at the battered wooden table and ate in silence. Maxie watched them with unblinking dark eyes of approval. She wouldn't ask questions about why they'd come. She would wait until they were ready to tell her. The Diné were good listeners and courteous. With her hands folded in front of her, she looked as if she was about to pray, but Chase knew she was merely waiting.

He told her about the events that had been occurring on the ranch. She didn't speak as he detailed Stevie's illness, the fires, and Paul's implication in the arson. Her dark eyes never wavered from his face, though she nodded several times.

"What has this to do with me?" Her tone was polite but interested.

Tess leaned forward. "We think someone who hates the Mastersons is behind the problems. We're trying to learn what we can about the original fire, the one that killed my parents and my uncle. What do you remember of that year? Was there anyone who might have had a grudge against one of them?"

"Mr. and Mrs. Garrett Masterson were much loved by the town."

Maxie often danced around a direct criticism of someone. Chase had learned to look past what she actually said. "What about Giles Masterson?"

She pursed her lips. "Mr. Giles was not so well loved," she admitted.

"Why? I know he could be authoritative. Did he push people in town around the way he did the family? Was there any one person who was particularly annoyed?" Tess's voice was eager.

Maxie looked down at her hands and frowned. The unhappiness in her eyes told Chase she didn't really want to talk about it, but he pressed her anyway. "We have to know, Maxie. The ranch's whole future is depending on the truth."

Maxie got up and went to the woodstove. She poked at the fire, then set a blackened coffeepot on to boil. "Coffee?"

"No thanks. Come on, Maxie. I know you care about Stevie and Tess." He exchanged a long look with Tess. She got up and went to where the Navajo woman stood with her back to them. The heat from the stove shimmered in the air, and he saw a damp sheen over Maxie's face when the woman finally turned.

Maxie came back to the table and sat down with a heaviness that she didn't try to hide. "Mr. Giles was a troubled man."

"Troubled?" he asked. *Troubled* seemed a strange word to describe a man Chase remembered as always playing practical jokes. He was never without a smile on his face.

"Darkness drove him."

"What kind of darkness?" Tess voiced Chase's own bewilderment.

"Search your memory, Tess. You know." Maxie clamped her lips together and twisted her hands in her lap. "Did you never wonder why I left you all when you needed me so much? I should have come back when he died, but I couldn't."

Could she be talking about sexual harassment? Chase wasn't sure how to ask the question.

Tess leaned over and took the older woman's callused hand. "Are you saying he touched you in a bad way?"

Maxie shook her head. "Not me. I could have put him in his place. He liked young girls. Like my Susan."

Something inside Chase clenched. He wasn't sure he believed it. Not of Giles Masterson. If such a thing was true, wouldn't there have been rumors?

Maxie must have seen his skepticism. She scowled and got up. "Talk to Genevieve Thomas in town."

"The hairdresser?" Tess shot Chase a doubtful look. "What's she got to do with this?"

The door opened, and Maxie's son Les walked in. His dark eyes swept the room. "What do you want?"

"Just to talk to your mother," Chase said.

"No more." Les waved his hand. "Leave now."

"Yes, yes," Maxie said. "Stirring up of bad memories. No more. I am beginning to feel anger again." Her shoulders were stiff, and her chin jutted forward. "I have work to do."

"Thanks for your help." Chase stood, and Tess joined him at the door. Maxie didn't raise her eyes from the floor as she told them good-bye. Les shut the door firmly behind them.

"You believe her?" Chase asked. A few chickens ran to peck at their feet. He pushed them gently away with his boot and got to the truck. Tess still didn't answer, and he turned to look at her. She was deep in thought as if she hadn't heard his question. Or maybe Maxie's claim had brought back some memories she didn't want to think about right now. The look of distaste on her face brought a feeling of unease.

He waited until they were inside with the doors shut. "Tess? You okay?"

"She just rocked everything I thought I knew about Uncle Giles. I was just remembering waking up in the night once and seeing him in my room."

"What did you do?" He wasn't sure it was right to ask the question. Imagining the scene, he wished he'd been there to thrash the man. Of course, he would have been a kid himself. Giles would have wiped the floor with him.

"He was standing there staring at me. I told him to go away, that I was sleepy. He finally left. I told Stevie about it, but she said he may have been sleepwalking, so I didn't think anything of it again."

"When was this?"

"About a week before the fire."

"Do you think he ever bothered Stevie?"

"Not his own niece." Tess shuddered.

Chase felt sick. "It happens, Tess. All the time. What other reason could he have had for being in your bedroom in the middle of the night?" Chase curled his hands into fists.

"I think Stevie would have told me to be careful around him. You know what a mother hen she is." Tess turned and looked out the window. "Do you ever regret staying at the ranch, Chase?" Her tone was wistful.

"You sound like you wish you hadn't left." His own reasons for staying were so complex he wasn't sure he could talk about them.

"On days when there are no wildfires and I'm lying on my bunk at the fire camp, I remember the smell of the sage mixed with pine, and I can feel Wildfire under me. I wonder why I ever left." She turned back and looked at him. "Do you really think I'm driven to fight fire because I want to die in one?"

"Guilt is a powerful motivator." The thought of her in the flames brought such a vivid sensation of fear and protectiveness that he jammed his hands into his pockets to resist the impulse to touch her.

She leaned against the truck and folded her arms across her chest. "Is that why you stay on the ranch? You used to talk about being a veterinarian."

Chase chuckled. "I didn't think you ever noticed anything I said back then, unless I gave you something to yell at me about." He was still wary of sharing his thoughts with her. As teens, when they'd speak on friendly terms, he'd often find she told her father what he said and twisted it to her own purposes.

"I was really bad, wasn't I?"

Listening to her soft, contrite voice, he understood the change in her was deep and fundamental. Something had happened to Tess when he wasn't looking. Maybe that something had happened to him too. Listening to her voice, he found it hard to remember a time when he wasn't fascinated by her. Maybe that had been part of the deep resentment he held toward her—her contempt hurt.

"You're supposed to say I wasn't that bad." A nervous laugh accompanied her words.

"Sorry, I was thinking about guilt. Maybe guilt made me stay the way it made you leave. I always knew I didn't deserve your family's kindness to me. I wanted to prove your dad's trust wasn't misplaced."

"Do you regret staying?"

"Not if it means we finally got to be friends." Did he really just say that? The dusty landscape stretched out in front of him, and he focused on it rather than look to see what her reaction was to his admission. He strained to hear her answer, but there was only silence, so he finally turned his head to look at her.

She was crying. Tears rolled down her cheeks, and she licked one away that sat on her lip. "I didn't mean to make you cry," he said.

"I was thinking about the lost years. So many things could have been different. I'm sure my attitude hurt my dad."

"He loved you very much, and he knew you loved him."

Her smile was sad. "And just because you came last didn't mean he didn't love you any less. I guess that's why I hated you. It didn't seem fair. I was there before you. But while Dad cared about family, he always said family was who you decided to let inside. He threw open the door where you were concerned."

"He changed my life." His throat felt thick, and he cleared it. "You want to go to a movie tonight?" he asked. "We could go see Genevieve, then take in a dinner and a flick."

"What are you asking?" Her steady gaze pinned him in place. "Is this a—a date?"

"Yeah." A long pause stretched between them. "You okay with that?"

She looked away and shook her head. "I don't know, Chase. I think there might be too much water under the bridge to go there."

His elation drained away. Maybe she hadn't changed all that much after all. He never knew where he stood with her. Apparently she liked to keep him guessing.

CHAPTER 17

*G*enevieve's Cut and Curl had been on the same corner for as long as Tess could remember. Her first haircut had been in the blue vinyl chair with the bank of mirrors all around. The door jangled as she and Chase stepped into the room smelling of perm solution underlaid with the herbal scent of shampoo and seasoned with years of gossip.

The harsh fluorescent lighting made the purple highlights in Genevieve's hair look garish. "Tess Masterson, as I live and breathe!"

She enveloped Tess in an embrace reeking of chemicals, but the fierceness of the hug warmed Tess. "You haven't changed a bit, Genevieve." Though she had to be nearing sixty, her brown eyes were just as warm and her smile just as bright as Tess remembered.

"Honey, you're a sight for sore eyes." Genevieve held Tess at arm's length and looked her over. "Who's doing your style? That cut's a little long for you. Your pixie face is lost in all the hair. You need it layered a little more. I've got time right now if you want me to fix it."

Tess laughed. "I'll make an appointment. I really stopped by to ask some questions."

Genevieve glanced at Chase, who stood by the door with his hands in his pockets. "I didn't think this was a social call with your archenemy in tow," she whispered.

Everyone probably knew how she'd felt about Chase. Once upon a time she spewed diatribes against him to anyone who would listen. No wonder he'd hated her. "We've buried the hatchet."

The hairdresser put her hand over her mouth and giggled like a sixteen-year-old. "There's a fine line between love and hate," she said too softly for Chase to hear.

At least Tess hoped Chase didn't hear. "You have a minute?"

"I've got fifteen of them. Want some coffee?"

"No thanks." Hair dryers lined the wall by the door, and Tess sat in one of the chairs. She motioned to Chase to join her, and he walked across the floor as if he expected a horde of women to come bursting into the room. She stifled a chuckle when he eased onto a chair but sat on its edge instead of leaning back.

"How's Stevie holding up?" Genevieve sat in her haircutting chair and crossed her legs.

"That's really why we're here. There's been another fire at the ranch, and we think Paul was framed by someone who hates one of us, maybe all of us. You know as much about the history of the town as anyone. We went to see Maxie. She told us to talk to you." Tess hesitated. "She said Uncle Giles liked young girls. Is it true?"

The color drained from Genevieve's face, and her smile fell. She plucked lint off her slacks, then stood and began to gather her hair clips from the tabletop. The purple glitter polish on her nails caught the light streaming through the skylight in the ceiling. "I really don't have time to talk now."

"You just said you had fifteen minutes," Chase said. "You were Willa's best friend. She'd want you to help her daughter."

"I know that," Genevieve snapped. "But it all happened a long time ago. Let the past stay buried, Tess. Your mother was my best friend, and I promised her—" She looked down and shook her head. "There's nothing to gain by digging it all up again."

"Except proving Paul's innocence. I'm sure the whole town knows he's been accused of the Wilson fire. Someone has a vendetta against our family." She told the hairdresser about the fires, the attempts on her life, and the note when she first arrived. There had to be a way to make Genevieve understand how dire the situation was. Unless they could uncover who was behind this, Paul would be going to jail. And while she didn't much like her brother-in-law, he was Mindy's father. The scandal would affect Mindy all her life. That couldn't happen—Tess wouldn't let it happen.

Genevieve sat back down in the chair. "It's not something I like to talk about." She clasped her arms around herself. The mirror reflected her anguished expression. "You have to promise never to talk about this."

Tess leaned forward. "You can trust us, Genevieve. We only want to understand so we can figure out how to help Paul."

Genevieve sighed. "I'm not going to destroy someone else in the process." She curled a lock of purple-tinted hair around her index finger.

"Maxie went to your mom and said Giles was bothering her girl. Willa didn't believe it, so Maxie left the ranch, just up and quit. God help me, I told your mother the girl had to be lying." Genevieve blinked rapidly and her voice quivered. "I was wrong."

"Why are you so sure she was telling the truth?" Tess glanced at Chase, and he must have seen the appeal in her face because he took her hand and held it. She clung to the warmth of his fingers. Talking about this made her feel dirty.

"My Natalie," Genevieve said simply.

Tess had adored sixteen-year-old Natalie, thinking her incredibly sophisticated and grown up. She used to watch her flirt with the boys on the school bus and wished she could be as self-confident. Natalie had an infectious laugh that turned heads. Cheerleader, homecoming queen, and president of the Home Ec Club, she was someone to be admired. Tess hadn't seen her in years.

"I couldn't believe it when she told me. I told Willa, and she finally went to your dad about it, and they had a big fight."

"I remember a blowup. Dad slept in the bunkhouse for three days."

"That's the one. He took his brother's side."

"Would Natalie talk to us? Where does she live now?"

"In Goodyear. The Stallion Pass subdivision off I-10. I can give you the address, but I don't know if she'll talk to you."

"What did her dad do?" Chase put in. "If that had been my daughter, I have raised a ruckus."

"He blamed me." Genevieve's mouth took on a pinched expression. "I blamed myself too. I should have seen it. Nate confronted Giles, but he never would tell me what went on. Our marriage disintegrated after that."

"Would he talk to us?"

"Honey, Nate Thomas is as close-mouthed as a Gila monster. You'd have better luck with Natalie."

Tess vaguely remembered a man with wisps of thin brown hair combed over his balding head. He usually wore a three-piece suit. "Isn't he a banker?"

Genevieve nodded. "He's a bank president now in Flagstaff."

I look up. The cave walls, slick with moisture, encircle me like a cocoon. The ceiling soars twelve feet above my head. If archaeologists knew about this place, they'd be swarming all over it, and the artifacts would be worth hundreds of thousands of dollars. But it's my special place, and no one will ever see it.

I step into the second chamber and look around to make sure my lair is still undiscovered, though no one would brave the brambles to find it. My own discovery of this place was a fluke. I was shooting rabbits when I was a kid and wiggled under the bushes after one. Standing here for the first time, it was like discovering a new world. The paintings on the walls dazzle my eyes, and I let my gaze linger on one after another. They are my secret treasure, my trove of delight. No one has seen them in centuries but me.

Everything seems undisturbed, and I sense solitude here—and approval. I can be myself here, no masks, no games. I grab the plastic bin and lift off the lid. Inside are my treasures, the trophies from each of my fires. The other boxes are full, but this one is reserved only for the Mastersons. The hay clippings join a charred boot from the Bar Q barn—the trophy that started the box—as well as a bridle from the Wilson barn, and a computer printout of the bank transaction. All is in order.

Touching each item strengthens me. Power feels good when you've always felt helpless. I settle myself on the hard rock with my legs crossed. Closing my eyes, the chant pours from my lips without effort, rising to crest and hum over my head. I am the wolf, crafty and powerful. Swifter than any human, with keen eyesight and smell. Nothing stands in my way. My back prickles, and I am sure hair is growing there. Soon my transformation will be complete, and I'll be able to roam the hills and valleys as a full-fledged skinwalker. And no man will stop me.

My first sighting of a skinwalker came when I was eleven. I'd been with Diamond on the rez. Night was falling, and we walked toward the truck to go home. The scent of wood smoke was sweet in my nostrils. I stood on the passenger side of the truck with my thumb on the door handle. A sort of growl or cry came from the woods. The back of my neck shivered. Eyes as red the Sedona dirt peered out at me. The shape was bigger than any dog or wolf I'd ever seen. I tried to call out to my dad, but my throat swelled shut. Then the animal disappeared. Diamond said I'd seen a skinwalker. The encounter made me hunger for more information. My life-long quest to learn all I could about the Navajo witches and what they could do began that day.

I examine my hands. Surely my nails have grown longer and more curved. Is that hair on them? There is no turning back. This is the culmination of a lifelong dream. And it feels very good.

The events of the night before were beginning to catch up with Tess. She leaned back against the headrest and closed her eyes. The drone of the wheels on the road lulled her. Chase wouldn't mind if she took a little nap.

She heard a bleep from her cell phone. Her purse was on the

floor, and her movements felt slow and thick as she dug in it for the phone. "Was I sleeping long?" she asked Chase.

"Nope. About fifteen minutes."

She found her phone and clicked it on. "Tess Masterson."

"Tess, it's Stevie."

"Hi, Stevie, Chase and I were just—"

"I need you to come back to the ranch right now."

"Stevie, calm down. What happened?"

"Our bank account is empty."

Tess opened the door and ran down the hall.

She peeked into Stevie's room, but it was empty. Bangs and thuds came from the office across the hall. Tess pushed open the door and found her sister at the big painted desk riffling through account books, shoving one aside and reaching for another. The room had been her father's, and Tess hadn't been in here yet. She could almost see her dad sitting at the desk, almost smell the aroma of his pipe tobacco.

Tess stepped into the room. "What's happened?"

Stevie didn't look up but continued to frantically flip through pages. "I called the bank to see about a loan for the feed we lost. The bank says we're overdrawn. That can't be right! You put some money in, and with what I had, we should have had thirty thousand dollars in there, enough to see us through until we sold some cattle in the spring." Stevie covered her face with her hands.

"There has to be an explanation. Could Paul have cleared it out?"

"Paul! That dog." Stevie's lips trembled. "We can't lose the ranch."

"What's going on?" Chase stood in the doorway.

"Our money's gone," Tess said.

Chase stepped to the desk and grabbed the mouse. "I've got online access set up. Let's take a look." The computer screen began to glow when he jiggled the mouse. He clicked through some menus and got to the bank's home page. "Here we go."

Tess stood behind him and watched the figures come up. All the money she had would have been in there as well. They'd all gambled everything on the ranch. She leaned over Chase's shoulder and stared at the screen. "It says we're a hundred and twenty dollars overdrawn, and the overdraft protection was activated. That must be it." She pointed to a large withdrawal.

"Let's find out." Chase clicked for more details. "It's an electronic withdrawal from this morning."

"Right after I kicked Paul out," Stevie muttered.

Chase's clicking stopped. "What? You kicked Paul out?"

"He's having an affair," Tess told him. "Has anyone seen him since he dropped by last night?"

"I doubt it," Stevie said. "You saw how angry he was when I told him he couldn't come back here. He threatened to sue for a share of the ranch. Maybe he thought he'd get away with more this way."

"Well, we already owe more than the ranch would ever be able to bring in a sale." Chase slumped in the chair.

"It might not be Paul," Tess said, honestly hoping. "Chase, Genevieve's ex-husband is a banker."

"You think he had something to do with this?"

"Maybe he's brooded all these years and decided to make the family pay," Tess said.

Stevie paced, ignoring them. "Could we be the victim of identity theft? Wouldn't that be icing on the cake? We have to get that money back, Chase."

Chase rose and put a hand on her shoulder. "I'll call the bank and ask them to research the transaction for us. We'll have to prove whoever took it did so without our authorization. And Tess, you and I can pay a visit to the Thomases tomorrow, see what we can figure out."

Tess, Chase, Stevie, and Whip ate a solemn dinner of leftover stew. Mindy played with her dolls in the living room. "I might be able to get a little money from my Jeep. It's paid for," Tess said. "Is there any other property we could hock?"

"I'll take a look around the barn, but I doubt it." Chase got up from the chair and took his bowl to the sink. "I guess we could sell some horses." He glanced at Tess. "Wildfire would bring at least fifty thousand all by himself."

"We're not selling my horse!" The idea was a black cavern yawning at her feet. Wildfire was her last real connection to her parents. She'd lost them because of her love of the horse. To sell him would be a final betrayal.

"It might be the only way," Chase said.

"He won't let anyone else ride him."

"No one would have to ride him. He's a magnificent stud animal." His stare grew more pointed. "You sacrificed your parents for him once, Tess. Don't sacrifice your sister too."

Tess wanted to throw something. "The ranch is not my sister."

"You can't sell Wildfire," Stevie put in. "Leave her alone, Chase."

"Son, you look like a cow with a missin' calf," Whip said, dabbing at his mouth with a napkin. "We ain't licked yet."

"And what great solution did you have in mind, Whip?"

The older man smiled, the expression causing his handlebar mustache to quiver. "I got me a bit of money set by. How 'bout I buy a share of the ranch?"

Tess gaped, and Chase's own mouth dangled open. Stevie seemed unruffled. Whip had offered money before, but he'd never asked to be part owner. Still, it was right.

Her gaze was steady as she studied Whip. "How much, Whip?"

"Fifty thousand. It ain't much, but it would get us by for now."

Stevie began to smile. "It would more than get us by. We could get some new stock. Are you sure you want to do this?"

"You sayin' you'll let me?" He tipped his coffee cup to his lips.

"You're family, Whip. I've never felt good about you being left out of the will. I thought you didn't want the responsibility of ownership though. That's what you always said."

"I'd have been willin' to invest anytime you asked."

Stevie nodded. "I had no idea you had any money. We haven't been able to pay you much."

Whip shrugged. "Don't cost much to live in the bunkhouse. I got my food and an old truck to drive. What else do I need?"

"I'll see a lawyer about drawing up papers," Chase said. "He can tell us what percentage fifty thousand will buy."

"I was thinkin' a fourth," Whip said.

"The ranch is worth more than two hundred thousand!" Tess put in.

Whip scratched his head. "That's the offer on the table."

Chase glanced at Tess and Stevie. "You want to talk about it?"

"I see no need to discuss it," Stevie said. "He deserves a share. Besides, what are our other options?"

Tess looked down. "Okay with me." She'd grasp at any straw to avoid selling Wildfire. "Thanks, Whip." The man's eyes glistened, and Tess would have sworn he was about to cry.

CHAPTER 18

"Tess, it's Dr. Wyrtzen. I wanted you to know the results of the testing we did. I'm sorry to say you're not a match."

Tess gripped her cell phone to her ear and shot a surprised glance at Chase, who was driving her Jeep as they headed toward Flagstaff Wednesday morning. "That can't be right! I'm her sister. Of course I'm a match."

His voice was heavy. "I'm sorry. Siblings are generally the best chance, but even they aren't always compatible. As in this case. I'm disappointed too."

"What does this mean for Stevie?" Tess already knew before the doctor answered.

"It means long-term dialysis. We'll put her on the list for a cadaver kidney. There generally isn't a rejection problem with them, but the wait can be pretty long. Just pray we get one in the next few years."

Tess's head was beginning to thump. "What will happen if it takes longer?"

"Nothing. I didn't mean to imply it would be bad news, but I know how restless Stevie can be when she wants to go where she likes and do what she wants."

"What about Mindy?"

"Stevie wouldn't even consider taking a kidney from her daughter. That's not an option."

Of course it wasn't. What was she thinking? If only there were more siblings to choose from. "Thanks for calling, Dr. Wyrtzen." Tess felt the burn of tears at the back of her throat as she clicked off the phone. She didn't want to tell Stevie and see the light of hope die in her eyes.

"Bad news?"

"I can't give Stevie a kidney. We're not a match." Chase reached over and took her hand. Who would ever have thought the man had so much compassion? She clung to his fingers with gratitude. "She'll have to be on dialysis until a cadaver kidney comes up. It could be years."

"We'll pray it's soon."

He was a rock, and all these years she didn't know it. What else had she misjudged? Her uncle for sure. What else?

The drive to Flagstaff went by slowly in spite of the Springsteen CD blaring out the speakers. Chase kept glancing at Tess as she sat with her forehead pressed against the glass. He knew she wasn't really watching the landscape rush past. Likely she was praying for her sister. Stevie would kick against the news Tess just received.

He parked the truck across the street from the bank. "We're here." The parking spaces were nearly all taken, and traffic moved at a steady clip. "You sure you want to do this?"

"Not really. I feel sick that we have to go in there and talk about this with a man we barely know." Tess swung open the door and got out.

Chase followed her across the street and hoped their timing would be good to talk to Nate Thomas. He approached the desk. "We'd like to speak to Mr. Thomas, please."

The young woman quit popping her gum long enough to ask their names. She nodded and picked up the phone. After speaking into it a few moments, she directed them to the hall. "Third door on the right," she said.

A cold sweat broke out on Chase's forehead as he led the way. How do you ask a man about the sexual abuse perpetrated on his teenage daughter? The door was open, and Nate Thomas sat behind a huge walnut desk that was polished enough to reflect his image. Nothing marred the shiny surface except for a black vertical file that held neat rows of papers.

Nate's hazel eyes didn't match the polite smile on his face. "Chase and Tess. What a surprise. Come in." His voice was expressionless, but he got up long enough to offer a limp handshake.

Chase squeezed the older man's fingers and sat down in one of the chairs opposite the desk. Tess did the same. "Sorry to disturb you. We should probably have called first, but our business was urgent."

Nate got up and went to close the door. "It sounds serious." He sat back down and opened the lap door and extracted a pen and a pad of paper. "What can I do for you?"

"It's not about a loan," Tess began. "Actually, it's about Natalie."

"I see." Nate put down the pen and folded his hands together. "I just talked to her this morning, and she didn't mention a problem." He nodded toward some pictures on the wall. "She is a doctor now, did you know?"

"No, I hadn't heard," Tess said. "She was always so smart that I'm not surprised. She'll be a great doctor. Anyway, this involves something in the past. Have you heard that Paul Granger was arrested for arson last week?"

"I'd heard something about that," Nate admitted. "I have to say it doesn't sound likely."

"Thank you. We're investigating the fire that killed my parents, and we heard something about Uncle Giles." Tess glanced at Chase with a plea in her eyes.

Chase didn't want to talk about it any more than she did. "What she's trying to say is that we heard Giles Masterson made inappropriate advances toward Natalie, and that you confronted him about it. We'd like to know about that conversation."

Nate's eyes narrowed. "That's none of your business."

"If the accusations are true, they might help us figure out who is targeting the Mastersons," Chase said.

"If it's true?" Anger starched his back. "Did you talk to my ex-wife? If she'd been the mother she should, Natalie wouldn't . . ." Nate stood as if he wanted to intimidate them, but since he was only five-six, his gesture lacked power. "You can leave now. I have nothing more to say to you. This isn't a topic for discussion. The last thing Natalie needs is for old wounds to be reopened."

Chase decided to go for broke. "Knowing what happened may help us uncover who has a vendetta against the Mastersons. Someone transferred thirty thousand dollars from their account yesterday."

Color suffused Nate's face. "Are you insinuating I would have stooped so low? Giles Masterson was a poor excuse for a human being, and I'm glad he's dead. But I have nothing against the rest of the Mastersons. For now, anyway." All the spunk drained out of Nate. "Please leave," he asked in a toneless voice.

Chase and Tess stood. "Thanks for your time," Chase said. They walked down the hall and out of the bank. "Now what?" he asked Tess.

"Now we talk to Natalie." She glanced at her watch. "But I'm too tired to drive all the way out there today. Can you go with me tomorrow evening? I'll need to work tomorrow. Coop's been really patient with me this week, but I can't expect that to last forever."

"Sure." Any time he got to spend with Tess was good, but he wondered if she'd give him the time of day when she heard how his spurs got in the barn. She hadn't asked him any more about it, but he was going to have to come clean sooner or later.

Gloom reigned at the Masterson's kitchen table. Most of them hadn't yet caught up on the sleep lost during Monday night's fire and had tried to work all day. Tess still hadn't told Stevie about the test results. Stevie was so hopeful she'd be well soon. Tess put a plate of roast beef and potatoes on the table and set out the corn casserole and bread. Chase sent her a smile of thanks, but the rest of the group began to pass the food without a word.

Tess glanced around at the men assembled at dinner. "Is Paul here?" Tess asked Stevie.

Her sister didn't raise her head. "No."

"Did the bank track down the problem?"

"They said they traced the transfer through several places to a Swiss bank account. They've filed a report, but the investigation could take months. It could be too late by then, if we ever get it back at all." Stevie finally raised her gaze to Tess. "Even Whip's money won't get us through the winter now that the feed hay is gone. We have to sell the ranch, Tess. I'm going to call the Realtor tomorrow."

"No! You can't do that." Tess sank onto a chair. "We can't let it go. There has to be a way." All these years, she'd taken for granted that the ranch would be here even if she roamed the world. It was the last link to her parents, to the old life. Besides, how would Stevie support herself? She was sick, and Paul was running around. The ranch was her lifeline.

"There is another way, but she'd never say so, Tess." Chase's voice was strained.

Tess began to shake her head. "Not Wildfire."

"We have an offer of a hundred thousand dollars for him. With that and Whip's investment, we could make it, get new stock, start fresh."

She didn't want to hear it, but she had to ask. "Who would pay that kind of money for Wildfire?"

Stevie and Chase exchanged glances, then Chase spoke. "There's a new ranch over by Kohl's Ranch. The man is raising racehorses. He's got more money than sense, but he wants Wildfire in the worst way."

"How did he even hear about him?" Tess glanced around the table. Only her smokejumper buddies would meet her eyes. They wouldn't have had anything to do with this.

Chase squared his shoulders. "I told him."

Her throat constricted with betrayal. Of course. Who else? She should have known better than to trust him. Their long history always ended up with her being hurt. She tried to swallow, but her mouth was too dry. "Why didn't you tell me when we were out today?"

"I just got the offer this afternoon. There was a message on my cell phone when we got home. I accidentally left it here this morning. I told Stevie, but she didn't want me to even tell you about it."

"You don't have to sell Wildfire," Stevie put in. "I'm not going to ask you to do that."

The room felt so hot and close that Tess couldn't breathe. She jumped to her feet and stumbled toward the door. She had to get out of here, away from the sympathetic eyes. Her choice was really no choice at all. If she insisted on keeping her horse, the ranch would pass out of Masterson hands. Stevie and Mindy would be on the street. All the hired help would be out of work. But how could she let go of her father's last gift, the last proof of his love?

Outside in the cool evening air, she lifted her face to catch the breeze. She went to the barn. Wildfire nickered when he smelled her. Her vision blurred, and she walked blindly across the wooden floor. She opened the stall and slipped inside. He thrust his head against her shoulder. She inhaled the scent of him and buried her face in his neck.

"I'm so sorry, Wildfire. But you'll have a good life. You'll get to make beautiful colts that run like the wind. I'll stop and check on you sometimes." But she wouldn't. It would be more than she could bear to see her horse in the possession of someone else. She wanted to fling herself down and drum her heels on the floor while she screamed that she would not sell him. But she wasn't two. Growing up was painful when it meant you had to give up what you loved to save what you loved even more.

Spirit whined and wiggled under the bottom rung of the stall. He nosed her leg. The horse snorted and pranced away. Tess's hand fell to her side, and she patted the dog's head. Wildfire came near and thrust his head into her shoulder again.

The barn door creaked open behind her, and she whirled, expecting to see Stevie. Chase stepped through the opening and pulled the door shut behind him. Clenching her fists, she turned her back on him. "Go away." She buried her face in Wildfire's mane. Her blood roared in her ears, and she didn't hear his approach until he put his hand on her back. She shrugged him off.

"I'm sorry, Tess, but I just didn't see any other way out of this."

She whirled and jabbed her finger in his chest. "You could have talked to me first, Chase. When did you do this? Weeks ago or after you asked me to go out with you?" Betrayal surged through her like a sandstorm.

He didn't back up. Grabbing her shoulders, he gave her a gentle shake. "Tess, listen to me. I didn't want to hurt you, but you have to think. This is the only way out. We're boxed into a corner. Wildfire will save us."

"He's *mine*, Chase." The words tore from her throat. Tears escaped from her eyes and rolled down her cheeks. "Dad gave him to me. He's all I have left of my father. He's been my comfort, my hope for a better future. And you're going to take him from me just like you've taken everything else. This is the hardest thing I've ever done."

"I know it's tough. I'd turn heaven and earth to find another way if I could. But there's just nothing. Nowhere to turn but to this. Will you do it?"

"I thought I could trust you, Chase. Did you do this to hurt me?" The tears came faster. She'd wanted to trust him, to believe they might have a future if she was brave enough to let it happen. Staring up into his eyes, she saw the pain flicker through his face. Maybe he did care.

"Since you're already mad at me, I might as well let you know what a real jerk I am." His eyes looked tortured. "You asked why my spurs were found in the barn."

Her anger went cold. It was going to be bad—she could read it in his face. "Yes."

He shut his eyes and wiped his hand over his face before opening them again. "Your dad and I had a fight, a bad one. We were in the barn. He demanded I take off the spurs. I refused, and he grabbed my arm, forcing me onto a bale of hay. I took off the spurs and threw them at him. One of them cut his head, and he started to bleed. I was too mad to care. I stormed out of the barn and went to see my brother. I didn't even care that your dad was hurt. Then when I got home, I found out he was dead, and I never got to say I was sorry." His voice broke on the last word, and he shuddered.

A week earlier she would have been livid that he'd cut her father's face. Now she saw his guilt. How far they'd come. His arm was hard under her fingers when she reached out and touched him. "It's okay, Chase. He knows."

He gathered her into his arms, and she went gladly. She inhaled the male scent of him that mingled with fabric softener and soap. Her fingers found their way into the fabric, and she clung to him, then pulled her head back and stared up into his face. His gaze searched hers, but she didn't look away. He bent his head, and his lips touched hers. She'd found herself looking at his lips over the past few days, wondering how they would taste and what they would feel like. The reality far surpassed her imagination. His breath smelled minty, but it mingled with a scent that was all Chase. His lips were firm and tender.

What was this rising sense of urgency she felt—love or just desire? Tess had been careful to avoid any entanglements that might lead her into the storm of emotion that now swept over her. The touch of flame in her belly moved through her, the first fire she'd ever welcomed instead of fought. The barn receded, and all that existed was Chase's lips on hers and his arms holding her close. Warnings clamored in her head, but she ignored them. They tumbled into a nearby hay mound, but she barely noticed. His hand moved down her back, and she burrowed closer, reaching up and clasping him around the neck.

Dimly she became aware of Spirit burrowing between them, whining. Then she was free. Chase rolled away and sat up with his back to her. The chill of the night air rushed across her heated skin. She could see him trembling. Her brain felt fuzzy and her movements languid. "Chase?"

"Sorry, Tess." His voice was hoarse. "Maybe we'd better go inside."

"I'd rather kiss you again." She put her hand over her mouth. Did she just say that?

"I'd rather kiss you too, but it's not . . . wise." He stood up and reached his hand down to her. The warmth in his blue eyes was gone, replaced with a careful distance.

Wise? Her eyes widened as she caught his meaning. For the first time she understood the power of passion. She grabbed his hand, and he hauled her to her feet. She lost her balance and tumbled against him. The way he recoiled almost made her laugh, but she was still angry with him. What had just happened between them?

She wanted nothing more than to go back into his arms. Awareness shimmered between them like a mirage in the desert, but this possibility was real. Tess didn't think they could ever go back to the way things used to be between them. It was going to have to be all or nothing. The way Chase was avoiding her gaze told her it was likely to be nothing.

Wildfire snorted and neighed. Tess tore her gaze from Chase and looked at the stallion. "What's the matter, boy?" The horse's agitation grew. He reared, snorting and neighing. His hoofs smote the ground again, and he began to move around his stall. Around and around he ran, tossing his head. His hooves kicked up chaff, and it floated in the air and made her sneeze. She wanted to get in the stall with him, but he was too upset.

"Could be a wolf outside," she told Chase.

"I haven't seen any in weeks."

"I heard one howling the other night." She shivered at the memory. The sound hadn't been like a normal wolf—this one had been so loud it seemed to be right outside her window. She thought again of the strange thing that had chased her on the way to Aunt Doty's. Was it the same animal?

"I heard it too." Chase went toward the door. "Try to calm him down while I take a look around. Don't get in the pen though."

She stood on the run of the fence and leaned over it with her hand outstretched. Wildfire rolled his eyes and reared again. The sound that came from him seemed nearly a scream. Foam stood out on his neck and withers. "Easy, boy, easy." He shied away from her hand, his agitation growing. Okay, this wasn't working. Wildfire wouldn't intentionally hurt her, but he was terrified.

She dropped her hand. Maybe Chase had found something. She hurried to the barn door and slid it open. "Chase?" The smell hit her first. A mixture of decay and something heavy like mud. Whatever it was, she recoiled at the odor.

"Shh." He stood at the corner of the barn. His arm snaked out and drew her to his side. "There's something out there."

His tone made gooseflesh rise on her back. "Something? What do you mean *something*?"

"It has red eyes."

She touched his arm. It was stiff. "Where?" The yard was a dark void where no moonlight illuminated. The night breeze had died, and the blackness echoed with a silent presence, an evil. Did she even believe in pure evil? She hadn't thought so, but standing in the darkness with Chase's breath touching her neck, she wasn't so sure anymore.

"There, under the tree house."

The tree house was in a huge cottonwood tree. She and Stevie had both played there as children, dreamed as teens, and now Mindy used it with her dolls. The yard's dark shadows only deepened in the recesses of the grove of trees. Then she heard a low growl. Wolves were something the ranchers dealt with often, but this sound was different from anything she'd ever heard. It felt *intelligent* and personal, as if whatever it was saw her and hated her. Her tongue stuck to the roof of her mouth.

"I've seen some animal in the past week or so. It chased me the day I went to my aunt's. What *is* that thing out there?" she whispered.

"I don't know. Maybe a skinwalker."

Tess had heard of the Navajo legend similar to that of a werewolf. A skinwalker was a Navajo witch who could change from man to animal and back again, the embodiment of evil. "You don't believe that, do you?"

"I believe in evil and demons." He gripped her hand and lifted his voice. "God, we ask your protection from this evil, whatever it is."

His deep voice rose and fell as he prayed for God to put a hedge around them. Little by little, Tess's terror receded. She kept her gaze pinned on the hulking thing with red eyes. The hair-raising growling died first, then moments later the eyes vanished. The sense of oppression she had been feeling seeped away, leaving her drained. Whatever it was, she hoped never to see it again.

CHAPTER 19

*O*nce Chase was sure Tess was safely inside the house and was all right, he went to the bunkhouse. Buck and Flint were up playing euchre at a battered wooden table. "Hey, Flint, you got a minute?" Chase pulled up a chair that was missing the back and straddled it.

Flint threw his cards on the table. "Buck just tromped me again. This is a good time to quit and save face." He rubbed Spirit's ears. "What's up?"

"You're an Apache. How much credence do you give the old myths about skinwalkers?" Chase felt stupid asking the question, but he couldn't imagine what that thing was.

Flint's expression didn't change, but a muscle twitched in his jaw.

Buck's feet hit the floor, and then he joined them. "What's a skinwalker?"

Flint's hands moved from his dog to the table, and he began to gather the cards. "A skinwalker is a Navajo witch, one who can change into an animal."

"How do they do it?" Buck asked.

Flint wrapped a rubber band around the cards. "Only a skinwalker knows. The rites to begin apprenticeship as a witch involve killing a close relative and eating them."

Chase felt faintly sick. "Do you believe that?" He didn't know what he believed. Whatever that thing had been out there tonight, it had filled him with the horror of the unknown.

Flint finally glanced up. "I have seen many unexplainable things among my people. I don't go looking for evil, but I believe it exists. There will always be men and women who want power at any cost, even if it means being a vessel for demons. Why are you asking these questions?"

Chase hesitated. He was bound to look like a fool in front of the other men if he admitted it, but at this point, he just wanted an explanation. "Tess and I saw something earlier tonight. It looked kind of like a large wolf, but it had red eyes. The way it growled was like nothing I've ever heard." He expected the men to laugh, but instead Buck looked toward the window with an uneasy expression.

Chase went on in a dogged tone. "Tess says she's seen it before. Several different times. At least she thinks it's the same animal. It chased her through the woods once, and she heard it outside her Jeep and outside her bedroom."

Flint gave a somber nod. "It might have been a skinwalker. They use the skin of the animal they wish to become like. They don't actually change into the animal, it's more that the animal's spirit takes over their human body. They walk and act like that animal.

And their eyes are weird. Red, I have heard the legends say. Did it threaten you?"

"No. I prayed and it left."

"I saw that thing too," Buck said. "It was looking in the window last night. I thought I was dreaming. Then I heard Spirit at the door trying to get out. He was growling." He looked at Flint. "Did you hear it? You called Spirit back."

"I heard." Flint's face was expressionless.

Chase wasn't ready to believe he'd seen something supernatural. A man dressed in a wolf hide he could believe. He pushed away the thought of the thing's red eyes. Maybe it was contacts or something. But whoever it was, the thing gave him the creeps.

Stallion Pass subdivision was just off I-10, and the distant hum of traffic, normally a soothing sound to Tess, did nothing to allay her trepidation as she and Chase got out of the truck and started toward Natalie's house. The sun had set an hour ago on their way in from Payson. A middle-class neighborhood filled with desert style homes on small lots, it was new and clean, but Tess would have expected a doctor to live in Scottsdale or one of the more expensive subdivisions.

Just as she got out of the vehicle, her cell phone rang.

Mrs. Stinson's voice came over the connection. "Tess, I told you I'd call. Allie is out of the coma."

"That's wonderful news! Can I come see her?"

There was a long pause. "I suppose. She's not really very responsive yet, but maybe seeing you will help."

"I'm in Goodyear. We'll stop at the hospital on our way back.

Thanks, Mrs. Stinson." She hung up and told Chase about the call. "Do you mind if we stop?"

"Nope."

Natalie's house, a two-story with an enclosed courtyard, had a green-tile roof and a river run in the front yard. They brushed past trimmed oleander bushes and beautiful mounds of bird-of-paradise that were illuminated by landscaping floodlights to the recessed front door. A TV blared from inside the house.

Chase rang the doorbell, covered with a lizard plate. Tess could barely look at him. Last night's kiss had made her feel like she didn't know him. Besides, she still hadn't forgiven him for arranging to sell Wildfire.

The door swung open, and a young girl stood framed in the doorway. Tess thought she looked around eleven or twelve. With her dark-brown hair and chocolate eyes, she looked so much like Natalie that Tess had to bite back a gasp.

"Hi, is your mom home? I'm an old friend of hers," Tess said.

"Yeah, she's in the kitchen." The girl stood aside to allow them to enter. "Mom, there's some people here to see you." She flashed a curious glance their way and went back toward the TV.

The entry opened into a great room that had terra-cotta tiled floors and a nine-foot ceiling lined with pot shelves. Kachina dolls and other Native American art decorated the shelves.

"Were you looking for me?" Natalie stood by the kitchen island with a dish towel in her hands. Her blank stare told Tess she didn't recognize her.

Tess smiled. "Natalie, it's Tess. Tess Masterson." She stretched out her hand. Natalie looked the same: dark brown hair and eyes, high cheekbones, slim and athletic.

Natalie's smile finally came, but it held a trace of uncertainty.

She clasped Tess's hand. "Tess, I should have recognized that hair. It's been so long." Her gaze shot to Chase. "And how could I miss Chase? What are you doing here? How did you find me?"

Tess decided not to answer part of the questions. She didn't want to get Natalie mad at her mother. "I'm sorry to just drop in, but could we talk to you for a minute? It's important."

"Sure." Natalie tossed the towel to the island. "Come into my office." She led the way to a set of double doors that opened off the great room. Shutting the doors behind her, she indicated the armchairs on either side of the window. "Have a seat and tell me what this is all about. How's Stevie?"

"She's been pretty sick. She has lupus," Tess said.

Natalie winced. "I'm a doctor, in case you didn't know. I hate to hear about this."

"Her kidneys are failing, and she's on dialysis while she waits for a cadaver kidney. I'm afraid I'm not a donor match."

"Too bad." Natalie pulled out the computer chair and sank into it. "So why have you looked me up after all these years?"

Tess wet her lips. She should probably handle this since it was a woman they were questioning. "Paul Granger has been arrested for arson. We think he's been framed by someone who has a vendetta against my family. I've been looking into the fire that killed my parents. During my investigation, I've heard some disturbing things about my uncle."

Natalie picked up a paper clip from the desk and began to play with it. "How does that involve me?"

She had a bit of her dad's poker face. Tess wasn't sure if Natalie would talk about it. "We heard he made inappropriate advances toward you when you were a teenager. Also toward Maxie's daughter, Susan."

Natalie's sigh was heavy. "Do we have to go into this, Tess? I see no purpose in raking up the past. Or are you saying I might have set the fires and have been doing it all these years?" Genuine amusement tipped her mouth.

"No, of course we don't suspect you," Chase said. "But if Giles was a child predator, maybe someone else he targeted decided to get revenge."

"Aren't most arsonists male? His victims would be unlikely suspects." Natalie shook her head. "As far as I know, Giles only had a taste for young female flesh."

"The girl might have had a brother or a father," Tess pointed out. "So you're saying it's true about Uncle Giles?" She'd hoped to disprove the accusation.

Natalie got up and moved toward the door. "I don't want to talk about it. I've put that part of my life behind me. It's too painful. Yes, it's true, but that's all I'm going to say. I hate to be rude, but my husband will be home for dinner soon, and we have dinner guests coming." She opened the double doors and headed toward the front door.

They had no choice but to follow her.

Tess stood by Allie's bed. Chase had to stay in the hall. Allie's eyes were open, but with all the tubes and contraptions attached to her, it was hard to see her face. Her legs were suspended in casts, and the skin around her eyes was bruised. "Allie? Can you hear me?"

"She can't talk," Mrs. Stinson said. "She's still on the respirator. But the doctors are hopeful there's no brain damage." Her husband stood in the corner but said nothing.

Allie's eyes fastened onto Tess. Recognition seemed to flash over her face, but Tess wasn't sure if it was her imagination. "Allie?" She leaned forward and picked up her friend's hand, careful not to disturb the IV snaking into her veins. Allie returned a slight pressure, then she began to thrash in the bed.

"You're agitating her." Mrs. Stinson tried to pull Allie's hand away, but Allie clutched it tighter and whipped her head around.

"I think she wants to talk to me," Tess said. "Allie, do you know who tampered with the parachute?" Allie's eyes widened, and she became more agitated when she couldn't communicate.

"You'd better get out of here," Mr. Stinson barked, emerging from the shadows. "You're just upsetting her." He wrenched Allie's grip away and pushed Tess toward the door.

Tess was sure Allie remembered something, but there seemed to be no way to get to the truth. She was going to have to be patient.

Friday passed in a blur of more demolition at the fire camp. Tess finished up the latest chute repairs while the men took turns running debris to the dump. Their good progress put Coop in high spirits, and the hours passed more quickly than Tess wished they would.

She returned to the ranch at the same time that a horse trailer lumbered up the graveled drive. Twilight shrouded the hills with purple and gold, but Tess noticed none of the beauty. She went straight from her Jeep to the corral and stood with her arms around Wildfire. She wouldn't cry, she wouldn't. But her eyes burned with the effort to hold back the tears. She already hated the man who was buying her horse. This Duffy Newcastle hadn't even bothered to come himself. He'd just sent lackeys. The lump in her throat grew to the size of the Castle Rock.

Wildfire snorted at the exhaust spewing from the truck. It

stopped in the glow of the security light. Tess smoothed his neck. "Easy, boy," she murmured. The stallion quieted at the touch. How could she let him go? She'd raised him, trained him to the saddle and halter, and nursed him through a rattlesnake bite. She buried her face in his neck and inhaled memories of him as she rubbed her cheek against his silky coat.

Stevie touched her shoulder. "They're ready for him. Tessie, you don't have to do this. We haven't cashed his check yet."

Her sister's tone held a telling lack of conviction. Tess raised her head and took a deep breath. She couldn't look at her sister. While it wasn't Stevie's fault the ranch was failing, it hurt that her sister had allowed this to go through. Tess knew her attitude was irrational—if there had been any other way out of the mess, her sister would have taken it—but none of the rationalizations comforted her now. Not with Wildfire about to be taken from her forever.

She kissed Wildfire's neck and backed away. Through a blur of tears, she saw Chase. He was clenching and unclenching his fists as he stared at the men coming to load the horse. She had a feeling he was about to try to stop them, but it was probably her imagination. After all, this was all his doing. She should hate him for it, but her emotions about him were still in turmoil.

Chase reached out to her, but she pretended not to see. She moved closer to Stevie, who put her arm around Tess as they watched the men try to load Wildfire in the trailer. The horse bucked and kicked one of the men in the knee. He went down, losing his grip on the lead. Wildfire reared, and his hooves narrowly missed the man's head when he came down. The other man grabbed hold of the rope before the horse could canter away, but Wildfire refused to go into the trailer.

Tess was going to have to load him herself. Supper would be ready soon, and this needed to be over. Wildfire wouldn't go in for anyone else. "Hey, boy," she called to him, and he settled. Was it her imagination that she heard a distinct *crack* in the region of her chest? Telling herself she had to hold it together for at least a little while longer, she took the lead and coaxed the horse up the ramp. Inside the metal enclosure, he bumped his head against her and pinned her into the front right corner. She didn't mind. With the straw under her feet and away from prying eyes, she could stay here forever with Wildfire's nose against her neck, his warm breath blowing across her.

"You okay?" Chase's voice interrupted her last moment with Wildfire.

"Be right there." She choked out the words and rubbed her horse's nose for the last time. She kissed his nose and went down his side, running her hands along his withers and belly. He moved out of the way, and she exited the trailer wishing it were all a nightmare. But hearing Wildfire neigh reminded her that this nightmare was all too real. It was like a baby's cry to a mother, but this was one appeal she couldn't answer, a problem she couldn't fix.

She put her hand over her mouth and ran for the orchard. She was burning up, so she shucked her jacket as she went and allowed the cool night air to wash over her. Chase called her name, but she didn't stop. The scent of apples that had fallen from the trees laced the air, and she slipped on a half-rotten one, nearly going down onto one knee. Catching herself, she continued to run until she was through the orchard and into the pines just beyond it. Only then did she let the tears fall. She flung herself onto a bed of pine needles. Pillowing her face in her discarded jacket, she unleashed her grief. She cried for all the things she'd lost in her life—her parents, her self-respect, her horse. When the tears were finally spent, she wiped her nose and sat up.

Where was her backbone? She'd survived worse than this. God would take care of her horse, and he would bring whoever was targeting her family to justice eventually. While she wanted judgment now, it was all in the Lord's hands. Hugging her knees to her chest, she listened to the night sounds. She needed to get it together for Stevie's sake. Nothing had changed, even if they had enough money to get by for now. The ranch would be lost in due time if they didn't find the arsonist. Tess had to figure out who was targeting them—and why.

She stood and turned to go back to the house when she heard something. A rustle of pine branches and the snap of a twig. Someone was coming. Maybe Chase had followed her, but the movements sounded furtive. Chase would be calling her name, not trying to be stealthy. She dove into a nearby bush, then told herself she was an idiot. It was likely one of the hands. But still, she stayed where she was with her head far back in the branches. Peering out at the shaft of moonlight that illuminated the clearing, she waited to see who was out there.

She smelled it before she saw it. The stink of wolf rolled off the figure that lumbered past her hideaway. A head full of sharp teeth looked around. She stuffed her fist into her mouth to keep from screaming when she saw the wolf's head atop a creature that walked upright. Then she peered closer and saw past the wolf pelts to a man's face under the animal head. She only caught a glimpse of a cheek inside the open mouth of the wolf pelt.

Though the realization it was a man should have reassured her, it didn't. Menace rolled off the figure as he crouched near where she lay and began to mutter. It sounded like a Native incantation of some kind, and it made her break out in a cold sweat. She began to tremble, and she wanted to plug her ears to drown out the guttural chant. *Go away, go away.* She should be looking at him more closely to try to figure out his identity, but her skin crawled at the smell, sight, and sound of him.

He cocked his head and looked toward her as if he knew she was there. Leaves crackled underfoot as he stepped toward her hiding place. She couldn't stay here. If he found her lying there, she'd be helpless. But if she moved, the rustling would alert him before she could get to her feet. It would take all her strength to face him, and right now she felt as weak as a newborn colt. Still, she had to try.

Her muscles coiled in her legs and arms. She sprang to her feet and leaped from the bushes. Shrieking an Apache war cry Flint once taught her, she bounded toward the figure as he snarled and backed away at her sudden appearance. She leaped past him, straining to reach the path where she could run more freely. The creature, man, or whatever it was sprang after her. His speed and agility seemed almost supernatural, but maybe it was her fear that made him appear so swift. She put forth a burst of speed and exited the trees.

She dared a glance back and saw the figure whirl and rush away. Pine boughs swayed as the figure passed, and she parted the needles and peered along the path. There was no sign of the man. How could she describe her experience to everyone? They'd think she was crazy. No. Chase would believe her. This man must have been what they'd seen last night. Could he have anything to do with all the trouble that had been befalling them?

I cross Dry Wash, desperate for my sanctuary. Once inside, I pace the cave, the wolf pelts swinging around me. Tess almost saw me. She shouldn't have gotten so close. What went wrong? I mentally tick off all my preparations, all the incantations and potions I've learned. There is nothing forgotten, nothing done incorrectly. No mistakes have been made.

My eyes burn and I sniffle, then wipe the back of my hand over my eyes. *Stupid, just like your mother.* I clap my hands over my ears to block out the sound of Diamond's voice, but the words come harder, faster. *You want to hit me, don't you? But you're too much of a coward. Slap, slap!* Curling down into myself in the corner, I cringe from the blows. The hard rock pokes my back.

Heaves shudder through my chest. How long have I been curled in the corner? I groan when I try to move my stiff arms and legs. The voices should have disappeared when he died. I took his power into myself. He shouldn't have the power to hurt me from the grave.

My sleeping legs come alive with pain when I stand. The lantern still glows. I turn up the wick, and the light gathers and throws the cave into sharp relief. My drawings decorate the northern wall. They're actually quite good. My mother always said I inherited her eye for scale. Seeing the images of myself with the wolf skin strengthens my courage. I am invincible. His words have no power to hurt me any longer.

A small leather pouch contains my potions and fetishes. I will arrange them around the fire. I will have a purifying ceremony and purge myself of the spirits from my past. I should have done it before now. The animal spirits need a clean, new home to dwell in. Then the past will be gone.

I arrange the logs in the fire pit and lay more wood to the side to add once the flames are hot. When the glow of fire illuminates the cave, I turn off the lantern and approach the fire. Muttering, I focus on the flame as it grows, feeding on the twigs and dry wood I carefully add. When it burns hot and bright, welcome heat seeps into my body. Feeling the sheen of perspiration, I revel in its cleansing power. The old hurts soak out of my body and into the dry soil as Mother Earth gives me solace.

"Hey-yah-hey." The chants pour from my mouth. I take the drum and beat it. The enclosed walls of the cave intensify the sound, thrumming it back to my ears. It makes my heart race. Free and clean. I am an empty vessel ready to be used and to use the spirits to take revenge on my enemies.

Sweat pours off me, and my vision narrows to a pinprick. I see myself as I will soon be: master of my fate. The vision intensifies. Mounted on Tess's horse, Wildfire, I am on top of Spider Rock. Graves litter the ground at my feet. The headstones all say Masterson. Looking out over the plains and arroyos, my gaze finds the ranch. It is empty now. Tumbleweeds pile against the door. The barn's roof has caved in, and weeds choke the path to the house and chicken coop.

My chants rise in the flickering firelight. Since the moment I was born, I have been moving toward this destination. Power flows along my muscles, and a sense of rightness, of belonging. It imbues my limbs with strength and determination as it moves through my veins and arteries.

When I rise from the fire, I am ten feet tall, and my shadow leaps on the wall, towering to the ceiling. Now they will pay, and not even prayers will make me run.

CHAPTER 20

*Y*ou're sure you didn't recognize him?" Chase handed Tess a
cup of coffee. A storm was rolling in, chasing the sunset. She still
looked pale, and the hand that took the coffee shook. He and Buck
had combed the area for an hour after she came flying back to the
barnyard. They'd found some barefoot prints, but it was hard to
know how long they'd been there or who they belonged to.

Tess gulped the hot drink. "His face was covered with the skins."
She shuddered and sat back against the couch cushions. Whining
with concern, Spirit pressed against her leg.

Mindy came running into the room and crawled into her lap,
and Tess cuddled the little girl close. "Hey, sweet girl."

"Don't cry, Aunt Tessie." Mindy patted Tess's wet cheeks.

"I'm okay, Mindy. Where's your mommy?"

"She went to town." *Meeting with Pastor and Paul,* Chase

mouthed. Tess gave a slight nod. Silence fell in the room. Mindy got her coloring book and crayons and settled on the sofa beside her aunt. Though she seemed absorbed by her task, Chase took care to ask questions without upsetting Mindy. He cleared his throat. "How did he walk?"

Tess glanced at Mindy. "He was running. Not familiar at all. Nothing was."

If only he'd been there. He lost her when she disappeared into the trees. "I called Eric. He's going to look around today." Tess nodded and put her coffee cup down on the table made from a tree trunk. Her hands had quit shaking, he noticed. She was a strong woman. This would just make her more determined to figure things out.

He needed to find out what he could about skinwalkers. Maxie would be the one to talk to. Flint seemed reticent to discuss it, but if Maxie knew they were in danger, she'd tell them what she knew. "I'm going to go see Maxie," he said.

"Now?" Chase nodded. "I want to come." Tess looked down at Mindy's bent head. "Mindy, you go get ready for bed. It's getting late.

"I want to watch Shirley Temple."

"Not enough time for that tonight, sweetie. But I'll read a story to you."

"Which one?"

"You pick." Mindy bounced out of the room.

Chase held out his hand to help up Tess. "You sure you're up to this?"

She took it. "I'm fine. Why talk to Maxie? You think it's a Navajo?"

He took her cup into the kitchen. "I'm wondering. It seems to be someone who thinks he's a skinwalker."

She shuddered. "I wish you'd seen it. It was downright creepy."

"Covering yourself up with wolf skins would do that."

"You don't think it was real?"

"I don't know, Tess." Last night he'd been sure it was real, but tonight, he wondered if the darkness was playing tricks on all of them. Still, the thing had disappeared when he prayed. Coincidence? Maybe. Chase wasn't ready to throw his vote in any particular direction.

"While you tuck Mindy in, I'll go find Whip to keep an eye on her."

Thunder rumbled overhead as Chase drove the truck over the rutted dirt road to the reservation. Driving up the track to Maxie's hogan, the darkness pressed in on them. He could barely see the outline of the dwelling when he parked. "Stay here, and I'll see if she's home."

"I'll come with you."

He shook his head. "She might be out feeding the animals. You watch the hillside for her, and I'll check if she's inside." He got out and went around the other side to the door. It stood open. "Maxie?" He peered inside, but the single room was empty.

He turned and nearly ran into the figure that loomed from the other side of the hogan. Darkness hid the man's face. "I'm looking for Maxie," he said.

The man stepped into the wash of light that spilled from the open doorway, and Chase saw it was her son Les. He took a step back, remembering the man's anger the last time they'd been here. "Is your mother home?"

Les brushed past him without speaking. At least he wasn't wading in with his fists pounding. Chase wasn't afraid of a fight, but he'd rather get the information peaceably. Les went inside the dwelling, but he left the door open. Chase took that as an invitation. He stepped in with him.

Les stared at him with dark, expressionless eyes. "Leave my family alone. You bring darkness with you."

"What do you mean?"

"The witch said if you came again, he would curse our family. My mother went to visit her sister to get away. Go away, and don't come back."

"Is this witch a skinwalker? We've seen something strange at the ranch, Les. I need your advice."

"I can answer nothing."

"We've seen a strange thing, a creature or man that walks upright and wears wolf skins."

A shudder, nearly imperceptible, shivered along Les's arms. "You leave. Now."

"I need some information first." Chase wasn't leaving without some idea of what he was facing.

Les gave him a long look, then walked past him and vanished through the door. Chase followed him, but the night had swallowed him up.

There was nothing like the blackness of an Arizona night. Clouds covered the stars, and a hint of rain freshened the air. The prairie stretched out without even the light from a house to illuminate the landscape. Tess strained to see something in the yard or the hills surrounding the hogan. There was no sign of Maxie or the sheep. What was taking Chase so long? She was tempted to get out and look for him.

She didn't see the figure coming until the door opened on the driver's side, and the cab light came on, nearly blinding her. She blinked away the spots in front of her eyes and turned to ask Chase what he'd found when she saw the figure wasn't Chase.

A young woman quickly shut the door behind her. "I must speak quickly before my brother sees me. He doesn't want me to talk to you."

"Susan?" It had been years since Tess had seen Susan. She was about Tess's age. Her long black hair was in a thick braid that hung over one shoulder. She wore jeans and a plaid flannel shirt. Tess had always thought Susan was beautiful, but today fear haunted her dark eyes.

Susan glanced toward the hogan. "Les will be angry. We have to hurry."

"Is your mother here?"

Susan shook her head. "There's no time. My mother told me you wanted to know about your uncle, that you were searching to find out about the fire. She didn't want to tell you the story. It is my story to tell, she says. Les wanted me to stay out of it, but I told my mother that I couldn't keep it any longer. It was time for the truth to come out." She cast a hurried glance toward the hogan.

Tess picked up on Susan's urgency. What would Les do if he caught her here? He'd been angry the other day when they'd tried to talk to his mother. What were they hiding? "You would have been around fourteen when your mother left the ranch. Were you there the night of the fire?"

Susan cast another glance toward the hogan, then shook her head. "He raped me. My mother went to your parents, but they did nothing, so my mother took me and left."

Tess closed her eyes and rubbed her forehead. Genevieve had already confirmed this story. In her own way, Natalie had too. She opened her eyes and reached over to take the other woman's hand. "I'm sorry, Susan, so sorry."

Susan did not return the pressure in Tess's hand. "The Mastersons owe me. Giles ruined my life."

Great, just great. Tess pulled away. "What do you want?"

"My village needs a nurse. I want to go to school and then return to help them. I need money to do that." Susan glanced again toward the hogan. She dove under the steering wheel. "It's Les," she whispered. "He must not see me. He will be angry."

Tess watched the man's stiff figure stalk past the truck without a glance. He disappeared over the hill. "He's gone."

Susan sat up. "Will you help me?"

"I'll have to talk to Stevie. The ranch isn't doing well." She heard Susan's intake of breath, an exasperated sound.

"You owe this to me," Susan hissed. She opened the door and got out, closing it without a sound. Moments later she was gone.

Was Susan just looking for a handout? Tess was inclined to believe her, especially after all she'd learned. Could Les or someone else in the family be out for revenge?

Someone tapped on the window, and she whirled again. A little girl was standing on tiptoe and peeking in the window. Tess leaned over and flipped the key onto auxiliary, then ran the window down. "Hello, who are you?" Who was this girl, and what was she doing out in the night?

The child smiled shyly. "I'm Mary."

Maxie's granddaughter. Susan's daughter, maybe? Before she could ask more questions, she heard the same howl she and Chase had heard last night. The child's eyes grew round and frightened. "The skinwalker," she gasped. She backed away from the car.

"Come inside the car," Tess urged.

The child stared into the darkness where Tess heard the sound of shifting rock. "He's coming!" She turned and ran in the opposite direction from the hogan.

"Wait!" Tess fumbled with the car door and got it open, half-falling out of the car onto the hard dirt. She had to get to the child, protect her. If only she had a gun or something. She reached down and felt along the ground. Her fingers closed around a rock, and she grabbed it up. It was a puny weapon, but it would have to do. "Mary, where are you?" She ran after the little girl.

Chase shut the door to the hogan behind him. The damp air cooled his skin, overheated from the shelter's wood stove. He heard a rustling, then something bumped him from behind in the dark, nearly buckling his knees. Flailing to keep his balance, his hand touched something warm and soft. When the animal moved and his fingers caught in the wool, his tension eased. The ewe thrust her nose into his hand. "Sorry, I don't have anything to feed you."

The animal meandered away with an indignant bleat, and he felt his way around the end of the building. It was like trying to move in black water. He couldn't see a thing. Stumbling over something on the ground, he nearly went down again. If he were a swearing man, he'd be saying a few choice words now. The rough logs under his fingers gave way to cool night air when he reached the end of the building. Where was the truck? He peered through the blackness and barely made out its dark form.

Stumbling toward it, he finally touched the hood then let the shape guide him around to the driver's door. It was like reaching home. He opened the door and practically fell into the seat. "Sorry I was so long. Everything okay?" Tess was gone. His pulse kicked into overdrive. It would be nearly impossible to find her in the dark. Wait, he had a flashlight. He dug around under the seat until his fingers touched the cool metal of the Maglite.

He pressed the rubber button and got back out of the truck. "Tess? Where are you?" The light's dancing beam made the discarded litter around the hogan appear to be alive. The beam swept over the seat ripped from the back of a car, an old toilet that was lying on its side, then moved on to an old bedspring. A slight impression of a path caught his eye. Maybe she'd gone this way.

Why had she wandered off? If she was going to get out of the truck, she should have come to find him. It would have taken powerful persuasion to coax her out of the truck in the pitch dark. Maybe she'd seen Maxie.

Or maybe the skinwalker had taken her.

Stupid thought. She'd know better than to get out and chase him. The thing terrified her, as well it should. Rocks slid away from his feet, and the surprise trickle of noise was as loud as an explosion. If only he'd paid more attention to the landscape the other day when they'd come.

The path meandered away from the hogan, down into a wash, then up again into thick vegetation. He swept his light around. "Tess!" He followed the path. It felt closed in here, and he knew if he could see, there would probably be canyon walls looming around him. Something loomed in the glow of his light. Another hogan perched on the hillside about ten feet above the bottom of the wash. Who lived down here? One of Maxie's relatives? Maybe Les? He wasn't eager for another run-in with the Navajo.

A small glow of light spilled out of the building. He went around to the east side and approached the door. A murmur of voices came through the wooden door. Straining his ears, he tried to make out the speakers, hoping Tess was one of them. He rapped on the rough wooden door. The voices ceased, and he heard the sound of someone shuffling to the door. It swung open, and he found himself face to face with a young woman. She looked familiar, and he recognized Susan.

She stared at him blankly. "Chase."

"Hi, Susan. I'm looking for Tess. She was supposed to wait for me in the truck, but she's gone. Is she here?"

"She's not here." Susan began to shut the door.

"Wait a minute, have you seen her?"

Susan looked away and darted a glance behind him, down the trail. She shook her head. "Go away now. Maybe she went for a walk." She shut the door in his face.

He was tempted to pound on the door again, but instead he turned and swept his light behind him. Steep rocks rose around the canyon. A rumble sounded, and he looked up. Lightning flickered across the sky, and he could smell the coming rain. A storm was no place to be caught outside. A flash flood was always a possibility in the hardpan dirt of Arizona. The lightning came again and illuminated a stand of trees. He needed to find her fast. Hurrying away from the hogan, he walked into the forest. A few drops of rain began to fall. Fifteen minutes later, he wallowed through a thick patch of brambles. A flash of lightning showed something lying up the path on the other side of the wash, just outside a cave. Was it Tess?

He cupped his hands and yelled over the rising wind. "Tess!" The flashlight beam began to dim, and he shook it, then aimed it up the path. The thin light illuminated a figure. It was definitely a person, but he couldn't tell if it was Tess. Boulders littered the wash, and past torrents of water had cut deep gouges in the bed. Picking his way across, he reached the other side and hurried up the path.

A moan echoed down the canyon as more thunder rumbled over-head. "Tess?" He crested the incline, and his light touched the figure lying in the path. Blood flowed from a gash on Tess's temple, mat-ting her hair on the left side. Her eyes fluttered but stayed closed when he knelt and touched her. He fished a handkerchief out of his pocket and stanched the blood flow. "Tess, it's Chase." He pressed his fingers to her throat and felt the pulse. It was strong and even. He should never have left her alone. What had she been doing wander-ing out here? If he wasn't so scared of losing her, he'd shake her.

Cradling her head and shoulders in his arms, he pressed his lips to the side of her face. "Wake up, Tess," he murmured. If only he had some water. There was a case of bottled water behind the seat of his truck, but he hadn't brought any with him. Lightning flashed again, and the thunder rolled in long waves. A splatter of rain began to fall.

She moaned. "Oh, my head." Her hand fluttered to the side of her head, and she opened her eyes. "What happened?"

"Only you can answer that." He propped her up and smoothed the matted hair back from her face. "Why did you leave the truck?"

"There was a little girl," she said faintly. "Mary. And that skin-walker thing was chasing her." She sat up as the skies opened, and a torrent of rain began to fall.

They were both drenched in seconds. Chase tried to shield Tess as much as he could. "We need to get across the wash before we're trapped over here. Can you stand?"

"I think so."

He helped her to her feet. Their clothing was soaked. Tess leaned heavily against him.

"I think I'm going to pass out," she muttered.

Sagging in his arms, she went to her knees. "I can't see. I have to wait for my head to clear," she muttered.

The rain only made the visibility worse. They couldn't delay long. Easing her back to the ground, he knelt in the pelting rain as the thunder rolled on. Lightning illuminated the scene with a ghastly glow. She closed her eyes and sagged against him. "Tess?" She didn't respond. If only he had brought his cell phone. Rain sluiced over them. He shone his light around the area, and the beam of light picked out an indentation under an overhanging rock. The ground there was dry. He half dragged, half carried her toward the sheltering rock.

As they reached it, he felt rather than heard a rumble under his feet. He peered through the sheets of rain and in the flicker of lightning saw a towering wave of water rush along the wash. Tossing rocks and sticks in its fury, it careened past. They were stuck here for a while. Leaning against the wall, he pulled Tess into his arms and held her.

Propping his chin against her head, he prayed for protection for them both and for Tess to awaken and be all right. What would he do if she wasn't? Holding her close, he knew she was way more important to him than he'd ever admitted. The rain began to slow, but he could still hear the thunder of the water raging over the wash. He rubbed his hand over Tess's cheek. "Wake up, Tess, wake up," he whispered. What if she had a concussion and needed to be hospitalized right away? They were stuck here. He'd never felt fear like this before, wishing he could gather her close and protect her from any harm. *Wake up, wake up.*

As if in answer to his silent plea, Tess opened her eyes. Maybe it was her befuddled state, but it seemed her gaze softened and tenderness blanketed her face. She reached up her hand and stroked his cheek. "Chase, are we dead?"

"No, sweetheart, we're very much alive." Did he really just call her sweetheart? The lightning must have touched him. Her eyes held an invitation, or at least he thought they did. He told himself not to take advantage of her weakened state, but his head went forward of its own accord, and he kissed her. She wrapped her arms around his neck, and her breath was warm against his face.

He closed his eyes and kissed her. The passion between them rose with his heartbeat. It felt right to hold her in his arms against the heart she'd occupied for so long without his realization. Her fingers tangled in his hair, and she kissed him back as though she never wanted to let him go.

Chase broke the kiss. What was he thinking? That was the problem—he hadn't been. He let her go, and she sat up slowly, putting a hand out for balance.

"Is it safe to go home?"

He reluctantly let her slip out of his arms. "Let me check." He crawled to the ledge and peered over. The sound of the water was slower now. Sweeping the beam of the flashlight over it, he saw it was still too deep and fast moving to cross. He moved back beside Tess. "Not yet. The water is going down, but we may be stuck here overnight."

A smile tugged at her lips. "You might have to make an honest woman out of me," she quipped.

"No one would imagine we'd be up to any shenanigans." He grinned. "Not with the way we fight."

"I don't think we've argued in at least a day. Is that a record?"

"I think it might be. You still haven't said what happened. How did you get hurt, and what happened to the little girl?"

Tess touched her head. "I remember following her, and I could hear that thing growling and howling. Scared me to death, but I was afraid for Mary. I think I got disoriented because I never saw Mary after she ran off. I went through the wash and was going up the slope, and I felt someone shove me. I fell over the side of something. I don't know how far."

"Someone tried to kill you." He hadn't wanted to consider it, but the fear had hovered at the back of his mind all evening. He pulled her into a protective embrace, and she came willingly. Her fingertips touched her lips. "You practice kissing often?"

The chemistry between them couldn't be denied. But was that all it was—simple magnetism and desire? Tess stroked his cheek with her palm tenderly. He took it, turned it over, and kissed the inside of her wrist.

"What is this, Chase?"

He wasn't ready to answer that question yet. What did he have to offer her? Everything he had in life was something he'd taken away from her. This truth was once a source of pride. He'd thought it pretty poetic that she'd gotten her comeuppance. Now he felt like a beggar, hat in hand. If he'd understood the true emotion hiding behind the screen of Tess's dislike, he would have never taken the inheritance. He would have given it back and gone out to prove himself to her.

When he didn't answer, the light in her eyes faded. She sat up and pulled away, "Do we have a relationship?"

He gave her a long look. "Yeah, but I have no idea where it's going to lead." The sweetness she offered was compelling, but he couldn't let himself be seduced by it. Not until he felt he could offer something she wouldn't have otherwise.

CHAPTER 21

I hadn't wanted to push Tess off the ledge. A firefighter should go to her Maker in blazing glory, not washed away in a flash flood like so much flotsam. Tess's passion mirrors my own. We deserve better. We will have better.

Nevertheless, the opportunity seemed God-given. Besides, if Tess were dead, she wouldn't have to bear the heartache of seeing what becomes of her family and her inheritance. It was a kindness, really.

The heater blows out full blast. My furs are in the backseat, too wet to wear. Chase is with Tess now, but only temporarily. She belongs to me. Her life and her death are my decisions. I dig out my lighter and flick it. The flame is soothing, calming all fears. Maybe I should go back and finish it now—with fire. The fire flickers out. I can bide my time. It will be all the sweeter for the wait.

Tess's headache had dulled to a gentle throb by the time the water went down, and they made it across the wash in the fresh moonlight. It was nearly three in the morning. All she wanted was to get to her bed and forget the way Chase had kissed her. He obviously had. He tried to help her over a boulder, but she jerked away.

"You seem grumpy and out of sorts," Chase said.

He would be too if she'd kissed him then acted like it was something she was ashamed of. She'd enjoyed every second of that kiss. In fact, she'd like to do it again. What was his problem? "My head hurts," she told him.

They'd reached the truck. "I should probably take you to the hospital."

"I'm fine. No double vision or anything. Just a headache. I want to go home and get some rest." She glanced around the truck. The storm was over, and the stars and moon illuminated the area enough to make out the shapes of things. "I wonder if we should try to see if Mary made it back safely."

"We don't even know where she lives," he pointed out.

"Probably with Maxie. She's her granddaughter."

"But Maxie's visiting relatives. You get in the car and stay put. I'll go check with Susan."

With the way her head was throbbing, she was more than happy to do that. He helped her sit, and she leaned her head back and closed her eyes.

Chase pressed the lock. "Don't open this, and don't get out," he warned. "I'll be right back."

She nodded without opening her eyes. If she looked at him, she might cry. Her emotions about him were as tangled as a tumble-weed. She must have slept because it seemed only seconds until the door beside her slammed. Blinking, she sat up.

Chase flicked water from his wet hair in her face. She flinched, and he smiled. "Just checking to make sure you're not unconscious."

"Did you find Mary?"

"Yeah, she's safe and snug. She's Les's daughter, not Susan's."

"Did you ask him about the skinwalker?"

"I tried earlier. Les refused to talk about it except to say a Navajo witch has been threatening Maxie. I guess it's taboo. Besides, they weren't exactly talkative after being rousted from bed at three in the morning."

Tess groaned. "I'll never get up on time. I'm supposed to have lunch with Buck and Esther today. She's bringing her dad. He went to school with Uncle Giles. Do you want to come?" As soon as she issued the invitation, she wanted to call it back. He would think she was just using it as an excuse to be around him. And maybe she was. She craved his presence like a drug. Maybe she was concussed.

"Sure. We need to get to the bottom of this. You could have died tonight."

He sounded grim as though losing her would have hurt him. The thought cheered her. Maybe he cared a little. But if so, why was he reluctant to show it? She wasn't used to dealing with men. Maybe his affection was just physical attraction.

Chase put his hand on the key, then pulled it back and turned to look at her. "Tess, I—I don't know what you're thinking, but I do care about you."

As a friend, a sister? He sure wasn't saying, and didn't seem will-ing to explore it more deeply. You didn't kiss a friend or a sister the way he'd kissed her. Her hand crept to her mouth, and she touched her lips without thinking.

His gaze followed her fingers, then he looked away. His voice was husky when he finally spoke. "You want to go see a movie tomorrow?"

Her mood lightened. "Okay."

He stared at her. "You're sure?"

Joy was bubbling over inside. She felt she could fly back to the house. "I'm sure."

Only firelight illuminated the house when Tess let herself in. Her headache had subsided, and bed didn't sound interesting when she wanted to mull over the evening's events. The welcoming snap and hiss of the flames devouring the logs enticed her to pause in the living room. The fire mesmerized her—the beauty, the raw passion. It was several seconds before she saw Stevie's familiar form in the chair. Her hands on the armrest and her head back, she sat perfectly still.

Tess peered at her sister and saw her eyes were open. "Why aren't you in bed?" she asked, stepping closer to the fire.

"I couldn't sleep." Stevie stirred and leaned forward with her elbows on her knees and her chin cupped in her palm. "It's nearly three in the morning. Where have you been?"

Tess wasn't sure she liked Stevie's accusatory tone. "We went to see Maxie and got trapped by a flash flood."

"At least it's more creative than the old running-out-of-gas excuse."

"Sarcasm from you, Stevie? You're not even curious if I'm all right?" Tess knew she should be angry, but Stevie's reaction was so out of character that she just wanted to understand it. She went around to the front of her sister's chair and knelt in front of her. "What's wrong?"

Stevie's expression softened. "Tess! Your head!" She gently touched Tess's matted hair, then moved to get up. "Let me help you with that."

Tess took Stevie's arm to stop her. "I'm fine, really. Just sit." Stevie acquiesced.

"I'm sorry, Tess. I shouldn't be taking my own problems out on you. Just remember, though, you can't trust a man."

"The session with Pastor and Paul didn't go well?"

"It went fine if you consider how penitent he acted. But it's all a sham." She dabbed at her eyes.

Though it pained Tess to defend Paul, she knew she had to. "Maybe not. God could have convicted him of his sin."

"So he said. But he was penitent last year too. I think he's just sorry he got caught."

"What did Pastor say?" Tess was still trying to get a handle on her sister's mood.

"He came down hard on Paul. But not hard enough, as far as I'm concerned."

"Did Paul promise to end things with Joni?"

Stevie's laugh held no real humor. "He says he already did, and that's she's going to move to Oregon with her sister. Pastor confirmed it."

"So are you thinking about giving this another shot?"

Stevie shrugged. "He's not who I thought he was. Until a year ago, I would have sworn that he would be faithful. I've tried, I really have. But he always wanted more than I could give."

"What do you mean? Can you talk about it?"

Stevie shook her head. "I'm too ashamed."

"You can tell me anything."

"Our marriage isn't right," Stevie blurted. "I—I just can't, you know. Every time he touches me, I just freeze up. I even saw a shrink about it, but nothing helps. I knew there was something wrong with me when we were dating. Paul was always so sweet and patient. I thought it would get better when we married. We made a special effort when we decided to have Mindy, but every night was like torture to me. He knew it too. I think things got worse between us after that. It's got to be hard to have a wife who cringes every time you come near."

Poor Paul. No man would be able to deal with that well. At least from what little Tess knew about men. She thought of her own reaction to Chase. "Maybe it's not you, Stevie. Maybe it's just that Paul never was the right man to make you feel something."

"No, it's me." Stevie leaned back and rested her head on the back of the chair. "Maybe it will all be better when I'm well and have a new kidney."

The kidney. If only Tess didn't have to tell her. The timing couldn't be worse, but she had to know. "I—I heard from Dr. Wyrtzen, Stevie. I'm not a match for you. I can't give you a kidney."

Stevie raised her head and stared. Her blue eyes reflected back the flickering light from the fire. "No," she whispered. "I'd hoped and prayed . . . " She buried her face in her hands and began to cry, hoarse, racking sobs that tore at Tess's composure.

"Don't, Stevie," Tess begged. She grabbed her sister's wrists and pulled her hands out of the way so she could look in her face. "We'll find you a donor. He's putting you on the list."

"It's hopeless." Stevie wept harder. "You have to promise you'll take care of Mindy for me. I don't want that—that woman to be around her."

"You'll be here to take care of her yourself. Don't talk crazy." Tess wanted to cry with her sister. She'd never seen Stevie so defeated. She didn't know how to be the caregiver when she'd always been on the receiving end of the equation. "It will be okay, Stevie. God has us in his hands." Giving assurance to her sister bolstered her own faith. If anyone deserved mercy from God, it was her sister.

Stevie swiped the moisture from her face and gave a tremulous smile. "You're right, I know you're right. I can do all things through Christ who strengthens me. We'll see our way through this. And don't let my problems affect your relationship with Chase. He's a great guy. I'm really happy for you." Her smile grew wistful.

"There's nothing to be happy about. We're just not enemies anymore." Tess got up and sat on the sofa where her face would be hidden in shadow. Stevie could read her way too well.

"You're not fooling me. You're falling for Chase."

"How do you know when you're in love, Stevie?" Tess stared into the fire and touched her fingertips to her lips.

Stevie's bark of laughter held bitterness. "I'm sure I wouldn't know, Tess, since I'm not sure I've ever felt it. I don't think I'm capable of love. Not the wholehearted kind anyway. I'm not like you. You'd charge hell with a water pistol. I'm afraid to risk that much of myself. I don't like to be hurt."

"Who ever hurt you that made you so afraid? Paul was your only boyfriend."

Stevie stood and stretched. "I need to get to bed. Good night."

Tess watched her sister stumble away in the dark and wondered what was so painful that Stevie couldn't talk about it.

"Out with the ice princess?" Jimmy asked.

His brother's voice startled him, and Chase tripped over a pair of boots lying in the way. He barked his shin on the cot. "Ouch," he said, rubbing his hand over the smarting skin. "Does Doty know you're here?"

"No. I can't stand her constant hovering. It's driving me crazy." Jimmy flipped on the light, and the bright glow chased the darkness from the bunkhouse room. Jimmy was sitting on a hardback chair. He looked wild-eyed. And scared.

"What's happened?" Chase demanded.

"I saw that thing again, that skinwalker thing." Jimmy shuddered. "It was totally creepy, man."

Chase sat on the edge of his bunk and pulled off his boots. A toe stuck through his sock. "Where was this?"

"I was crossing the bridge over the creek behind Doty's place to come here when I heard this growl. I beat it out of there, man." He wrinkled his nose. "It smelled bad, too, like old skins. The thing chased me all the way home. Sometimes I could feel its breath on my neck. Creepy." He shivered again.

"What were you doing out at that hour? We all should have been in bed." Chase couldn't help the suspicion in his voice. If he found out Jimmy was stealing cars again, he didn't know what he was going to do.

Jimmy's head drooped, and he dropped the cocky hoodlum facade. "Thinking. I'm going to jail, aren't I, Chase?"

Chase could have soothed it all over, made some promise that would be impossible to keep, but he refused to do that. "I think so, Jimmy. I wish it were different."

Jimmy snapped off the light and plunged the room into darkness. He went to the door and opened it. "I've messed up, big time."

"You can take this correction from God and let it shape you into a better man, Jimmy. Or you can let it push you further down the wrong path. The choice is up to you. You know you deserve what's coming."

Jimmy's answer at first was a long pause, then, "I know."

There was a snuffle from his brother. Chase ached to get out of bed and comfort him, but something kept him on his own cot. God needed to be his brother's comforter this time. Chase had messed it up too many times. "I'm praying for you, Jimmy," he whispered.

Jimmy snuffled again. 'Thanks, Chase." The door shut behind him.

Tess scanned the Rim Cafe for Esther's brunette head. "Do you see her?" she asked Buck. Chase was supposed to show up too, and she found herself watching for his wide-brimmed cowboy hat.

"I don't think they've arrived. I'll ask." Buck approached the waitress, who shook her head. Buck rejoined her. "They're not here yet, but she said to sit wherever we like. They should be along any minute."

They found a corner table that was covered with a red and white checked tablecloth and decorated with a vase of wildflowers. Tess settled into the chair by the window so she could peek out the red café curtains. They'd gotten a lot done at the fire camp this morning, and she was ready for a break.

"Thanks for doing so much to make Esther comfortable and part of the group," Buck said. "It means a lot to her. And to me."

The poor guy was really smitten. Tess hoped the new Esther would really appreciate him. She toyed with her napkin. "How do you know you're in love, Buck?"

A grin spread over his face. "Flint and I have a bet on how long it will take you two boneheads to figure it out. I said any day now. Flint thinks it will be another two weeks."

Heat spread up Tess's neck. "You're a lot of help."

"You're a goner, Tess. You've loved the guy for years, you just didn't know it. Give the poor man a break and just say so."

"I thought guys liked to do the chasing."

"We do, but we need some feedback on how we're doing. At least give him a longing gaze once in a while."

She couldn't help the giggle that bubbled to the surface. "What if he doesn't feel the same way?"

He barked out a laugh. "Are you blind, woman? The poor sap doesn't have a chance. He only has eyes for you."

"I hope you're right," she said in a low voice. She looked back to the entrance of the café. She saw Esther and her father enter the café. "There they are." She smiled and waved, and the two came toward them. The door opened again, and Chase came in right behind them.

Esther was dressed in a knee-length skirted suit, a navy one. Her hair and makeup were flawless as usual. Tess's gaze shot to Chase. Was he attracted to that type of woman? He glanced at Esther, then his gaze fastened on Tess, and a smile tugged at his lips.

Buck stood and kissed Esther when she and her father reached the table. He introduced Mr. Sanchez to Tess and Chase, and they shook hands. Once they were seated, the waitress brought them water and menus.

"It's amazing to me that a woman is a smokejumper," Rob Sanchez said. "How do you carry all those heavy packs around?"

Tess got that question often. "I work out all the time. I'm stronger than I look. Once I get it on my back, carrying it is no problem." The man was just as supercilious as she'd expected. He'd been a state senator for six years, and she saw his name in the paper nearly every week. It seemed he was always pushing something she was opposed to.

"Esther said you wanted to talk to me about your uncle," he said, getting right to the point once they'd placed their orders. "I'm not sure what you're looking for."

"How well did you know my uncle Giles?" Tess asked.

"We were good friends in high school, played basketball together. When I went away to college, we lost touch for a while, but we reconnected in our twenties and often had lunch."

"Did he date much in school?"

He smiled. "The girls were always after him. Giles was an imposing figure on the court. His three-point record still stands. But Giles never seemed interested. I can't think of anyone he dated seriously." He hesitated. "Other than your mother. He was crazy about her, and it about killed him when she married your dad."

Tess gasped. "My mom and Uncle Giles?"

Rob shrugged. "I sometimes wondered if your mom regretted her decision. She and your dad split up for a while. I can't remember exactly, but I think it was a year or so before you were born."

Tess couldn't quite wrap her mind around this new revelation. She'd never heard her parents fight. *About a year before you were born.* The words echoed in her head. Siblings were usually a match for organ donation, weren't they? She and Stevie weren't compatible. Was it possible her dad wasn't her dad? *She wouldn't think that way.*

"How about as an adult?" Chase put in. "Did Giles date anyone later?"

Rob shook his head. "I fixed him up with women from time to time, but it never went beyond the first date. I don't think he ever got over Willa."

Tess took a drink of her water. "Um, did you ever notice that he liked adolescent girls?"

Rob raised his eyebrows. "Whoa, where did that come from?" He took a sip of his coffee, then set it down. "Look, I don't want to get involved in something this ugly. I've got a career to protect."

"Are you saying you know something?"

"That's not what I'm saying at all. I just don't want to be pulled into a witch hunt that might adversely affect my political career. Do you have any idea what innuendoes like that can do to a man? And you have no proof, do you?"

"I have accusations." She thought about telling him what Susan and Natalie had said, but decided not to pull in the women.

"Accusations," he scoffed. "Look, let's talk about something else. Like the upcoming wedding." He turned a full-wattage smile on Buck and his daughter. "I hear you've set the date."

Tess hadn't heard the news. "When is it?"

"June tenth." Esther's smile beamed out. She laced her fingers with Buck's and gave him an adoring smile.

As they began to talk about the plans for the ceremony, Tess glanced out the window. Was that Jimmy in the shadow of a doorway across the street? She squinted as the figure moved and sunlight shone on the man's face. Yes, that was Jimmy's scowling mug, looking down the street. What was he doing in town, and where was Aunt Doty?

"Excuse me a minute," she murmured. Buck nodded, but his

gaze didn't stray from Esther's face as she expounded on the color scheme and how many bridesmaids she planned to have. Tess rose and laid her napkin on her chair. She pushed past a group who had just entered the café, then stepped outside. Careful to stay in the shadows of the doorway, she stared across the street. Where did he go? The doorway was empty, and she didn't see his flashy car parked along the street.

"What's wrong?" Chase had followed her out.

"I saw Jimmy over there."

Chase frowned. "He was out last night too. Doty will be furious."

A car engine revved, then sped by them. They turned to see Jimmy's red Pontiac tear down the street. A black sedan followed it, also traveling over the speed limit. Jimmy made a sharp right turn, and the Solstice disappeared down the alley. The other car tried to do the same, but it was larger and less agile. It missed the turn and almost hit a street lamp. The driver started to back up but was blocked by two cars who'd stopped to avoid a wreck. Tess heard the driver curse at their honks as he drove away.

"You recognize the car?" she asked Chase.

"It looks like the same one that was parked outside the Zane Grey cabin the day I caught Jimmy." He clenched and unclenched his fists. "I'd better go find him."

"You want me to come with you?" *Please say yes.* She longed to be at his side to help in any way she could. What did that say about how she really felt about him? Examining that question would be something she'd have to do in the middle of the night.

Her cell phone rang, and she answered it even as Chase shook his head. Coop's voice was loud with agitation.

"Tess, get Buck. We've got a big fire blazing up the mountain. We're going in."

"Be right there." She clicked off her phone. "I might not be back for the movie," she told Chase. "I've got a fire to fight." When his face darkened, she hoped it meant he was disappointed. "I've got to get Buck."

Chase put his hand on her arm. "Be careful."

"I'm always careful."

He bent his head and his lips brushed hers. "When you get back . . . " He hesitated.

She didn't have time to wait for him to decide what he wanted to do when she returned. He'd have to figure it out.

CHAPTER 22

Chase drove along the dusty back road with his eyes on the horizon. He was sure Jimmy had gone this way. After last night's talk, he'd hoped Jimmy had seen the error of his ways and was actually listening. Maybe there was no hope for his brother, but he wasn't ready to give up on him quite yet.

He rounded a curve in the road and spied a plume of dust ahead. The wind began to blow the cloud away, and he saw Jimmy's car canted with its nose in the ditch, the back tire still spinning. Two men were standing by the open door. They saw Chase's truck coming and slammed the door, then got back in their car and drove away. Chase accelerated toward the accident. His fists were so tight on the wheel it was hard to steer. He strained to see any sign of movement in the car.

He saw Jimmy's head move, and he closed his eyes and blew out his breath. At least he was alive. The truck shimmied in the dirt when he jammed on the brakes behind the red car. The truck had barely stopped moving when his boots hit the dirt. "Jimmy?" He jerked on the door, but it was stuck. Bits of the driver's window lay shattered on the ground, and he was afraid to hammer on the window for fear of showering Jimmy with more glass.

Jimmy's head moved, and he moaned. Blood poured from a gash on his forehead, and his lips had begun to swell around a cut. Chase tugged on the door handle again, and it finally swung open with a shriek of protest. He pulled out his handkerchief and stanched the wound on his brother's head. He slapped his hip pocket. No cell phone again. Maybe Jimmy had one. He reached over and rummaged along the floor and seat for Jimmy's phone.

His hand touched a notebook, and he tossed it onto the seat when he found the cell phone under it. He called for an ambulance, then he crouched beside Jimmy and prayed. If only he'd come to. His gaze fell on the notebook, a bright orange spiral-bound. Curious, he picked it up and flipped it open. A list of names and dollar amounts in Jimmy's familiar scrawl ran down the page. None of the names was familiar, but all the addresses were fairly local. He looked closer. A type of car was jotted down next to each name. Was this a list of the stolen vehicles? Eric might be able to tell him.

Jimmy moaned again, and his eyes opened. "Chase?" He put his hand to his head. "What happened?"

"You had an accident. I saw a black car chasing you."

"Oh yeah." Jimmy lifted his head off the back of the seat. "Ow." He probed at the cut on his head. "They didn't want me to give the money back."

"What money?"

Jimmy looked toward the floor on the passenger side. "It's gone," he said, his eyes dull. "I took the briefcase of money from their office. I was going to give it back to the people we robbed."

Chase wasn't sure he should believe his brother. Jimmy's whoppers were legendary. His gaze went back to the notebook. "Did you give any money back?"

Jimmy held his head in his hands. "The first two on the list."

There was a checkmark beside the first two names. "Why?" Chase asked.

"I'd thought maybe if I gave it back, God would let me go."

Chase put a hand on his brother's arm. "You can't bargain with God, Jimmy. He already knows your heart, whether or not you're really sorry. He doesn't play games. Sometimes even when we're sorry, we have to pay the piper."

Jimmy shrugged and closed his eyes. The faint sound of a distant siren floated toward Chase as he watched his brother's bloodied face. Maybe there was hope for Jimmy yet.

"Okay, listen up," Coop shouted over the roar of the plane's engines. "The wind is driving this bad boy, and we've got to get in there and stop it before it gobbles up Dry Wash and the surrounding ranches. We've already got two hundred acres burned."

"What caused it?" Tess asked. She still felt breathless from the helter skelter pace of getting ready. Her face felt hot, and she fanned herself with her hand.

"Probably lightning from last night's storm. We might be able to tell when we get to the head." Coop grabbed hold of a handhold as the plane began to taxi down the runway.

"You look tired, Coop," Tess told him as the plane went airborne. His eyes drooped, and the lines in his face seemed more pronounced.

"I had a hard time sleeping last night. Some coyote was howling outside the window. You got in pretty late yourself. You and Chase." He winked.

Tess's cheeks burned, and she looked away. "Yeah, we were out investigating the fires."

"Looks like a pretty rough investigation." He pointed to her bruised and scabbed forehead.

"I'll be all right."

"Find anything?"

She shook her head. "No one wants to talk about skinwalkers."

"Skinwalkers? What do Navajo witches have to do with the fire?"

"Maybe nothing. But I think one has been following me."

Coop grinned. "Sure you're not having a nightmare?"

She could understand his skepticism. If she hadn't seen it with her own eyes, she'd be doubting it too. "It's real all right. Some guy dressed in animal skins."

"Maybe it's a caveman." Coop's smile was widening. "He wants to impress you with his muscles."

Tess laughed. "He's going about it the wrong way." Chase had the only muscles she liked to watch, but she'd never say that to Coop.

They reached the drop point, and the team prepared to make the jump. Coop would be strike-team leader, and Tess had landed the sought-after role of cutter. She'd get to use the chainsaw today and cut brush out of the fire's path.

With the door open, she could see the smoke column rising from the green forest. It towered above the plane, disappearing into the blue as a smudge of gray. Closer to the ground it was black, then blurred to a marbled yellow-gray. Tess snapped on her helmet and got in line to jump. She would be in the third stick out the door. Flint was her partner today. Buck and Coop were jumping just ahead of them.

It was their turn. She and Flint sat on the floor. The heat from the fire brushed against her face, and she smelled the wood smoke, an enticing odor that made her want to see the beauty of the fire. Her vision filled with the forest below, and she looked for the jump spot. There it was—a clearing in the aspen, oak, and pine trees. The spotter slapped her on the shoulder, and she rolled out of the plane. Then she was falling through the drift of smoke as it cast its shadow over the land. The fire looked voracious, crowning in the trees.

Thunder cracked and lightning arced out of the top of the ominous smoke cloud. Tess counted off the seconds aloud, "Jump-thousand, look-thousand, reach-thousand, wait-thousand, pull-thousand." She yanked on her rip cord and was jerked upward. She looked up to see the beautiful sight of the canopy opening over her head. Pulling on the toggles, she negotiated the currents in the air as if she were in a canoe and navigating the river. She was going to land right in the middle of the clearing. The other smokejumpers were beginning to unpack their gear.

She drifted toward the earth, then the wind shifted, and a head wind pushed against her. The gust eddied around her, and she saw she was heading toward the small pond on the right side of the clearing. Tugging on the steering toggles, she attempted to move to the west of the pond, but the capricious wind moved her back toward it. She reefed the right toggle, but no matter how much she monkeyed with the steering, the wind drove her right to the pond.

She hit the water four feet from the shore. The warm wetness soaked her to the waist. Grimacing, she dragged herself and her chute out of the pond and onto shore. Flint and Buck catcalled and cheered as she made landfall.

Flint came toward her to help. "How was your jump?" His grin was cheeky.

"What's it look like?" she grumbled. "I'm soaked."

"Any jump you walk away from is a good one," Buck chimed in.

Both men were laughing so hard they could barely stand. Tess gave Buck a shove. "I'll push you in and see how you like working in wet clothes."

"You'll dry fast in the heat," he chortled.

"I'll hang you out in the heat," she said, shoving him again. He kept grinning as he went to start unpacking the gear that the plane was dropping.

"Enough clowning around." Coop gave them a quelling look. "We're above the fire now, and we're going to control this bad boy today. Tess, you get to work cutting. Buck, I want you on the dozer. Flint and the rest of you, come with me."

Tess gathered up her chute and her gear and stowed it, then found the chainsaw the plane had dropped. She trudged to the cutting area and fired up the saw. The work wasn't as hard as some that the others were doing. Row after row of trees fell as she cut them. Other firefighters hauled the debris out of the way of the fire. When it got here, it would find no fuel to continue.

By late afternoon, her chest hurt from breathing smoke, her muscles ached, and her head throbbed from the smell of the gasoline and soot. The smoke seemed to have intensified as the fire moved toward them. The roar of the flames was louder now, echoing up the canyon. It was hard to see with all the smoke.

"The monster is gaining strength!" Coop shouted. "The head is coming this way. I want you all to move to the right flank. We may have to RTO, and our escape route to the lake is down the right flank."

RTO meant "reverse tool order," which meant to get the heck out of Dodge. Tess cut off her saw and picked up her tools, her movements efficient and economical from having performed the duties hundreds of times. She wasn't worried, not yet, though the smoke thickened and the heat built like a blast furnace.

Then a roar went up the mountain, and flames shot thirty feet in the air. The fire came at a sprinter's pace, the flames crowning in the treetops, leaping from tree to tree in seconds. The smoke-jumpers and the hotshots turned and ran up the hill away from the fire. Tess stumbled and went to one knee. Buck grabbed her and hauled her to her feet.

"Drop the saw." He took it from her hand and tossed it down, then grabbed her hand and pulled her up the hill.

The heat grew unbearable almost instantly, and Tess could hear the pulsing roar of a fire gone berserk. She kept stumbling over tools the firefighters had dropped in their haste to escape. Then the flames began to whip overhead. They weren't going to make it.

Once Jimmy was checked out, bandaged, and sent home with Doty to rest, Chase roamed the ranch restlessly for a few minutes, then decided to drive to town. His truck seemed to have a mind of its own as it turned down the street the Diamond house had occupied. He parked and looked at the burned-out house. The fire had carved a *V* out of the center of the roof. Charred timbers were exposed to the harsh sunlight. The desolation depressed him. He got out and walked up the steps. Why was he even here? Hoping to find a connection to the other fires, maybe. The sheriff and an arson investigator would have gone over the place timber by timber.

The scent of smoke was still strong. Ash and soot rose from his boots as he walked through charred remains. It was probably dangerous to be walking here. How did Tess bear to breathe this stuff all summer long? He'd never understand her compulsion to fight fire. The center of the house around the chimney had collapsed and fallen all the way down. One wall canted. It looked like the remains of an attic closet with sloped walls. An old chest lay on its side, the contents spilled out with the wind riffling the old clothing inside.

Hundreds of children had passed through these walls. One of them had likely fired this house, killing the old man. Jimmy? Chase didn't want to believe it, and maybe that was really why he'd come, hoping to find evidence one way or the other. Jimmy had given him a lot of grief, but the kid had endured a hard life up to now.

Chase scuffed through the debris with the pointed toe of his boot. Some of these clothes were from the seventies and eighties. He kicked aside platform shoes, pink jelly shoes, and a partially-melted cassette of Michael Jackson's *Thriller*. His gaze landed on a neon-green T-shirt badly burned and stained with soot. Protruding from under it was a skateboard that was about the same color. It was hand-painted, and the design looked familiar. He'd seen it somewhere. It looked vaguely Native American, but had some stylistic differences in the elongated lightning bolt. Where had he seen it before?

He was tempted to take the skateboard with him, but Eric might take issue with removal of evidence. Chase picked it up and turned it over. The word on the back was inscribed in neon-blue lettering. *Retribution.* It seemed an odd word. Another word was partially obscured by soot, but his fingernail rubbed away the black mark. *CJ*. The *C* had a characteristic scroll on both ends that was hard to miss.

Cooper Johnston.

His mind tried to reject the evidence in his hands. Did Coop pass through these walls? And even if he did, that didn't mean he was the arsonist. Chase dropped the skateboard back into the pile of rubble. There was one way to find out. He was going to have to go through Coop's belongings.

As he drove through town, he saw a man wave him down. Duffy Newcastle got out of his big dually truck and stepped to the window when Chase stopped. "Hey, Chase. Have you seen an extra stallion at your place?" He was about six-four and had to weigh three hundred and fifty pounds.

"Wildfire has run off?"

Duffy nodded. "He broke down the fence last night. My crew has looked for him all day. We thought he might have headed your way."

"I've been gone a while. I'll take a look when I get home. How's he settling in?"

"He's not. My men can't handle him. I think he misses Tess."

"They're close," Chase admitted.

"I have to admit I feel bad. When you look him in the eye, he almost seems to be suffering."

It must be bad if Duffy had noticed it already. Wildfire was probably trying to get to Tess. Chase should never have told the man about the stallion. "I'll be on the lookout."

"Appreciate it." Duffy tipped his hat and went back to his big truck.

Chase watched for the horse all along the drive home, but he saw nothing but cattle and rolling hills. Whip was in the corral, and Chase got out of the truck and waved him over. "You seen Wildfire?"

"Nope. He broke out?"

"Yeah, I ran into Newcastle in town. Wildfire was missing this morning."

"We better tell Tess."

"Yeah, I will." Chase looked toward the bunkhouse then back at Whip. "Do you know if Coop ever stayed at the Diamond house?"

Whip raised his bushy gray brows. "Why you asking such a tomfool question? You know he did."

"No, no I didn't. He doesn't talk about his past much. What do you know about him?"

"Why you asking?" Whip lit a cigarette and puffed on it, his brow wrinkled. "'A talebearer reveals secrets, but he who is of a faithful spirit conceals a matter.'"

"I was out at the house today. I saw a skateboard that had the letters *CJ* on it. They were in Coop's handwriting."

Whip puffed on his cigarette. "Coop's mom used to work here when she was a teenager. She got pregnant, and old lady Masterson, Garrett and Giles's mom, kicked her out. She moved to an old shack at the edge of our property. It burned down a few years ago."

Chase nodded. He remembered the shack.

"She was barely able to feed Coop. One winter, a real bitter one, Coop came walking to the ranch and said his mom wouldn't wake up. She'd died in the night. Could've been starvation or maybe the cold. She always made sure Coop got whatever she had. Garrett wanted to take in Coop, but old Mrs. Masterson would have none of it. The state moved in and put him in foster care. He was about nine or ten, as I recollect. He landed at the Diamond house, but he lit out the day he turned eighteen. The old man was mighty hard on Coop. Locked him in the attic closet more than once. Coop hated him."

"Enough to kill him?"

Whip didn't answer for a minute. "What're you saying?"

"I want to look through Coop's things. Will you help me?"

Whip's flinty gaze stared him down, then he finally nodded. "Okay. I think you're barking up the wrong tree though."

"I'd like to look at his house up in Flagstaff too."

"I think he keeps a key in his duffel."

They went to the bunkhouse and pulled Coop's duffel bag out from under the bunk. Chase unzipped it. A man's things ought to be private, but he had to know. Coop's jeans and T-shirts were neatly folded. The side pockets were stuffed with toiletries and a couple of books. He pulled out a dog-eared copy of *Skinwalkers* by Tony Hillerman. Flipping open the cover, he saw where Coop had written on the title page.

ALL THE OLD KNIVES THAT HAVE RUSTED IN MY BACK, I NOW DRIVE IN YOURS.

Phaedrus (Thrace of Macedonia)

Coop was with Tess. Chase knew he needed to warn her. There was enough here to assume the worst.

CHAPTER 23

*T*he roar of the flames filled Tess's head until she couldn't think, couldn't focus. She thought she heard a voice on her radio, but she couldn't tell, and there was no time to pause to answer it anyway. The fire gobbled up everything as it chased her up the hill. She didn't know if she could outrun it. The intense heat seared her skin and dried her eyes. Buck's hand had been tight to hers, but she didn't feel it anymore.

"Buck!" Peering through the thick smoke, she tried to see her friend. Embers rained around her in a fire show that would have been dazzling if she weren't caught in it. Her foot hit something yielding, and she knelt and felt the object. It was Buck. "Get up." She grabbed his arm, but he was unresponsive. He must have hit his head when he fell. The fire had nearly reached them. Her self-preservation instinct urged her to flee, but she wouldn't leave Buck to die out here alone, not even if she had to die with him. The area where he'd fallen was smoldering already. The fire had burned away the vegetation along the hillside, and she spied a cave. Could she get him into it? She had to try. Grabbing his shoulders, she began to tug him toward the opening. The fire was roaring toward her, and she somehow found the strength to drag him into the cave.

She eased his shoulders onto the ground, then pulled her fire tent from a belt pouch at her waist. She dropped to the dirt and pulled the aluminized Mylar fabric around her and Buck, making sure to tuck the anchoring strips under them both so the firestorm wouldn't whip it away. A strange sense of calm drained away her panic. This was the moment she'd always thought would come— the day she would pay for saving her horse instead of her parents. The day God exacted justice. At least she would be with him and with her parents.

The heat grew intense. Buck's inert body lay prone, his face turned toward the tent. She pressed her face into the soot on the ground and tried to draw in a cool breath, but the stink of charred soil and smoke mingled with the building heat and made it feel like she was breathing liquid smoke. The dragon roared outside the cave, and she knew the fire was on top of them. Though there was nothing flammable inside the cave, the heat was intense. Her eyes shut, she prayed for it to be over fast. The choking heat and smoke filled her lungs until all she could feel was the fight to draw in enough oxygen.

Then the ravenous fire roared away. The ear-popping sound began to diminish, and Tess could think again. She pressed her fingers to Buck's neck. His pulse beat strongly. They were alive? It didn't seem possible. She drew in a breath, then another and another. Each lungful of air held a little more oxygen, a little less heat.

Why had God spared her when she deserved his judgment? Her gratitude flowed toward the heavens. So this was what mercy felt like. Had she been serving God out of fear when what he wanted from her was this love she felt welling up, this thankful awe for his mercy? Waiting for the air outside the tent to cool, she prayed for the rest of the team, that God would be as merciful to them as he had been to her and Buck.

When she finally decided it was safe, she inched her hand out from under the shelter to test the air temperature. It was still hot, but not too hot to get up and get moving. She sat up and peeled back the tent. More oxygen rushed to her starving lungs. Throwing off the shelter, she stood. "Buck, we're alive." She rushed to the cave's mouth and peeked outside at the devastation around them. The fire had gobbled up anything flammable for as far as she could see in the still-smoking ruins.

Buck moaned, and she bent to touch him. "Buck?" She touched his shoulder, then rolled him onto his back. Her gaze landed on his right cheek, which had been up against the tent. Oh no. The tent must have come up a bit on that side. His cheek was badly burned, but at least he was alive. The pulse in his neck still beat strong against her fingertips, but he wasn't stirring. She would have to radio in for help. She raised Coop on the radio and told him what had happened and her location. He promised to get there right away.

Buck groaned, and she got a bottle of water out for him. His eyes fluttered, and he opened them. "Here, have some water." He managed to swallow a few drops, then licked his cracked and bleeding lips. "We're still alive."

He didn't seem to notice his burned face, which was bad news. The nerve endings must be dead, so he had some third degree burns in there. "We made it. I put the fire tent over us."

"And I wasn't awake to see it in action." He struggled to sit up, but she pressed him back against the ground.

"Lie still until we get some help." She wanted to wash his burned cheek but knew she shouldn't touch it yet. Buck closed his eyes and didn't answer. "Buck?" He didn't respond. She looked around. There were sealed containers around the perimeter of the cave, and her flashlight illuminated drawings on the walls. Animal skins were heaped in the back corner. Some of the pictures were new—a man wearing wolf skins. They made her flesh crawl.

She walked to the back corner and examined the animal skins. They seemed to have survived the heat, though soot came away on her glove when she touched them. Kneeling by the boxes, she pulled the top one toward her and lifted the lid, which had melted and warped from the heat. It resisted her efforts, but she managed to tear it off.

A charred boot? Something about the boot looked familiar. Her father once had a pair just like them. She tried to remember what the investigation papers said. Her father wore only one boot when he was found. She'd always assumed the other one came off in the barn and was incinerated or buried in the rubble. Carefully setting the boot aside, she continued to look through the box. There was a bridle with a *W* engraved in the silver. From the Wilson's barn? She picked up a paper and glanced over it. It was the confirmation of a bank transfer from the Masterson bank account through several other accounts.

Her stomach roiled. Could this be the arsonist's trophies? There was also a Baggie here with bits of vegetation inside. Hay. From their hay field? She poked further into the box. A child's charred doll, burned wood, a locket bent and twisted from heat. There was a photo album in the bottom. Black and heavy, it looked old. The first picture was an eight by ten of the Mastersons. It had been taken just before the fire that killed her parents. Black marker obscured most of her parents' faces with an X.

She shuddered, not wanting to see any more, but she had to know who hated them so much. And why. Flipping the pages, she looked at page after page of Masterson pictures sprinkled with the photos of other area ranchers who had been affected by the arsonist. There were photos of blackened fields, burned barns and houses, and an occasional obituary. She closed the album and looked at the skins. Jeans, boots, and a belt lay under them. A rodeo buckle on the belt caught her eye. Picking it up, she turned it over and saw the engraving on the back. Cooper Johnston.

Not Coop. She wouldn't believe it. Was the arsonist after Coop next? But even as her heart rejected the evidence, her mind clicked through the things she knew. Coop had been in foster care, and he'd had ties to the family since he was a child. It was a known fact that sometimes arsonists gravitated to firefighting.

"Put that down."

She looked up to see Coop staring at her. He yanked off his helmet, revealing a soot-streaked face that was pale under the black smudges. Letting the belt fall from her fingers back into the heap of clothing and furs, she studied his face. "Why, Coop?" He'd been her friend, her mentor. It didn't seem possible that he would have held such animosity toward the family all these years.

Coop approached her with a hard smile that didn't reach his eyes. "Don't look so shocked, Tess. We're soul mates, both craving the relief from our pain that fire brings. I know you can feel it. Neither of us can resist the fascination of fire. Can you tell me you've never thought about setting a fire yourself?"

"I fight fires, I don't start them."

"You're lying. All of us are the same. Like moths to a porch light, we crave the fire and are driven to seek it."

She shook her head at his odd talk but didn't argue with him. "Why us, Coop? We're your friends."

"Giles ruined my mother's life. And mine. He's my real father, you know." Sincerity shone out of his eyes. "He seduced my mother when she was fifteen. When she told him about the pregnancy, he told her no one would believe her. He was from a good family, and she was poor white trash. She struggled to support me, but in the end she was too weak. She died one winter after making sure I had the last bit of bread and milk in the house. When she died, *he* let me rot in the state's foster-care system." His eyes burned with resentment.

"But Uncle Giles is dead. Why blame the rest of us?" He'd killed her parents, her uncle. How many others? "Were you angry you were left out of the will?"

"I would have given you a chance if your father had given me my fair share of the ranch. You're my sister, after all. He knew who I was, and said he'd change the will. When he died, and I found out I was left out, I knew I had to exact my own justice. On the Mastersons and the whole area. They'd all scorned my mother and left me to rot in that house. Now I'll have my justice."

She shuddered. *Justice*—she was beginning to hate the word. "Sister? What do you mean?" Her legs trembled.

"You never suspected you didn't belong to Garrett Masterson? You look like him, you know. Your eyes especially. Big greenish-gold eyes like a cougar."

"How do you know this?" she whispered.

"I heard your mother talking to Maxie one night."

Tess gulped back her pain. There would be time to deal with

who she was later. Right now she had to get away from him. And save Buck. "I can see you've been wronged, Coop. But another wrong doesn't make a right. I've done nothing to you but love you as a friend and mentor." The hard rock she sat on was making her leg go numb. She stood and faced Coop.

The harshness in his face softened for a moment. "I've always liked you, Tess. It was hard to make the decision that you had to die too. You and Stevie. But justice must be served. I knew it was a sign when the fire killed your parents."

"Wait, are you saying you didn't plan for them to die?" None of this made sense. How could the man she'd looked up to have been so full of hate all these years? "Was the fire an accident?"

Coop looked down at Buck without answering. "He's going to be badly scarred."

Did that mean Coop intended to let him live? "Can we do anything for him?"

"He needs to have the wound cleaned."

Tess's radio crackled to life. "Tess, it's Chase. I've been trying to get in touch with you. Stay away from Coop. He's the arsonist." The urgency in his voice came through in spite of the way the radio cut in and out.

She flicked on the radio and ran toward the cave entrance. "He's here, Chase!"

Coop pounced after her and knocked the radio to the ground, where it shattered against a rock. "How could he have figured it out?" He pulled a gun out of his belt. "No more tricks, Tess. I'd rather not shoot you. Fire is much cleaner."

Tess nodded. "No more tricks." At least Chase knew she was in danger. But he wouldn't know where she was.

Coop grabbed her arm and hustled her toward the door. "We'll go together, Tess. Like I've always dreamed we would. Like a brother and sister should."

While this isn't the way I'd planned it, all things work together for good. I've heard that somewhere. If Chase knows, he has probably already told the sheriff. That means plans have to change. Tess and I will dance with the fire together, a waltz of such beauty and power that the thought of it brings tears to my eyes. How fitting, how right.

She tries to pull back, but I push her on and dream of this night. Another beautiful barn fire. The house too. Everything the Mastersons own and love will go up in flames with us. She tries to jerk away again, but waving my gun convinces her to cooperate. "I'll shoot Buck if you don't come along quietly." If there is one thing you can count on with Tess, it's her loyalty.

She gets to her feet and nods. A wave of love pours through me, fierce and pure as cleansing fire. Of all my firefighter friends, I've loved her the most. My sister, the feminine version of me. There is no one else I'd rather die beside. We'll cross the golden strand of fire together, arm in arm. From the knowing look in her eyes, she understands and approves my plan. We are more than siblings, we are soul mates.

Once her hands are tied and lashed to the big chest, I push deeper into the cave. A wise man prepares for every eventuality, and our quick getaway is ready. Back through the cave is an entrance to another room where I've stashed an ATV. It rolls easily over the cave floor to the mouth. Buck jerks at the sound of the engine, but still doesn't awaken.

Once Tess is on the back with me, her hands tied together around my waist, I put it in gear and we ride along the charred and bleak landscape toward the ranch.

"What about Buck?" Tess shouts above the sound of the motor.

"Someone will be along to find him." It will take at least an hour to get down out of the hills, a pleasant jaunt together, just the two of us. It will be nightfall by the time we get to the ranch. They'll be looking for us on foot. Even if Whip and some of the rest are at the ranch, once we're in the barn, no one can stop me.

My heart races in time with the engine as I contemplate the coming conflagration. It will be the biggest, grandest one yet. No one will ever forget it—or me. My fame will be eternal.

Chase stood with the firefighters on the edge of the blackened ruin of forest. Already his lungs and nose felt coated with soot from the last traces of smoke that lingered in the air. Several men were loading Buck onto the chopper.

"We know Tess was with Buck," Flint said. "Some of her equipment is still in the cave. The last I heard, Coop was heading to help Tess," Flint said. His hand swept the landscape. "They could be anywhere."

The sun's rays slanted low in the sky. It would be dark soon. It had been several hours now since he'd understood the danger and convinced Eric to commandeer a chopper and get out here. Too long. Who knew how cold the trail was? Tess had to be all right. Coop had always seemed to have a special kinship with Tess. Surely he wouldn't hurt her. But why had he taken her with him?

He tried to think through what Coop would do next. "You know

Coop well, Flint. Why do you think he took her—just as a hostage? And where would he go?"

"From the looks of what he has stashed in the cave, it was his sanctuary. He's been driven from here, and I'd say he's desperate." Flint knelt and poked through the rubble at the cave mouth.

Chase watched him study the ground. He was supposed to be good at arson investigation. "He hates the Mastersons. What could he do to get back at them now that we know his plan?"

"I don't know. Coop's not the man I thought he was," Flint said.

Eric was listening. "I'll get some men out to watch the ranch. Close down the roads leading in and out of there. I don't think there's any worry though. They're on foot, and it will take them hours to get to civilization to get a car."

"They've already got a head start of several hours."

"They're still tromping these woods somewhere. Take it easy, Chase. I've called out choppers with lights to search by air. Search dogs will be here shortly as well. We'll find them."

"I hope you're right. I've got a bad feeling about this, Eric." Chase turned toward the waiting chopper. "Could you get me to the ranch? I think he'll head there with her."

"We can go as soon as the dogs get here and I give the search teams some instructions. I don't think there's any way they'll make it as far as the ranch." Eric's cell phone rang, and he answered it. After listening a few moments, he clicked it off. "Allie Stinson started talking as soon as they took her off the respirator. She saw Coop hanging up Tess's chute. A little late, but now we know he's targeted her all along."

"Tess will be glad to hear she's alert." Chase knew finding them in the dark would be difficult, if not impossible. He stood watching the sun sinking lower and the charred forest growing more bleak. If only he could get into Coop's head. The man had some kind of plan. Tess's abduction didn't feel like a random act of desperation. Coop knew Chase had discovered his identity and that the law would be after him. He could head for Mexico to escape, but why take Tess? She would only slow Coop down if he was trying to get away.

Maybe he wasn't trying to get away.

Chase examined the idea from different angles. He didn't like the implications. "Do you think there's a chance he isn't trying to escape? Maybe he wants to go out in a big way—and take the Mastersons with him."

Flint paled behind the soot on his face. "Coop's whole life is fire. He's studied it and knows it better than anyone. I hope you're wrong."

"Get me to the ranch!" Chase grabbed Eric's arm.

"You're jumping to conclusions. I need to stay here and get the dog teams searching. Go to the ranch if you want, but I think you're wasting your time. They're out here somewhere." Eric waved his hand toward the forest.

Chase stalked to the chopper and got in. When had it happened? He was completely and totally in love with Tess Masterson. She had to be all right. He had to trust that God would protect her.

CHAPTER 24

$\mathcal{T}$ess felt as bruised as the apples on the ground in the orchard. Bouncing over potholes and fallen tree limbs had jarred every bone. She peered around Coop's shoulder and saw the ranch house approaching. Light spilled from the windows. With so many lights blazing, Stevie had to be home. Tess had hoped her sister might have gone to town, though with the way she'd been so sick lately, she'd known it was a vain hope.

At least Mindy wasn't there. Paul had taken her to his parents' home with him for the weekend. She prayed Whip was there. Maybe he could help her. Most of the ranch hands had Saturday nights off, but Whip generally stuck around. If there was no one home but Stevie, they were in a lot of trouble.

The ATV bounced over a final rut near the back of the barn. Coop turned off the engine. He untied her wrists but held on. "Get off."

Tess tried to swing her leg over the machine. She tried again and finally managed to get off, though she nearly fell. Coop's grip saved her from a tumble in the mud. What did he have in mind? His expression was hard to read in the dark. Why come here? It seemed insane. She'd expected him to try to escape, to use her as a hostage.

"What are you going to do?" she asked.

"You know." He took her arm and propelled her around the barn.

She knew? Tess didn't like the sound of that. She could see the shine of his teeth as he smiled, and the almost euphoric way he bounced on the balls of his feet as he moved her toward the house. She gulped back her fear and stepped around the cow patties in the back pasture.

The wind chimes tinkled as they moved to the barn. Coop's grip loosened as he shoved open the door to the barn. Tess took the opportunity to wrench her arm from his fingers and run toward the house. "Whip!" she screamed. She prayed Stevie would look outside as well and call the sheriff.

Coop tackled her from behind, and her body slammed into the ground, driving the air from her lungs. Sand stung her cheek. She spit grit out of her mouth and tasted blood on her lip from the impact. Coop still didn't speak. He dragged her to her feet and shoved her back toward the barn door, which stood open like the mouth of a grave. He meant to kill her. She could feel the truth of it in the hardness of his hands and the implacable way he pushed her.

Whip didn't answer, and she feared he was gone. She couldn't see his truck beside the barn. There was no response from inside the house either. Stevie could be in bed, exhausted by dialysis and discouragement.

"Let me go, Coop. You don't want to hurt me."

"It won't hurt for long, Tess. Haven't you ever wanted to walk into the flames, to be one with the fire? I know you have. I've seen the longing in your eyes. I'm just going to grant your wish. We'll do it together." The glow from the caged light overhead cast his face in a sickly yellow glow. His eyes glittered, and his smile was exalted.

She heard a familiar whinny and looked to the doorway. Wildfire blew air out from his nostrils. What was he doing here? Coop hadn't shut the door, and the stallion pranced toward her. If only she could vault to his back and get away. He moved toward his old stall as if he wanted to be fed.

Coop's grip on her arm tightened as though he'd felt her involuntary move toward the horse. "Don't try anything else, Tess. I'd like our final moments to be ones of harmony."

"Please, let Wildfire out. I don't want anything to happen to him."

Coop smiled. "Typical Tess. Always thinking of her horse." He took out his gun. Waving it casually, he motioned for her to sit on a straw bale. "This is our time, Tess. I know you've been waiting for this for years too."

She sank onto the straw, glancing around furtively for some kind of weapon.

A shadow passed between the outside light and the open barn door. Stevie stood in the doorway. Pale and swaying, she grabbed the doorway for support. "What's going on?" Her gaze went to the gun in Coop's hand. "Coop?"

Tess sprang to her feet. "Stevie, run!"

Her sister's eyes widened, and her gaze went to the gun in Coop's hand.

Coop pointed the gun at Tess. "Come join us, Stevie. It seems appropriate, I think." Stevie took a few steps inside the barn. "Shut the door," he said.

Stevie tried to slide the door, but she wasn't strong enough. Panting, she leaned against the wall.

"Never mind. Sit by your sister." He waited while Stevie stumbled to the bale and sank beside Tess.

Tess could feel her sister trembling. "We'll get out of this," she murmured.

"Wrong, Tess. We're going to have a beautiful fire tonight. It will light up the sky for miles around." Coop nodded toward the can of gasoline on the ground. "Pick that up and splash it around."

"No." Tess laced her fingers together and gave him a defiant stare.

"Oh, I think you will." His smile was almost gentle, but his eyes were hard. He raised the gun barrel and pointed it at Stevie's head. "I can shoot her first if you'd rather."

Tess glanced at her sister. Stevie's eyes were saying *no*. Tess crossed her arms over her chest. "A gunshot would be better than dying in the fire. You're going to kill us anyway, so what difference does it make?"

Coop's mouth grew tight. Muttering under his breath, he grabbed up the gasoline can and began to splash it around. The heavy fumes filled the air. Wildfire snorted and kicked at the wall.

"Put him away," Coop said. "Otherwise, I'll splash it on him and he can be our fuel."

Tess rose and grabbed the horse's dangling halter. She led him toward the open door. Her glove strap caught in the halter and pulled from her clothes.

"Put him in the stall!"

But Tess ignored Coop. Let him shoot her in the back. She dropped the reins and slapped Wildfire on the rump. He shot through the door and out into the night. "Find Chase!" she shouted.

Coop laughed. "Your horse doesn't know any name but yours. And Chase is still tromping the woods looking for us. Don't pin your hopes on him." He stepped to her side and yanked her back away from the door, then slammed it.

Tess had been so close to freedom. The night air leaking around the door smelled of hope. If Stevie weren't there she might have dared to jerk open the door and run for her life. But she couldn't leave her sister. Turning slowly, she went back.

"You should have gone with Wildfire," Stevie whispered.

"I wouldn't leave you." Tess reached over and held Stevie's right hand in both of hers. They were both cold and shaking.

"I knew it would come to this someday." Stevie seemed almost eerily calm.

"What do you mean?"

Coop gave a burst of laughter and put down the gas can. The bang it made sounded empty. "Yes, tell your sister how you killed your uncle and your parents, Stevie."

Tess couldn't breathe, couldn't move. It couldn't be true. A terrible resignation settled over her sister's face. "Stevie?" Tess whispered. "What's he talking about?"

"Tell her how you killed your uncle with a pitchfork and set fire to the barn." Coop's voice was mocking. "You've let me take responsibility for it all these years. But I saw you, Stevie." Coop took out his lighter and began to flip the top open and closed. "I helped you that night. He wasn't dead, you know. So I locked the door."

All the saliva in Tess's mouth dried up. The tiniest spark and the place would go up like a Roman candle. Stevie was rocking back and forth. Grief radiated from her like heat from hot coals.

"I'm sorry, Tess, so sorry," she moaned.

"He molested you, didn't he?" Tess whispered. "Uncle Giles. That's why you killed him."

Stevie nodded. "I was afraid he was going to start on you next, Tess. You told me he was in your room, remember? I didn't know any other way to protect you. He raped me, and I couldn't let him ruin your life like he'd ruined mine. I asked him to meet me in the barn when I thought Dad would be gone. Mom hardly ever came to the barn. I thought it was safe. He came in smiling so smugly, like I *wanted* to see him, wanted him to . . . to touch me. He shut the padlock behind him."

"Why didn't you tell Dad? He would have made Giles leave again."

"Giles said Mom wouldn't believe me, and I remembered that they hadn't believed Maxie. I was so scared." Shudders passed through her, wave after wave of them. "There was a pitchfork, and I—I just grabbed it. I didn't think. When he was dead, I had to cover it up. I couldn't talk about it or tell anyone what had happened. I set the hay on fire, and it just spread." Tears were streaming down Stevie's face. "I didn't know Mom would come in. Dad must have gotten back from town early and smelled the smoke, heard Mom scream."

Tess closed her eyes.

"I should have been strong enough to tell you. I'll answer for that too—for letting you suffer so much guilt when I'm the one to blame."

Tess put her arm around Stevie. "You only wanted to protect me. Mom and Dad—it was an accident." Her throat was thick. So many secrets, and they'd all led to tragedy.

"Sarah, losing Sarah was my punishment from God. He knew she was an abomination, a result of incest."

"No, no, Stevie. I'm sure God loved Sarah more than any of us ever could have. She was special to him." Tess inhaled. "Giles was Sarah's father? Is that why you married Paul?"

"I loved Paul. As much as I was able. He knew about Giles and promised to take care of me, to never let me be hurt like that again. That's why his affair hurt so much," Stevie whispered. She buried her head in Tess's shoulder.

Coop sneered at their embrace. He unzipped his satchel and pulled a wolf skin around him. With the fur embracing him, he seemed bigger, taller.

Maybe it was her imagination, but he seemed to be growing right in front of her eyes. He began to mutter some incantation, and his eyes glittered with a light that made her shudder.

Coop's whispered spells fell silent. He raised his hands. "The time has come. We really can't wait any longer." He held out the lighter and flicked it.

CHAPTER 25

The chopper landed in town, and Chase ran to his truck. Eric had decided not to come with him. The sheriff was sure the dogs would find Tess and Coop in the woods, but Chase didn't think so. Coop was bound to go back to the ranch. The Mastersons seemed to be the target for his wrath, and Chase couldn't imagine that Coop would just walk away.

The display on his dash said eight o'clock. His headlights swept across the dark road. There was no other vehicle in sight, and no other ranches were out this way, so the landscape was vacant as far as he could see. He started down into a wash that ran across the road but stopped at the roar of black current. The water was four feet high and flowing rapidly. No way could his truck get across that.

"No!" He pounded the wheel. Glancing in the rearview mirror, he saw another vehicle coming up fast behind him. Only when it drew nearer did he recognize Whip's beat-up Dodge. Chase got out and jogged back to the other truck.

"Where you goin' to in such an all-fired hurry?" Whip huffed, hitching up his jeans as he joined Chase between the two vehicles.

"Coop's taken Tess hostage. I have a feeling he's heading to the ranch for a final fire."

"You're funnin' me, Chase. Even when I saw the stuff in his gear, I thought we was barkin' up the wrong tree."

"No joke, Whip."

Whip was frowning. His gaze sharpened, and he looked over Chase's left shoulder. "Is that Wildfire?"

Chase turned to stare into the darkness. A horse stood atop a nearby mesa. The moon illuminated the animal, and there was no mistaking the stallion's superb lines and flowing mane. "Sure is."

The horse turned his head and began to pick his way down the mesa toward them. "Hey, boy." Chase held out his hand and approached Wildfire as he neared.

Something was caught in the stallion's bridle. Chase ran a soothing hand over Wildfire's neck and withers as he peered at it. "Looks like a strap of some kind."

He'd seen something like it before—attached to Tess's firefighting gloves. Which could only mean the horse had seen Tess when she was dressed in her gear. "They're at the ranch!" The road was impassable—how could he get there?

Wildfire snorted and pranced in the road. No one but Tess had ever managed to stay on him. Chase ran his hand over the stallion's neck. "Easy, boy." No saddle. Could he do it? Would the horse let him? "Tess needs us, Wildfire," he whispered. He ran his hand over the horse's withers the way he'd often seen Tess do. Wildfire shuddered but calmed down. Chase wrapped his hand around the stallion's mane and vaulted onto Wildfire's back. Rather than take a bronc-busting stance with the horse, he leaned forward and ran his other hand down Wildfire's neck.

"Steady, boy. We need to help Tess." The horse must have felt Chase's urgency. He pranced in the dirt and whinnied, but he didn't buck. He snorted and stilled. "Good boy," Chase whispered. He sat upright and grabbed handfuls of mane. "Let's go home, Wildfire. Go to Tess." The horse's neigh rang out on the wind, then they galloped off into the night to find their way around the flood.

The lighter in Coop's hand flared to life. He tossed it onto the ground. Tess watched the flicker of light drop through the air. She should move, but she froze and watched the lighter tumble end over end, illuminating the dust motes. Before it hit the ground, a soft *whump* rocked her eardrums. The flame ignited the gas fumes. The flare of fire raced along the floor in both directions, running toward the straw bale where Tess sat with Stevie.

The fire gobbled up debris, gasoline, and floor. Coop's smile grew broader and more exalted as it ran toward him. He raised his hands in the air like a prophet in a furry mantle, then looked heavenward. "Dance with me!" he called to them. "Come, Tess." He began a mad shuffle around the floor, capering toward them with his arms open wide.

The wolf head came down over his face, obscuring most of his features. Tess could almost believe he was changing in front of her eyes. Even his walk was different, jerky and wooden.

"We have to get out!" Tess screamed. Flames and smoke obscured the door as the flames circled them. She tugged on her sister's arm and dragged her toward the door. Stevie moved like a zombie. Tess gripped the hard wood under her fingers. She shoved the sliding door open.

"Nooo!" Coop ran at them with outstretched arms. Tess looked into the clear night air and saw Chase thundering toward her on top of Wildfire. Time slowed as Tess tried to move out of the barn, tried to drag Stevie with her. She felt she was mired in quicksand. Chase vaulted off the horse toward her, but he was too far to help yet. Tess stood half in and half out of the barn. They had only seconds as the roof above her head blazed and embers rained down.

"All three, all three!" Coop howled. The flames had overtaken him, but he didn't seem to feel them. He tottered toward them with his arms out.

"No!" Stevie shoved Tess the rest of the way out of the barn, then turned to run toward Coop.

Tess tried to snatch her sister back, but her fingers touched only empty air. Stevie launched herself at Coop, and they were both encircled in flames. Chase reached the barn as Tess started toward her sister. A flaming timber fell from the ceiling and blocked her path. "Stevie!" she screamed. Chase grabbed her arm and dragged her to safety as more timbers began to fall.

"No!" Tess struggled to free herself. "Let me go. I have to save Stevie."

Chase's iron grip pulled her close. "I'm sorry, sweetheart, it's too late."

The roar of the flames intensified. Glass in the windows broke from the heat, and smoke as black as the night billowed out. Summoning all her strength, Tess jerked herself free. She turned and ran toward the shed.

"Tess, stop!" Chase called after her.

She ignored him and ran faster. There was a chainsaw in there. She could use it to cut through the wood and drag her sister to safety. She slid open the shed door and spotted the saw on the workbench. She grabbed it up and turned to run back toward the barn. As she stepped out of the shed, she saw the flames shooting high into the night sky. She was fifteen years old again, watching her family burn.

But this event had to end differently. She knelt with the saw on the ground and primed it, then pulled the cord. It sputtered, then kicked to life. Hefting it, she started across the driveway as the entire barn roof collapsed. Soot and burning embers rained around Tess as she stood transfixed by the calamity. The saw dropped from her numb fingers and died as the pressure on the handle let off.

"No," she moaned. She dropped to her knees. Her vision blurred. "Go to God, Stevie." Her tears joined the heat of the ash falling onto her face. Her sister's spirit was even now rising skyward. How could she live without Stevie? This wasn't justice. Watching helplessly as the fire consumed the barn as if it were made of paper, she wished she could have told Stevie that God was a God of mercy. She didn't have to be looking over her shoulder for him to strike her down.

"Oh Stevie," she whispered. The hole in her heart was never going to be filled—it would always carry the shadow of Stevie's face and smile. Her sister had always put her first. She'd been father, mother, friend, and confidante. No one else would ever take her place.

Chase knelt beside her. She longed for his arms, his support. She clung to him, both of them weeping. They knelt with their arms entwined and watched the building burn. In the distance, she heard the wail of sirens as the volunteer fire truck came careening down the lane.

The beep of the monitor echoed off the tile floors, adding to Tess's chill. She stood beside Chase and Flint and looked down at Buck in the hospital bed. Allie sat in a wheelchair beside the bed. Both legs were in casts and stuck out in front of her. Her arms were in casts as well. Four friends had gone into the fire this season, and only two came out unscathed.

Bandages covered Buck's face, but his pain-filled eyes peered out from under the swath of gauze. At least he was still alive. Her vision blurred as she thought about the funeral two days ago. She'd never get over Stevie's death.

"Ready, Buck?" the doctor asked, his voice a fake cheery tone.

Esther stood on the other side of the bed, out of place among these jeans-clad friends in a copper-colored wool pantsuit. She held Buck's hand, but her gaze darted from his face to the scissors in the doctor's hand. Her skin held a green cast, and her mouth twisted in a revolted half smile. Tess wasn't sure if the woman would stay to watch the reveal or bolt. If Esther dumped Buck, Tess would personally hurt her.

"Let's get it over with." Buck's vocal chords had been damaged by the heat as well, and he spoke in a harsh whisper.

Esther flinched at the sound. "I'd better step out of the way." She pulled her fingers from Buck's grasp and moved back two steps. Tess moved to the other side of the bed and grabbed Esther's arms, ostensibly for support, but mostly to make sure she stayed with Buck. This would be hard.

The doctor began to snip at the swathing that encircled Buck's head. Esther dug her fingernails into Tess's arm, but Tess managed not to flinch. She was barely breathing herself. She'd been telling herself to expect the worst, but even she wasn't prepared when the doctor finally revealed Buck's face.

Angry red ridges marred the right side of Buck's face from his temple to his chin. He was going to be horribly scarred.

Esther gave a low moan. "No, no." She started to stumble back but ran up against Tess, who refused to budge.

"Don't you dare run," Tess whispered. "Smile, kiss him."

Allie saw what was happening and sent a warning glance toward Esther too. Esther took a deep breath and started toward Buck. He turned toward her, revealing more of his face, all the more hideous because of the smooth handsomeness of the other side. "I—I can't." She wrenched off her ring and threw it on the bed. "I'm sorry, Buck. So sorry." She tore her arm from Tess's grasp and ran from the room. Her sobs echoed down the hall then faded.

Fury rose in Tess. Nothing she could say would heal the wound. Buck's eyes had the closed-down look she'd come to recognize as pain. "Buck, I—"

"It's okay, Tess. I was expecting it." He picked up the ring and handed it to Tess. "Hang on to it for me, will you?" His fingers went to his face, but the doctor took his hand and moved it gently away.

"Don't touch it, Buck. There's still the risk of infection." The doctor handed the scissors to the nurse. "Don't be discouraged. We've got more work we can do on this. I've spoken to a top-notch plastic surgeon about you, and he'll see you next week."

Buck's hand dropped away. "I don't want any surgery. Looks aren't everything. Can I have a mirror?"

Tess's gaze met Chase's. Chase stepped to the bed and handed Buck the mirror that was lying beside it.

Buck held it out and peered into it. He paled and handed it back. "When can I get out of here? I've got a business to run."

"In a couple of days. We want to watch for infection."

"Today. I can come back and have you take a look. I want out of here." His low, tight voice was hard to hear.

The doctor nodded slowly. "I understand. We'll process the paperwork." He and the nurse left the room.

The silence echoed with fear of the future. "I guess that's it then. If you all will leave, I'll get dressed," Buck said.

"I'll be outside to take you home," Tess said.

"You brought my truck, didn't you?" he asked. When she nodded, he shrugged. "I'm deformed, not incapacitated. I'll drive myself."

Tess didn't like it. Not one bit. But there was nothing she could do. He was like an animal going off to lick his wounds. "Call me if you need me."

"I'll be fine." He glanced at Flint. "Hey, buddy, could you hang around and help me get into my clothes?" Flint nodded, and Buck nodded toward the door. "See you later, Tess. Allie, it's great to see you doing so well. Thanks for coming. You too, Chase." His voice was heavy.

Tess propelled Allie's wheelchair out the door. She wouldn't cry. It would make Buck feel worse. Her eyes felt gritty from all the tears she'd shed over the past week. Mindy was wan and silent, and Paul was a changed man. He walked around the ranch with a suffering expression. Tess understood their problems better now. In spite of his infidelity, he'd loved Stevie.

"I want to go to the cemetery," she told Chase once she got Allie back in her room and they were outside the hospital.

"You were just there this morning. I'm not sure it's healthy, Tess."

She'd haunted Stevie's gravesite ever since the funeral. Stevie felt just a breath away when Tess was standing beside the mounded dirt that scarred the placid setting. "Please," she whispered.

CHAPTER 26

A woodpecker clocked away on a nearby tree, the *rat-a-tat-tat* the only sound disturbing the quiet as they got out of the truck. Chase watched Tess as her gaze took in the quiet ranch, then ranged over to the burned-out remains of the barn. Her shoulders slumped, and she turned away. Her face was still white and strained from the visit to the cemetery.

He started toward her, then stopped and jammed his hands into the pockets of his jeans. He was no good for her now. God alone could heal her heart—and even then it would take time.

"I'm not sure what to do next, Chase," she said, her voice barely above a whisper. "Wildfire is gone, the ranch is in serious trouble, and I've lost my passion for firefighting. I'm not even who I thought I was. Tell me what to do."

She was asking *him?* He wished he had an answer for her. "It's going to take some hard work to save the ranch," he admitted. "We've got Whip's money to help out, but it's not enough. Maybe we'll see a return of the money Coop stole sooner than later, but it's hard to say. Fifty thousand would have fed the cattle for the winter, just barely, but we need nearly a hundred thousand now that the hay is gone. I think we should sell some cattle to start off with. Maybe half the herd. Then we start building back next spring. It's not what I want to do, but I don't see a better way."

"But what about the money we got for Wildfire?"

"I have something to show you." At least he was able to do this much. He took her arm and guided her toward the back pasture. "Look."

Wildfire stood at the top of the mesa. His black mane flowed in the wind. His head turned, and he whinnied when he saw Tess. The mesa sloped toward them, and he trotted down the hillside.

"Did he run away again?" Tess's voice held a hopeless note.

"Nope. This is his home now."

She looked up at him then. "What are you saying?"

"Newcastle couldn't keep him penned in anyway. He took back the money with a grateful smile and a good riddance."

"Wildfire—he's mine?" Hope shimmered in her eyes. "You— you aren't just teasing?"

"Would I tease about something this important?"

She flung her leg over the fence and ran to meet her horse. He whinnied again and broke into a gallop. His hooves kicked up sand when he stopped in front of her. Bumping his head against her shoulder, he blew into her hair. If Chase were a woman, he knew he'd be crying about now. As it was, a lump formed in his throat. Tess's arms encircled Wildfire's neck, then she leaped onto his back, and they took off over the field. Watching them was like watching her parachute from a plane. A beautiful thing.

When they came back to the fence, lather coated the horse's withers, and Wildfire panted. Tess slid from his back and ran back toward Chase. She vaulted the fence and launched into his arms. Cupping her hands to either side of his face, she pressed her lips to his. She smelled of horse, sunshine, and pine, an intoxicating aroma to him.

Before he could react, she pulled back. "How can we afford this, Chase?"

She was still standing close, so he gathered her in his arms and buried his face in her neck. "I couldn't let you make the sacrifice, Tess, not after losing Stevie," he whispered in her hair. "It was a shortcut we shouldn't have taken. There's no way around hard work and dedication. God will help us through this."

She pulled away and looked into his face. "Chase Huston admits to taking a shortcut?"

"It went awry," he reminded her.

"You just have to pick the right shortcut." Her smile dimmed, and her gaze searched his. He couldn't mistake this welcome in her face.

He bent his head and kissed her. She entwined her fingers in the fabric of his shirt and kissed him back with a passion that surprised him. When she finally pulled away, he didn't want to let go of her. "You have to marry me, you know," he said, tracing the curve of her chin with his thumb. He never knew how Tess would react. She might run away again, flee all she'd faced in this past month.

She stilled and a small gasp escaped her lips. "Marry you?"

"Don't tell me you always kiss a guy like this." He bent his head and kissed her again, reveling in her response. If she didn't know she loved him yet, he'd have to prove she did. He relinquished her lips with reluctance. "You love me and you know it. We were meant to be together from the first time you threw a cow pie at me."

"It was your fault." A smile tugged at her lips, and her face shone.

He cupped her face in his hands. "I love you, Tess Masterson. I love the way you fight for what you believe in. I love your passion for life and your family. I want to be one of your passions."

"You already are," she whispered. Tears shimmered on her lashes. She bit her lip. "How can I be this happy about your loving me when I've just lost Stevie? It doesn't seem right." She gulped and looked toward the barn. "And who am I, Chase? I'm not Garrett Masterson's daughter."

"Yes you are. I never showed you this because I thought it would make you mad." He put his hand in his pocket and pulled out his pocket watch.

"Dad's watch," she whispered. "It's been handed down from my great-grandfather."

"When he gave it to me, he said he always wanted me to remember that a man's family is who he lets into his heart. You've heard him say it too." She gave a nearly imperceptible nod, and he continued. "He *knew* you were Giles's child by blood, Tess. But you were his because he chose to love you, to let you inside. You're still his kid, and nothing will change that."

She fingered the watch he laid in her hand. "Thank you, Chase. I know he loved me just as much as he loved Stevie. And you." She put the watch back in his hand and closed his fingers over it. "We'll give it to our child someday." She looked back toward the barn's remains. "I miss Stevie so much."

Joy surged. He tipped her head back toward him. "We'll never forget Stevie, Tess. She'll always be part of us. But you know she's looking down from heaven with approval. She would be the first to tell us to grab our happiness with both hands because life is fleeting. We can't live in fear of what the next day will bring, but we can take each day as it comes and thank God for the privilege of sharing it together."

"Thank you for saying that," she said softly. "Stevie would want this." She laid her cheek against his chest. "I do love you."

"I know," he said, allowing a trace of smugness to enter his voice. "What's not to love? I'm poor, an orphan, and ugly to boot."

She laughed and hugged him before raising her head. "You know perfectly well you're a handsome devil. And we'll be paupers together, at least for a while. We're going to make it no matter what happens though."

He searched her face. "What happens if we lose the ranch, Tess? Will you blame me?"

"Will you blame me? I'm the one who ran away when I should have stayed to work it. But I don't want the ranch anymore, Chase. Stevie isn't here. My parents are gone. It's not that important anymore." She took a deep breath. "I'll only marry you on one condition—that you go back to school and become a vet."

She was offering him the desire of his heart, but he couldn't let her make the sacrifice. "You don't mean this, Tess. The ranch has been in the Masterson family for generations. We can't let it go."

"We'll let Whip run the ranch—he's going to own a fourth of it anyway. He's better at it than both of us put together. He can sell some stock and get it to a level he can handle with a couple of ranch hands and build it from there. Paul will be here to work, and I can help out too. It just isn't as important as I thought it was. There are more important things in life than land and money."

"What about your firefighting? You love it." The thought of her jumping into danger made his heart hiccup, but she was giving him his desire, and it wasn't fair that she should give up what made her feel alive.

"I can still do it until we have kids."

"We'll get right to work on that then," he said, grinning.

A hint of color touched her cheeks. "You don't want me to jump?"

"The thought of jumping out of a plane sounds about as much fun as stepping in a cow pie," he admitted. "I don't like to think of you in danger."

She nodded, but he could tell her thoughts were far away when her gaze wandered back to the burned remains. "Do you know what today is?" she asked.

He did, but he hadn't wanted to bring it up in case it would make her somber mood worse. "It's your birthday."

Her gaze turned back to him. "I think I can finally let go of the past, Chase. Now when my birthday comes around, I'll remember it was the first time you told me you loved me."

"But it won't be the last," he said, gathering her in his arms. "I've got a present for you." He pulled out a tiny box. Her eyes widened. "It's not as big a diamond as you deserve," he said.

"It's beautiful," she breathed. She put it on her finger and slipped into his arms. "It fits just right."

The roar of the plane's engines filled Tess's head. The spotter had already opened the door, and she could see the tops of the trees, touched with orange and gold, spread out before her like a painting. The tree cover broke, and she saw the clearing. Cars, trucks, and

SUVs crowded the parking lot of the Zane Grey cabin. Their friends waited below, as did the pastor.

"I can't believe I agreed to this," Chase moaned.

"You look a little green," Whip observed. "'Death and life *are* in the power of the tongue, and those who love it will eat its fruit.' It ain't fair that your tongue got us both into this mess."

"We'll take care of you, old man." Flint slapped Whip on the back.

Buck smiled, and though the twisting of his ruined cheek made him look angry, there was no mistaking the amused glint in his eyes. Tess thanked him with her eyes for making the effort to come join the joy of the day, though she knew he had to be remembering his own lost love.

Chase grinned. "You can drop him any time, guys. I've taken enough of his guff today."

Whip raised his brows, an expression of alarm spreading over his face. "I think I changed my mind. You can get by without a best man."

"No way," Chase said. "If I'm going through with this, so are you. You guys go first."

Whip looked pale, but he stepped to the doorway with the two firefighters. Flint snapped the tandem harness around him. "See you on the ground," Flint said with a backward glance at Chase and Tess. The men vanished through the open doorway. Buck went out right after them.

"I guess there's no turning back now. Whip would kill me if he jumped and I didn't," Chase said.

She'd never seen Chase out of jeans, boots, and hat, but he looked very appealing in his orange jumpsuit with the parachute strapped to his back. "It will be fun. You'll see. I won't let go of you." She stepped closer and snapped the tandem harness around them. "Don't look down, just look at me." He followed her to the open door.

He gave a weak smile. "It will be the only thing that saves me from a heart attack." Gathering her into his arms, he kissed her until she was breathless. "Though having you so close is enough to stop my heart."

She pushed him away. "Stop, or I won't be able to jump."

"That was the general idea. We can radio down and tell them we'll land and drive out."

"Chicken."

"Bwack-bwak-bwak."

She chuckled. "You'll be addicted after this jump."

"I can promise you I won't be."

"Ready?" She cast a longing look toward the open doorway.

"I'm ready to marry you. I'm not so sure about the jump."

"Love makes us do crazy things." She put her hand over her mouth to hide her smile.

"You can say that again," he grumbled. He exhaled then nodded. "If it means we get to go on our honeymoon, I'm all for it."

She laughed aloud then. "I can tell what's important to you."

His grin softened, and he cupped her face in his hands. *"You're* what's important to me, Tess. I'll do anything to see that smile in your eyes." He kissed her quickly, then released her and moved to the doorway with her.

They sat on the floor of the plane with their feet dangling into the slipstream. Tess looked at the man she loved and let her love shine out toward him. "Blue skies, Chase," she said, repeating the universal mantra of skydivers. He smiled back at her, and they leaned forward, tipping into nothingness. The blue sky swirled above them, and they flew out to meet their destiny.

ACKNOWLEDGMENTS

*H*ave I ever mentioned I love Arizona? Writing this book was an act of passion. I have Native American blood in me, and this story poured from my heart almost without effort. Notice I said *almost*.

I'm blessed beyond all measure to work with my WestBow family: editor Ami McConnell, who has taught me so much with every book; Natalie Hanemann, who keeps us all on schedule and smiling while we do it; visionary publisher Allen Arnold; his assistant and my fellow Hoosier and friend Lisa Young; publicist extraordinaire Caroline Craddock; creative marketing genius Jennifer Deshler; and amazing cover designers Mark Ross and Belinda Bass. And while I don't work directly with Amanda Bostic now, she and I still exchange e-mails, and she brightens my life with her support. I've grown to love and appreciate the Thomas Nelson sales staff more and more. I'm so blessed to work with the Dream Team of WestBohemians!

Erin Healy is the polish behind my books. Anyone who thinks all they have to do is write a book and it's done has never worked with a good editor. I have two of the best in the industry! Ami and Erin both bring so much to the finished product. I'm a revision junkie now. If you like my books, thank them!

Thanks to my agent, Karen Solem, who is only a phone call or an e-mail away when I wonder if I can really do this. Thanks, Karen, for your friendship, your insight, and your wisdom.

To my critique partners, Kristin Billerbeck, Diann Hunt, and Denise Hunter, who took time out of their own writing days to go over my manuscript and make sure I got this right. Thanks a bunch, friends! And thanks to friend Robin Miller, who was the first to read the entire manuscript in one gulp. You're a great encourager, Robin!

And as always, my heartfelt thanks to my wonderful family. My husband Dave, my son David, and my daughter Kara have been my cheering section from the first day I sat at the computer to write, even during those long first seven years when no one wanted to buy anything. I love you!

And to my Constant Companion, the Lord Jesus Christ, who has put me in my "sweet spot" and allowed me to write the stories of my heart, thank you.

READING GROUP GUIDE

1. Tess reluctantly returns home for the first time in twelve years and discovers that her elder sister, Stevie, is seriously ill. She confronts Chase, her foster brother, about not letting her know but he says that if she were a good sister and not so busy running, she would have known. Tess justifies her actions by telling Chase he did not know how many fires she had fought and how many lives she had saved that year. But Chase stands his ground and says he believes it would have been braver for her to have "done her duty by the ones she loved." Do you agree with Chase? (P 25)

2. Infuriated with Tess, Chase asks Whip whether he was ever jealous that Garrett, and not Whip, inherited the ranch even

though he had just as much right to it. Whip says that he is not going to complain about his situation because "a sound heart is life to the body, but envy is rottenness to the bones." What do you think makes Whip able to be so sensible in comparison to Tess's mistaken envy of Chase, and Coop's deserved resentment of the Mastertons? (P 27)

3. Tess is immensely jealous of Chase because she believes her father loved him more than her, and that he had taken her place. Stevie on the other hand, wanted a brother and knew that her father yearned for a son. She immediately accepted Chase as her brother, and saw that that Chase gave her father joy. What do you think makes Tess and Stevie react so differently to their father's fostering Chase? (P 48)

4. Justice plays a large role in this book. Coop is driven by the belief that he can only forgive the Mastersons once he has made them pay for their sins. Chase struggles to decide whether he should bail his delinquent brother, Jimmy, out of jail. Tess believes she is pursuing justice in her search for the truth about her parents' death. Buddy Havelin, the owner of the Rim Café, tells Tess that she will come to understand that life is not about what is deserved, but about what is not deserved. Which character in the book do you think had the correct understanding of justice?

5. Stevie wants to believe that God will not give her more than she can handle, but she feels she is at the end of her endurance. Her life is a vicious cycle of tragedy and its unfortunate results. What can be learned from Stevie's life? (P 69)

6. When Chase is crossing the street to the jail to bail Jimmy out, Dr. Tally drives by. He offers Chase a job as his assistant and says he will pay for him to get his veterinary license. The vet tells him he has a gift with animals he should not ignore. But Chase feels he is obligated to help out at the struggling ranch. Do you think it is right to let the circumstances of life prevent the pursuit of using God's gifts to the fullest? (P 83)

7. The grassy field where the barn in which Tess's parents died stands is described as having a healing effect that is almost artistic. Chase supposes it is God the great Physician and Painter's way of "brushing green strokes across the black and bringing new life to what was ruined." How else does God bring healing and new life in the book? (P 105)

8. Buck and Tess narrowly survive the last forest fire in the book by sheltering in the cave in which Coop has been hiding. Once the fire has passed over them, Tess cannot believe she is still alive. She believed she deserved to die for saving her horse instead of her parents. Tess tangibly feels God's mercy and realizes she has been serving God out of fear instead of love. Has there been a time when you tangibly experienced God's mercy? (P 263)

9. Coop eventually captures Tess and Stevie, and sets the new barn on fire with him and the sisters in it. Stevie manages to push Tess out of the barn to safety, but when Tess reaches in to pull her sister out, Stevie launches herself at Coop, who is engulfed in flames. Why do you think Stevie chooses to die rather than be saved? (P 285)

10. Tess feels as if her heart is breaking when she gives up her horse, Wildfire. She believes it is the only way to save the ranch. So it is to her complete surprise and absolute joy when Chase returns Wildfire to her. Have you ever had to give up something precious, only to have it returned you? (P 290)

11. Garrett always told Chase and Tess "a man's family is who he lets into his heart." Tess ironically believes she is Garrett's daughter and that she was replaced in his heart by Chase, "the foster child." What are other examples of how the love of family makes a difference to the lives of characters in the book? (P 292)

12. Upon discovering and proclaiming their love for each other, Chase tells Tess he believes Stevie would want them to grab their happiness with both hands because life is fleeting. "We can't live in fear of what the next day will bring, but we can take each day as it comes and thank God for the privilege of sharing it together," he says. What other valuable life lessons has Tess learned during her summer at the ranch? (P 292)

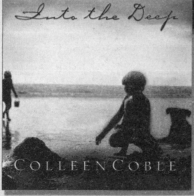

WestBow
PRESS

A Division of Thomas Nelson Publishers
Since 1798

visit us at www.westbowpress.com

Alaska
Twilight

COLLEEN COBLE

EXCERPT FROM
DANGEROUS DEPTHS

Koma Hamai sat in the warm Hawaiian sun with his fishing net strung out on the volcanic rock. He muttered an ancient chant as he mended the net with gnarled fingers. Hansen's disease had numbed the nerve endings in his fingers, and net mending was a hard job but one he found satisfying. There was nothing better than seeing something broken become useful again.

The ocean boiled and foamed with blue-green ire as it spent its power on the rocks, then came to lap at his feet with a cooling touch. He heard a sound behind him, back by the fishpond, probably one of the many axis deer that romped the jungle along the edge of the sea. When it came again, the furtiveness of the sound penetrated his contentment.

He stood and turned to investigate. The apparition staring back at him was like nothing else he'd ever seen in this life. From the head to the hips, the thing was round. Dark eyes stared out of a hard helmet, and the rest of its body was covered with some kind of green skin that looked as tough as a lizard's. Koma backed away, forgetting his fishing net, then bolted and ran for his cabin. As he ran, he prayed his ninety-five-year-old legs would run as fast as they did when he was twenty, but with the limp from his broken hip, he knew he'd never outrun the monster. He didn't want to end his life as food for Ku. Surely the thing chasing him was the Hawaiian god who built the first fishpond.

A predatory hiss sounded behind him, and he spared one final glance at the strange being. Ku aimed what looked like a speargun at Koma. He fired. The old man stumbled and the spear barely missed his back. He recovered his balance and ran for his life to his cabin.

Tree branches whipped at his face when he entered the jungle, but he was safe here. He knew these trees and paths the way he knew his one-room cabin in the dark. He paused, sensing no pursuit. He peeked through the leafy canopy and saw the being moving off in the opposite direction. Ku never looked back as he moved off through the trees. Why not follow him to his lair? Koma was able to move without a noise through the jungle. He hurried after Ku along an almost impassable path to a cabin so overgrown with vines it was nearly invisible.

By the time Koma returned to his own cabin, the creature had grown in his mind to a height of fifteen feet and sprouted fangs.